RAVE REVIEWS FOR DOUGLAS CLEGG!

"One of horror's brightest lights."

—*Publishers Weekly*

"Douglas Clegg has become the new star in horror fiction."
—Peter Straub

"Douglas Clegg is clearly and without any doubt one of the best horror writers in the business."

—*Cinescape*

"Clegg gets high marks on the terror scale."
—*Daily News* (New York)

"Douglas Clegg is one of horror's most captivating voices."
—*BookLovers*

"Clegg has cooler ideas and is much more of a stylist than either [John] Saul or [Dean] Koontz. Think Robert Frost if he were being strangled by H. P. Lovecraft."
—*Dallas Morning News*

NIGHTMARE HOUSE
"Clegg's modern sensibility shows that tales in the classic horror tradition can still entertain."

—*Publishers Weekly*

THE INFINITE
"A cavalcade of nightmares. Memorable for its evocative, disturbing imagery and haunting emotional insights, this novel adds a new chapter to horror's tradition of haunted house fiction."

—*Publishers Weekly*

"A master~~ful~~ ... *finite* is undoubtedly Cl ... ing the growing literary ... n full control of his tale ...

—*Rue Morgue*

MORE PRAISE FOR DOUGLAS CLEGG!

MISCHIEF

"Clegg has earned the right to be judged against nobody's work but his own. On that basis, *Mischief* is an important addition to his oeuvre."

—*Hellnotes*

"[Clegg] draws eerily plausible parallels between the arcane rituals of academic institutions and esoteric occultists, and imbues Harrow with an atmosphere of menace thick enough to support further flights of dark fantasy."

—*Publishers Weekly*

THE HOUR BEFORE DARK

"*The Hour Before Dark* works well. I was compelled to keep turning the pages as fear gnawed a hollow in my stomach and raised my pulse to racing level from cover to cover."

—*Cemetery Dance*

"Gripping to the end. An ever-tightening ballet of suspense."

—*Chiaroscuro*

YOU COME WHEN I CALL YOU

"This is horror at its finest."

—*Publishers Weekly* (starred review)

"A brilliant achievement of occult fiction."

—*Cemetery Dance*

THE NIGHTMARE CHRONICLES

"Douglas Clegg's short stories can chill the spine so effectively that the reader should keep paramedics on standby."

—Dean Koontz

"Clegg's use of innovative metaphors catapults each story beyond a landscape crowded with the horror genre's usual monsters and madmen into a territory he alone can claim."

—*Publishers Weekly*

THE CHILD ON THE STAIRS

Stepping over the threshold, into Harrow, Ethan saw a brief flash of smoke along the stairs.

Something was on fire—with all the candles, constantly burning, he was sure something had caught fire while he was out.

He dashed for the staircase, drawing off his wet jacket to douse any flames. As he took the first step up, Ethan saw, not smoke or fire, but what seemed like frost in the air, or a thickened chalk dust hanging in an unnatural stillness.

In the next second, it was no longer there, and in its stead was a young child—not the boy he had seen running among the trees, but another.

A strange child . . .

DOUGLAS CLEGG

NIGHTMARE HOUSE

LEISURE BOOKS NEW YORK CITY

LEISURE BOOKS ®

May 2004

Published by

Dorchester Publishing Co., Inc.
200 Madison Avenue
New York, NY 10016

ISBN 0-8439-5177-X

The name "Leisure Books" and the stylized "L" with design are trademarks of Dorchester Publishing Co., Inc.

Printed in the United States of America.

Visit us on the web at www.dorchesterpub.com.

TABLE OF CONTENTS

For Ed Gorman—two short novels for one fine writer.
I can't thank you enough for what you've done for me.

Nightmare House

STET FORTUNA DOMUS.

It was the carving above the keystone of the house: *May the House's Fortune Stand.*

The old man had stolen that phrase from another Harrow, but it fit this place. At least it fit his wishes for his Harrow.

A telling moment: When I was six years old and on one of my infrequent but wonderful stays at my grandfather's estate, he told me that there were three things to watch for in the world.

While I could not—ten minutes later—remember a single one, what I remember now is the warmth of his hand, the musty smell of the ill-fitting suit that must've lived most of the year within a closet full of mothballs, and the way he could not stop looking at me as if I were the most important child in the world even with my lies and games and pouts and stolen gingerbread men from the kitchen. It was the only time I felt this in my childhood.

I never forgot that moment.

Even now, I can't judge him beyond knowing that my grandfather loved me and wanted all this for me. It was the house. What the house held. I would never call a work of architecture evil. Nor would I suggest that a house could be anything but a benign presence; it is always the human element that corrodes the stones and the wood and the brick and the foundation. It is the human heart that bends the floors and burns the rooms and imbues the structure with the spirit of error and false remembrance.

Imagine this house, this estate, this property: the acreage, the river, the trees, the gardens, the entire world captured within a home.

It sits on a slope, surrounded by woods; beyond the house, a village, and beyond the gently sloping hills and the woods and the village, the Hudson River. It was built over many years, unfinished in some respects even after my grandfather's death. All anyone really knew of the property was what they'd heard of the rumors and the gossip and the newspaper accounts now and then of an eccentric collector living up the Hudson.

The house had a name, and as with everything that possesses a name, it had a personality as well.

Rumor had it that treasure was buried within its walls; rumor had it that screams had come from it more than once; rumor had it that a madman had built it for his own tomb; rumor had it that no one willingly remained overnight in the house; and rumor had it that a child could still be heard keening from within on an October night.

The year was 1926 when I arrived at Harrow and claimed my birthright.

* * *

My name is Esteban, and lest you think I'm from some fascinating heritage, I will tell you what I knew of my parents. My father was from solid New England stock. He could trace his line right back to Cornwall, and what was not English was French from my grandmother's side. My mother, whose maiden name was Juliet Chambers, was from an English-Irish-Germanic background.

Esteban, they said, came from a promise my mother had made to the midwife at my birth—who had rushed to her side when the carriage she'd been riding in overturned and nearly killed her.

The midwife delivered the baby—which was, of course, me—and asked my mother to name it for the Saint Esteban, which was enough of an aristocratic-sounding name that my father begrudgingly allowed it.

My mother told me that without this mysterious woman, I would never have burst into the world with all my limbs intact, nor would she have lived beyond my first cry. Esteban sounded romantic to her ears, and seemed a very suitable and exotic name for someone who had the dark hair that neither parent possessed, although a maternal great-grandmother—who had been Irish—had those looks as well.

My mother often told me that she wanted to name me Zebediah, and given that as an alternative, I was more than happy to be known as Esteban. My father apparently wanted to anglicize the name to Steven, but fate intervened. Other children could not pronounce "Esteban," so, since the age of four or so, I'd been briefly known simply as Easton, another unusual name but falling on the Anglo-Saxon side of the chain for my father. I mispronounced the name with my childhood lisp as "Ethan," and when my father got hold of that name he ran as far as he could with it. It was to become official. It was New England; it was Old England; it was acceptable to him, although my mother was noticeably irked, and would occasionally, right up until her death, call me Esteban now and again.

Thus, by third grade I finally had a name with which everyone (but my mother) felt comfortable, and one that didn't raise the specter of some family scandal purely by its foreignness to Bostonians.

But Esteban has been my secret, true name, so you must know it and remember it.

So Ethan I became.

My young life was uneventful save for my naming.

My mother, since the accident that had precipitated my birth, had been sickly much of her life. She claimed a weak heart, and her many medications were famous among us: She could not leave her bed without a spoon of some remedy; she could not kiss my father good morning without some wee dram of medical potion to get her heart to its normal capacity; and she often spent months at spas in Saratoga and across the sea—leaving me with a nanny and my father, neither of whom I had particular fondness for. Once, I saw my mother laugh and nearly run across the rocky shoreline, but I felt immediately afterward that I must have dreamed this, for I never witnessed such a burst of energy again. I joked with her that her doctor was her real family, and I learned quickly never to make that kind of insensitive joke again.

But mostly I remember her remaining in the shuttered room of Balmoral, the house along the Cape that my father inherited after his mother had died. I knew little of the world other than Boston and Cape Cod and the Hudson Valley and all the intermediate destinations, until I took a trip to New York City when I was nineteen; then, I wanted to be in no other place than that exciting citadel to ambition, power, and promise. Boston began to seem small and provincial to me.

After my mother died, my father disinherited me over a minor skirmish regarding what he felt, as a son, I should be doing with my life; he felt I should be playing politics and amassing a fortune by taking advantage of "deals" and "opportunities" and "the way the world works for men" and such. I felt I should be pursuing my dreams and ambitions. I went to live in New York, and my life as an adult began.

But I had only seen Harrow in brief spurts of summer vacations or spring weekends. It was the house my grandfather owned and lived in along the Hudson River; I remembered it in flashes and in shadows of thought, of a few moments as a child when my father and I had gone there on short and—as far as my father was concerned—unpleasant visits.

I remember my grandfather intensely.

I remember wanting to be there in my dreams.

To me, it had seemed like a magical place, a palace of wonder and confusion.

To me, Harrow was Mystery.

Part One

The Inheritor

"There is a real world, but it is beyond this glamour and this vision. . . . You may think this all strange nonsense; it may be strange, but it is true, and the ancients knew what lifting the veil means. . . ."
—Arthur Machen, *The Great God Pan*

Chapter One

1

My dreams are there now. You can go in any room, any secret chamber, and you will find them—shadows of dreams, like smoke from a fire that has only just died. They are no longer with me—I do not dream. I live now in stark reality. In light. In a harsh sun. Did I leave them on purpose? Of course not.

They were taken from me by Harrow.

You know the place; you read of it in the papers, in the pulps, the little legends that have grown there. They are calling it Nightmare House now in the papers, but back then it was just Harrow.

Once, one can suppose, there was some innocence on this land, but my research has shown that the earth from which the stones were taken was bloody ground, that not a window—not a piece of glass—was added without some knowledge of the glass's history, of the wood and stone's prior existence as tree, as cave, as lair.

And the abbey.

My grandfather liked that kind of touch. Smuggling artifacts and entire structures from the Old World to the New.

He liked owning ancient things.

Harrow was ancient.

Harrow existed, for all I knew, before the world had been created.

2

And the world was still young to me then.

I was born to the century's end; 1897 to be precise; I was born to the Modern Age.

Soon men could fly, could live dozens of stories above the earth, and could speak to each other through a tube or wire. By the time I was ten, I had already seen automobiles begin to replace carriages; while still a teenager, I had gone to war in Europe, and returned having seen only the slightest bit of action. I had my grandfather to thank for that, for he arranged that I should be an ambulance driver, and he had the connections for it. I had always suffered small strokes of ill health since battling pneumonia as a child (a weakling, my father had said, from the beginning), and I was not quite fit for battle. I married by the time I was twenty-three, worked at a book publisher in the city called Foxworth & Sons; although I was not a Foxworth, I had grown up with the "& Sons" and they rewarded me with the sheer glamorous drudgery of publishing books on what was then the hot item: crossword puzzles. I made a good living. In fact, I thought I was happy until Madeleine, my wife, left me.

And then Harrow changed my life.

My grandfather died in May of 1926, but it took me until October of that year to find my way to his house along the Hudson Valley, to a town called Watch Point—it grew as if the stones had been washed up by the river in just such an array. The place looked ancient and quaint, and it saddened me—just looking at it.

Justin Gravesend, my grandfather, had been first a wealthy businessman and then a wealthy antiquarian. This means, as my father had always said, he collected ancient things and did not much of anything else his entire life. This was not entirely true, since in his youth my grandfather had commanded railroading and shipping interests, but once a fortune had been made, he happily sold off his businesses and retired to the country.

I had not seen the house since I was very young. Now that both my father and grandfather were gone, it was my duty as the sole heir to make the day's drive up from the city and go through things, to decide what to sell and what to keep, to find just what my grandfather had been up to in the last years of his life—those years when my father and he had refused to patch up their differences.

Now they were both dead.

I had to stop to turn the crank only half a dozen times in the course of the trip—the car I owned had been my father's and was still of the old-fashioned va-

15

riety of my childhood. We called them jalopies then; my father had paid a pretty penny for that Model T when I was young, adding to it with whatever were the most modern accessories as the years went on, until it resembled a mess more than a Model T. But the wipers my father had added in 1920 worked well, and I was thankful for them. This, despite the fact that everyone on the road seemed to be driving the new Chrysler, the McLaughlin Buick, the Overland, or the newer Ford touring car, so that my tin lizzie looked like a throwback to the age of dinosaurs. Still, it did the job, with more bumps and a good deal more bother than another car; yet, as long as I could get out of the city, I was happy.

The day began full of good omens. This included the money I now had in my grubby little fingers—more wealth than some of my superiors at the publishing house even had. It felt good to be alive and free, and on the road. The weather was magnificent and balmy for the last days in October, but by the time I found the Hudson Valley on muddy roads in areas where people apparently had not yet discovered pavement or cobblestone, driving slowly through villages and towns with no markers (I have always been a fool with a map or directions, I admit, and my wife never failed to point this out), a summer storm was brewing along the horizon.

Driving to Watch Point, with its scattered stone houses surrounding what I can best describe as a hamlet, became nerve-wracking as sheets of rain came down, my wipers barely drawing off one spray of water when another blinded my view, my jacket soaked, all a blur—and by the time I found the narrow muddy road that led to Harrow and the beginning of the wooded enclave that was the invisible fence surrounding my grandfather's property, I was sure I'd be skidding off the road into some rocky ledge.

A chill descended with the rain.

I should have taken a train up and then hired a car to Harrow, I thought, as the water soaked through the cracks and gaping wounds in the old jalopy and into my shirt and trousers. *You are a fool.* I heard my father's admonition in my head. *You will always be a fool.*

A queer sort of folk occupied Watch Point—even as a child I had noticed their difference, their eyes that seemed too far apart by a quarter inch or so, their complexions too olive and ash—and their bodies mostly covered with an oily sort of cloth. The closest material I could imagine would be sealskin, but I knew, even as a child, this might not be possible. In the rain, they milled about, a dozen or so of these creatures (all right, these people, but there were times, in these small villages isolated by thirty miles and a hundred years from the rest of civilization that they seemed to have nothing in common with those of us from the city, as if they had once been fish flung from the river below). They went about their business as if the storm were not battering at them, as if the flashes of lightning were nothing. "Queer folk," my mother had pronounced when I was a child and we had come through to spend one of the holidays.

And then, the woods, a golden darkness within the storm, branches waving violently, entire trees listing to one side or another with the sudden winds, brilliantly colored leaves like flags battering at the windshield—

And then the house, in the dark of the storm, illuminated by a lightning flash.

The house I had not seen in so many years.

Even in the blinding rain, I could see it. I wept. I wept as I hadn't even for my father, who had died two years before in an automobile wreck outside Boston. I wept as I hadn't in many years; and the feeling I had was that someone had just kicked me in the gut, that something at the very core of my being had been pummeled.

I remembered some happiness here at this great house, this English manor house my grandfather had built to remind him of his native land.

Although he had been raised a poor boy, circumstances had changed in his twenties, and it had been as if money could not avoid him in his prime as he amassed wealth.

He had a mania for old things; he had gone on strange expeditions throughout the ancient and modern world, with men who had names like Schliemann and Kempler and Orinda. He had managed to find a crumbling abbey in France, located through one of his many collectors—and he was rich enough to bring that building over, stone by stone, until he had—not a beautiful, lovely complete structure, but a crumbling abbey within which he could wander and grow his gardens and be alone, as he had been since my grandmother's death.

The house had always had a name; that's what my father had said.

"It's called Harrow," he told me. "For a school in England. A place where your granddad very much wanted to go. A place he dreamed of going."

"Why didn't he?" I had asked when I was eight.

"It wasn't a school that poor boys went to," my father said.

"But Granddaddy's rich," I protested. "Mommy said—"

"He hasn't always been rich. He grew up very, very poor. He grew up dreaming of having all the things he came to have in his life."

"I dream of things I want, too," I said.

My father said, so quietly I could barely hear him, "Better you should never dream at all."

And now, nearly twenty-one years later, I parked my Ford before the house that had become mine.

"Harrow." I said it aloud, against the elements. "Harrow, you belong to me."

But I was to learn that this house belonged to no man.

3

Let me mention this now: My grandfather had never lived in the Modern Age, despite the fact that he was somewhat responsible for creating the Modern Age, what with his cattle, railroad, and shipping businesses—all of which he had completely abandoned to others by his forty-sixth year. He turned inward; he began avoiding the modern world and turned to the ancient; he began, in my father's words, "refusing to acknowledge the present or future."

He used gas lamps in his rooms. Candles in wall sconces; great hearths in each room, yes, even in summer, for the house got quite cold. Heat could not enter it easily. He owned a candlestick telephone most popular twenty years before, and a large battery-operated radio that nearly took up half the parlor, and these were his only connections to the outside world as I then knew it.

The rain stopped by seven, and I was too exhausted to go through all the papers in my grandfather's great library—piles of them still sitting there after all this time.

Mrs. Wentworth came in with a late supper—just as we had discussed on the telephone before I drove up. She had been Granddad's companion in many ways, and I had no doubt she felt badly used after having taken care of the man for thirty-one years and then to have been shut out of his will. But she bore this well—I felt no evidence of jealousy or anger about the woman, whose exuberance had not been dulled by his death or his wishes.

"Lamb stew for the chill," she said, heating up a small saucepan on the ancient Easter Range that looked like the kind I had last seen at the age of six—in the grand kitchen that seemed made to serve banquets. "And a bit of fresh salad. I grew the lettuce out in the Holy Land and the peppers and shallots, too. All fresh. One more week and we'll lose them all to this chill."

The Holy Land was, of course, the ruins that stretched behind the house just to the west.

Wentworth was a round woman whose eyes never seemed to close as she spoke of missing the old man and of the days when he was his usual self. She reminded me a bit of a character from Dickens, the well-fed dowager with no dowage.

"He had been in such pain for the past year, it was a blessing he got called," she said.

"Mrs. Wentworth," I said when she brought a cup of black currant tea into the drawing room for me. "Are you doing all right yourself?"

"Fine, sir," she said. It was almost refreshing to be alive in the year 1926 and to be called "sir" by a woman who had a good three decades on me if not more. She was easily sixty years old. My father's generation had been called "sir" with regularity, but I had grown up with Jazz Age men and women who believed that was part of the dead past.

"I know my grandfather didn't provide for your retirement. . . ." I began. With a pang of guilt at the sudden wealth handed to me, I noticed the china cup from which I drank—expensive beyond what I could imagine.

"Oh, sir!" She laughed, sitting herself before the fire. "Good lord, he provided me well enough over the years. Didn't you know?"

"Know?"

"He paid me twice the going rate for housework and cooking. And then he taught me how to take care of it," she said, a wistful quality overtaking her voice. "But . . . I do miss the old badger."

21

"Badger?"

"That's what I called him. He was my old badger, and I was his shrew."

"Did you love him?" I asked impulsively, feeling that I had broken some barrier with her, that we'd created intimacy in this moment . . . and I had known my grandfather so little that I wanted to find out more about him from someone.

Mrs. Wentworth blushed, shaking her head. She rose, brushing her hands against her skirt. She grabbed a poker and pushed at the kindling beneath the logs—sparks danced up the flue. "No, sir. I cared for him, but he was as unlovable as a badger, your grandfather was. He had claws. He dug down and hid. Whether it was those books of his or those letters he wrote to Lord knows whom, what went on between us was hardly love. But I did care for him, and I knew he needed me here."

"I thought, perhaps . . ." Again I had not thought this through. Something in Wentworth's manner had gone cold.

She set the poker back down against the hearth. "A fire like this can burn all night, but its beauty is when it dies. When it's ash, that's when you can get near it. Like your grandfather, I suppose." She chuckled, then left me alone again. I heard her later, just before I went to bed, washing up in the kitchen. I stopped in, and said, "I'd like very much to keep you on. At least until I know what I'm going to do with this place."

"Did you leave your wife then?"

"Months ago," I said, not wishing to correct her.

Madeleine had, in fact, left me. But that was in the city—that life. That worry. That hurt.

That emptiness.

She nodded as if agreeing that not being married was good. "Well, I will be happy to come work here for as long as you need me. But my feet hurt some days."

"I don't want you to hurt—"

"No, sir, I don't mean I don't want to keep coming here. Harrow is as much in my blood as in my dreams. I couldn't leave this place if I wanted to. Just that some days . . ." She hesitated, and I detected that now she was lying.

"Some days I just am not up to coming here. My feet and sometimes my hands get cold. They swell. Maggie comes in some days. Maggie's good at washing and dusting, but you must watch her when it comes to keys. She is sticky with keys."

"There's a Maggie as well as a Wentworth?" I asked, grinning.

"There's even an Arthur who comes twice a week for the grounds." She nodded. "He's good with a gun should you like to hunt. There's good game about these woods. Wild turkeys, excellent geese this time of year."

"I'm afraid I'm not much of a hunter."

"And then," Wentworth said, not having heard my feeble comment, her eyes closing for a moment as if in prayer, "there are folks that are no longer with us."

We had a moment of silence between us. While I loved my grandfather dearly, I did not know him well enough to even pray for his soul. Weep for him, mourn a bit, and wish that I had known him better, yes. But pray? I had not believed in God since the war. Prayer was for the naive and the deluded; it was for the mass of people who refused to face reality. Madeleine had been a devout Catholic; she had thought I would go to hell for my lack of faith. But even she had left her faith when she left me for another man. I had come to the conclusion that all religious faith was lost as the years went on, and it was to keep children obedient.

I thought then that the only hell was knowing what men did to one another in war, and how we managed to destroy ourselves in peace. God was a dream. Faith was a foolishness. However, I respected Wentworth in her prayer. She needed it.

When the moment had passed, I said, "Of course. When you're feeling well, I would love to have the help. Particularly going through his things. His papers."

"Burn that lot," she snapped, a change of mood overcoming her pleasant features with wrinkles and winces. She turned back to her business. "I'll lock up, sir. You seem tired. The bed is all fresh and ready for you, and I'll be back by eight to fix breakfast and show you the grounds."

Sensing a new bitterness in the air like the scent of burnt cooking oil, I withdrew from the kitchen and went to the small wine cellar beneath the back stairs. Very quickly, and without much of a search, I grabbed an old cask of amontillado with a light amber color to it and the scent of walnut and brown sugar at its cork, and went back up to the drawing room. I lay before the fire, thinking of Madeleine, trying to erase the images of my wife in the arms of the man who had enchanted her, and managed to drink myself into a coma fairly quickly.

The fire was red ash when I awoke, having heard someone whisper something in my ear.

Then, I fell back to sleep, the liquor still swirling in my head.

4

I awoke again when I felt a crawling in my ear. It terrified me all the more because I heard a gentle buzz along with the crawling, and knew some insect had crawled up my neck and along my earlobe. I slapped at my ear, and the feeling ceased. I had fallen asleep, drunk, on the red oriental carpet with the fleur-de-lis–like designs; the room was cast into darkness. For a moment I believed I was back in my apartment in the city; but within seconds I remembered I was at Harrow, in my grandfather's drawing room.

I heard a clock in the hallway chime three times, and sat up so that I could find my way to my bedroom. The alcohol pulsed in my blood, causing me to grasp at walls and doorways.

The house was completely dark—pitch black—and I stumbled, stubbed my toe as I went, turned this way and that, opened doors, reached for lamps and switches but could not find any, until finally it came to me that I was dreaming and not walking through the

25

house at all. Then another stubbed toe, and I knew that no dream was this bad.

I came to the great glass door to the conservatory finally, and opened it on to a cloud-shrouded moon, and there, the abbey, a haunted skeleton of some unknown history, fittingly preserved in its decadent state.

The moon emerged fully from the clouds and grew brilliant, casting a coat of light across the world of Harrow.

Granddad—the Badger—had cut away the world, had finally collected a graveyard to keep life and death both back from the door.

Wandering the property alongside the ruins in the hours before dawn was like moving slowly through another century, another world.

As I went I felt a presence with me, a warm presence, a benevolent presence, a presence that made me think my grandfather was still there, a ruin among his ruins—

I turned toward that presence, to look it in the face.

5

I was dreaming, wasn't I?

But this could be no dream: I was awake in a haze of alcohol and sleep and exhaustion and, even, mourning. For how could I be out, drunk still, in the darkening garden with its halo of moonglow, stumbling through these ruins?

The moon streamed across the forms and monoliths that defined the abbey. In the shabby but pure light, a woman—who may have been perhaps not the most beautiful creature I had ever seen, but one of the most mysterious—stood in the half light of the moon as it moved slowly like a white veil being drawn back. She seemed to be carrying something on her back. Her face was obscured, but I saw that she was naked yet not naked, that she wore a gown so tightly wound about her form that very little was left to my imagination—

But you are drunk, I told myself. What wild creature is this who stands so still, not ten feet away from me? No wonder, I reasoned, there was such a thing as the Eighteenth Amendment, this Prohibition that was so easily ignored and so rarely enforced. For drink made men see angels in the moonlight! It led men like myself down a literal garden path to see visions of heaven and beauty, flickering faerie temptresses with breasts and wings and the shadows of night—before us, before men, who, according to my ex-wife, were unworthy of even the lowest rungs of hell. So said my drunken mind that might even have been shouting this out loud.

For it was neither woman nor creature, but a statue of an angel, the burden on its shoulders, wings; there was no gown at all to allow the figure any modesty; it was a beautifully sculpted nude.

And as my eyes finally adjusted to the ambient light of shadow and moon and the whiteness within the darkness, I saw that I stood—as I had begun to hazard in my liquored mindfog—in a garden.

It was a place I remembered from my childhood visits. One would think I could never forget this wonderland. It was what my grandfather had called his Garden of Earthly Delights, a sunken statue garden bordering the abbey. It had a long narrow path between the miniature wilderness that had been growing and twisting within it for a quarter of a century. Among the weeds and the grass and the flowers gone wild were several statues.

The angel before me seemed to shimmer in the light. I sensed the other figures in murky darkness— and then it came to me: I had played Blind Man's Bluff with my grandfather here in this very garden, and had hidden behind a statue of the god Pan, and had sought brief refuge beside a representation of the Greek goddess Athena before my grandfather had managed to grab me and I had lost the game. Once, as a child, I had begun crying in the garden and had looked up at the turret that extended from the east wing of Harrow. There, I saw my grandfather standing at the window within the turret room, looking down at me. He dried my tears with his stern but loving presence. I could not remember much of the afternoon spent in this special retreat of my grandfather's, but at least I felt at home somewhere in the world.

The memories were coming back. That was good. I had been back at Harrow for one evening only, but soon I would remember the small things about my grandfather, the wonderful things. My father and mother had despised him, and I had been kept away often from him and from Harrow; but now it would be different. I cautioned myself that I need not remember only the bad, but the good as well. There was great good in Justin Gravesend. I was thankful to him for those brief memories of happiness in my childhood, of seeing him at the tower window, or playing in the garden with him nearby, of knowing now that he had saved me from work that bored and frustrated me, and had, through this inheritance, brought me to his own greatest love: Harrow.

And then, I saw some creature stir among the fern and ivy, and there, a shadow, and then another, low to the ground, so small that at first I thought I was imagining it, all around the statue of the angel . . . creatures, moving . . .

7

Cats.

I counted six of them, and I went over to see why there was a lost city of felines in this garden of angels and remembrances; they began yowling as I approached, all running in and out of the arbor and around the statues. I thought: My hands are full here. I need to burn down the garden, get rid of these feral cats, and probably sell the whole damn property and just get a house closer to the city.

I lingered by the angel a bit, laughing at my foolishness. Who was I to rid a place of cats? I always liked cats, and no doubt they would kill a few mice.

The chill of October began to seep into my bones,

and I even heard a mockingbird—an early riser—in a nearby tree. I felt sleepy and somewhat happy and ready to take on the ownership of this estate and all that went with it. Cats and angels and moonlight, as well.

And then, one of the statues moved.

8

All right, she was a vision, I'll admit, but not of an angel or of a goddess or even a statue. She had stood so still for the longest time that I had been positive she was some shepherdess carved in alabaster from a pastoral scene. She was perhaps five-foot-four, at the tallest, and in her right hand she carried a lantern that had as poor a light within it as I'd ever seen.

She had, in fact, been standing there for several minutes, and I saw at once that there were two cats at her feet. The Queen of Cats, I thought, and here she is. Unlike the angel, she was not a nude, but wore a heavy jacket that went past her knees, and in the feeble glow of her lantern, I could practically see fire in her red hair. Also, unlike the angel, she was flesh and blood, and even shivered a bit to prove it.

After a moment's hesitation when she wasn't sure whether I had really seen her, she stepped around the cats and the ivy, and looked at me as if I were the one trespassing on her property. As she got closer to me, I began to smell fresh shallots, the kind my grandfather grew in the Holy Land garden.

"Who are you?" I asked as calmly as I could, given my wobbly feet and my feeling of having just gone from seeing an angel to seeing something too human. I could not take my eyes off the lantern—not that her face was not lovely in shadow, but the lantern looked so ridiculous. "What kind of contraption is that?" I pointed at it before she had a chance to answer my first question.

"It's a lantern. A bicycle lantern," she added as if this first explanation weren't enough for my enfeebled brain. I detected a slight brogue, a charming bit of Irish in her, and I laughed so loud I was afraid to wake people in the village.

Cats scattered through the underbrush at the honking sound of my laugh.

"I used to have one of those," I said. "Give it to me, let me see."

She looked at me as if I were ready for the nut house. And some part of me thought: Bless the night and the moon—it clothes us with something more provocative than mere flesh—it gives us a glimpse of our souls. She was there, near the angel statue, and the moonlight made her seem as fierce and beautiful as any of the figures standing nearby.

"Please," I said. "I won't bite."

She took a few more steps in my direction, and I went in hers—nearly stumbling across a thick patch of weed and roughhewn stone—and soon I held up the lantern.

"This is so . . . old-fashioned." I grinned as I hefted it and remembered the one my father once had in his workroom in Boston. "An Eveready Clover Leaf lantern. Good lord. Is anything modern in this village?"

I glanced over to her again, her face now lit with the quavering whiteness of the lantern's light while the moon spent its efforts elsewhere.

"Don't tromp around at night scaring people," she said.

Before I could say much else, she lit into me with words and perhaps even some foul language that sounded funny coming from her maddeningly sweet lips. Somewhere in her tirade, I began to realize that she was the "Maggie" Wentworth had warned me about—and now, here she was—spitting venom about sneaking up on her in the night; again, I distinctly smelled fresh onion and shallots, and in fact, was positive I saw some twisted scallions in her hair. Had she been lying in the dirt, staring up at the moon? Digging for something? Needing sustenance from the garden? I wondered what she could possibly have been doing at that time of the morning, with her old-fashioned lantern and the cats 'round her ankles—digging for shallots and turnips on my grandfather's property? Part of me thought it a lark to imagine a servant girl digging away at all hours for food; part of me felt sad. Was she so poor and destitute that she was reduced to this? Part of me was self-righteously enraged for my dear grandfather that the very people he had hired to work for him would steal, but this was ridiculous. Who cared if the young woman took from the garden—and in October, no less!

It was funny and sad, but this woman before me was furious because somehow she could read my mind or my face or the way I grinned and she became more enraged, for she seemed to know all the things of which I had begun mentally accusing her.

9

"Your grandfather let me take vegetables and fruit from the garden, and it's October so why would I be sneaking over here," she said, stumbling over her words, obviously guessing at my suspicions. "And I'm not out here at three A.M. for the wild onions," she added. "And furthermore—" she wagged a finger practically in my face—"I'm not some trollop digging for weeds. I have plenty, thank you, and I only take what's going to waste here, so wipe that look of judge, jury, and executioner off that snotty face of yours."

The woman had a mouth on her. I was stunned. All I could think to say was: "Why are you here at this time of night—or morning—Maggie?"

"Mrs. Barrow to you."

"All right, Mrs. Barrow," I conceded.

She calmed a bit. Something about the way she explained herself led me to believe that she was used to being accused of all kinds of minor crimes.

"It was the cats. I thought one of them was hurt," she said. "And then . . ."

"Then?"

"I don't live that far from the property. Sound travels long distances this time of the morning. And I couldn't sleep," she said.

I felt she was holding something back. "Was it just the cats?"

"They're going at it, the devils," she said. "They sound like babies crying when they're in season. It's a racket like you've never heard."

"If they're wild, I'll see to it that they're gotten rid of," I said, not really meaning it, but I was unsure of any other solution. "They might carry disease."

"You, the new master of Harrow, ready to rid the place of the cats that have been here longer than you'll ever stay. Diseased! These are healthy cats living on healthy country mice," she spat. "Murder innocent cats, will you?"

I had to catch my breath. I didn't want servants; I didn't even want Wentworth. But I supposed they, too, were part of what I'd inherited. I was no longer a working man; I had just become everything I had always loathed in my father: a gentleman of leisure.

"All right," I said. "Mrs. Barrow—Maggie—I'm very sleepy, and I've had bad dreams and need to go back to bed and have some more. You're welcome to the shallots in this garden. I will ignore the cats as best I can. Is that fair?"

She eyed me suspiciously. I had thought her quite beautiful at first, but between her temper and her intolerance of anything I had to say, she was beginning to seem less than lovely. "Give me back my lantern," was all she said. When I did, she smiled briefly. "You scared me half to death, coming out here like you did, weaving in and out of the path with that wild look," she said. "I thought you were some kind of ghost."

Then she turned and seemed to flit along the path,

back into the darkness, no doubt returning along some narrow road known only to her, across a break in the stone wall that surrounded Harrow, back to her little apartment in the village, back to her husband may-he-be-spared-the-smell-of-shallots.

I shrugged it all off and felt a small ache along the back of my head, and knew I must try to get some rest. I would be no good for the morning or even the afternoon if I stayed up all night long.

As I walked back to the house, I thought I heard the sound of a child wailing, but I knew it must be the cats, the cats whose Irish Faerie Queen I had just met, the Faerie Queen Maggie, Our Lady of Shallots.

I wanted to look up at the side of Harrow, half expecting to see my grandfather there (as I had when I was a little boy), standing at the window of the turret room, watching me as if I were the most important thing in the world to him.

I say "I wanted to" because part of me was fearful that he might be there, that he had somehow not left Harrow, that he had called me back to him even in death, and that I would look up at the window and see him there, glowing in some ghostly white smoke, and I would feel a chill and never sleep in Harrow again. It was juvenile of me, I know—but the fear had crept into me as I returned to the house, and I dared not look up at that window.

It became very real to me at that ungodly hour of the morning that I must not look up at the window, because what if I saw him there—what if he were still there—what if I could never live in Harrow without sensing his presence, for good or ill, at every turn, every remembered instant?

Finally, I looked up to the turret, overcoming my silly fear, knowing that he would not be standing at the window, watching me.

What I saw felt more shocking. More violent. More jarring, in some indescribable way.

I saw that the window of that room no longer existed.

Brick and mortar had filled the place where the window should have been. I imagined that I had remembered it wrong, that my grandfather had never stood there looking down at me, that the window itself had never existed, but that what had seemed a tower window had been sealed since its beginning.

Chapter Two

1

I, the one you know as Ethan, am writing this account of that time at Harrow as a warning to you. It is the year 2000, and it is a wonder I can write—or think—or breathe—at all, as my nurse says.

I am in my room. I am ancient—I feel ancient, anyway. The body is a vehicle for consciousness, one supposes. My brain still has its daily fevers. My hands curl in pain at times, but I will keep writing for whoever comes after. I still smoke unfiltered cigarettes, rolled for me daily. I defy Mr. Death to come take me, although I know Mr. Death will arrive soon enough.

Still, another smoke, a sip of thick coffee, spattered with cinnamon and nutmeg, and I will write more in my journal of that early time at Harrow.

I am now looking back on what I considered the prime of my life, although I was probably just around the curve of it at twenty-nine—for I would soon grow serious with the shadows that emerged from Harrow.

I have lived through wars and peace and technological furies the likes of which I could not imagine in my youth; I am more than one hundred years old. Can you imagine what I saw then? The wonders in the sky—for we had begun what was then a miracle, called Air-Mail, by which an airplane could transport packages and letters from one end of the country to another in a few days, whereas it would take weeks for letters to travel before this marvelous change. And the radio—I was completely mesmerized by it, would even close the newspaper with my beloved Krazy Kat and the funny pages to listen to the news of the world or the broadcast of a boxing match. And the movies! I was in Harrow one night only and already wished that I could rush out to one of the great movie palaces in Manhattan to catch the latest Charlie Chaplin.

Certainly, we had terrors in the world then. We had the fears and paranoia of menaces and foreign evils, we had serial killers the likes of which would curl your hair, we had all the good and bad that is forgotten and years later sifted through for moments to be relished as quaint and sentimental. There never has been an innocent time in human history—I suppose Harrow, in many ways, stood for that idea alone. There was no innocence in the world, and to pretend so is to bring a veil across one's face and never look beyond it. The 1920s was no golden age; it was no calm before the storm. We even had boredom and craziness. It was a different time, another world; it was beyond anything you can probably imagine, you who are alive and reading this now; and yet, I tell you, it resembled this world now, near enough to the birth of yet another century. These were the years I felt most alive. They were imperfect years; they were years of absolute confusion for me, between the end of my marriage, the losses of both my parents, and the loss of my distant but beloved grandfather. But they were my years, and I won't give them up without a struggle.

These were the years I often return to in order to feel that breath on my face again, that tender kiss of all life takes from us as we grow beyond what life is meant to allow us.

Yes, I have been accused of clinging to life—but why shouldn't I?

Yes, I return in my mind to my discovery of Harrow, my ownership of it, my legacy.

But in those days, I was young in that way in which the last year of one's twenties is still young. I was nearly as young as the century itself.

Do you know the Hudson River and its beauty? Have you been there?

I imagine the beginnings of Watch Point and Harrow—not when it became known as Camden's Hundred under a Dutch-English family—but in those eras going further into prehistory. The glacial movement created the worm-holes that became the river thousands of years ago; the primeval forest grew, the strange creatures that inhabited that realm arrived, the valley flourished. And then, something happened. Nothing cataclysmic, but something happened, and the land where the house would be built acquired a sense of being unclean.

There is even a story—though no doubt created by some local wit—that Henry Hudson paused somewhere on his exploration of the river that would later bear his name, and mentioned, "This is a very bad land to fall with, and an unpleasant land to see." He was, according to local wags of Watch Point—none of whom are to be believed in this—referring to the property that would become Harrow. In the 1620s, the Dutch West India company sent families to settle the river. Watch Point was largely overlooked, owing, it was suggested, to the way it jutted into the water and of the menace of the natives in the area.

When the land that became Watch Point was first known, it was settled by Mahanowacks, a variant spelling of what we know as Mohican, but nonetheless, this group was distinct and more closely related to the nearby tribe known as the Wappings and somewhat related to the Schaghticokes. The Mahanowacks were distinct from the other tribes of natives in that they were not welcoming to the invader.

Warlike and unwilling to transact business with the Dutch, the Mahanowacks along the river by Watch Point ended up being massacred in an event that was all but erased from the history books. Some of the survivors, no doubt, went up the river to join the tribes of Mohicans, some went east to share space with the Pequots and the Mohegans (again, a separate but similar group), others west across the river. Many were killed and one can only suppose this killing took place near Harrow.

This is purely my own conjecture from what I know

now about the property and from my grandfather's collection of artifacts.

But I won't get ahead of myself.

It was 1926 when I arrived, and it was October, and my body was still strong and invulnerable, and my hair was thick and dark and my skin was perhaps too pale except where it was ruddy around my face, and I didn't know that the feeling of being young would ever end. My first full day at Harrow, I woke up late in the morning surrounded by such luxury as I had never seen before.

I truly was Ethan then.

Think of me thusly: Ethan with his snobbish up-bringing; his outmoded ideas of women and wealth and his silly fears of what will come and what might come to pass; Ethan with his thoughts that are not thoughts at all, but the accumulated grease and gunk of a mind filled with the emptiness around him. Ethan, with his then-strong body, from playing tennis and what little boxing instruction he'd had at school. Ethan: a man who I would not necessarily like were I to meet him today, but in those days, he represented the least of society's ills—an inheritor, a man without accomplishment, a man who had spent his entire young life "getting out of the way of things."

Harrow, I believe, taught him much.

Harrow changed him. I can see myself as him now; I can slip down into that world gone by and watch him move through it, unaware of what waits for him.

I will tell you of him as if he were not me at all. As if he were there, within a dream, living in Harrow—

watch him as he sleeps, now, watch him in that dreadful place. . . .

2

The drapes around his bed were shut. At first, when he opened his eyes, Ethan had the sensation of being buried alive. He had dreams of being entombed like this when he was younger, and in times of stress, the dreams often returned.

It was an unpleasant feeling, to say the least, but one he knew was pure fantasy on his part. The curtaining about the enormous bed was wall-like and seemingly impenetrable—thick, red velvet drapes. Above his head, a large mahogany monstrosity that arched from the four posts, in which were carved snakes entwined with vines and a rabbit or other small creature.

The mattress was stuffed with eiderdown and did not bend as had his cheap bed at his equally cheap apartment in New York; instead, it felt thick and fat and it seemed to conform to his body perfectly. He felt rich for the first time in his adult life.

Rich as a king, for a moment anyway, although he knew that the books of the estate would need some serious going-over, but the fantasy was in his head. He imagined the women who would throw themselves at him, his ex-wife calling to express remorse, the shirts he would buy as had Jay Gatsby in the recent novel by Fitzgerald; in fact, he very much felt like Gatsby, lying beneath a ton of covers and sheets with the musty smell of unlaundered luxury surrounding him.

Harrow was his domain; Ethan Gravesend was king here; he could do anything now with his life. He could pursue the dreams he'd always had of . . . And then, grinning, he pressed the half dreams from his mind. Ethan heard a bird singing, somewhere beyond the red drapes that enshrouded the bed.

He pulled off the sheets, feeling sticky and overslept. He sat up, feeling that awful scratchiness of still occupying the shirt that he'd worn for nearly twenty-four hours before going to bed; he remembered—vaguely—crawling up the stairs, dizzy and sleepy, and nearly able to fall asleep at the top step, but managing to find—as if by magic—a bedroom with candles lit and a bed waiting. His throat dry and his stomach growling, he tore open the smothering drapes.

The light was blinding for a moment; the sunlight blasted him. When his eyes adjusted to the light, he saw from the open window of the bedroom that he must have slept right through the best of the day.

It was noon.

Mrs. Wentworth stood in the doorway—no, she blocked it with her form, bedecked in a long dark dress of somber demeanor. She was, he assumed, still in mourning, and these were widow's weeds she had donned, but this mourning was one accompanied by food.

She had probably been waiting for the new master of Harrow to rise since dawn. On a small table beside the door to the room: a plate of cold fried eggs and a pot of no-doubt lukewarm coffee. She had one of the most suspicious looks he'd ever seen on a human being. Ethan was on his feet, feeling a curious draft now that he was free of the bed.

He realized in seconds that she glared at him not (merely) out of impatience, anger, and general contempt:

He was naked from the waist down.

3

He made it to the elegant bathroom at the end of the hall in seconds—in fact, he ran from the bedroom as fast as his embarrassment could carry him.

Still, he laughed too loudly while sponging off a hangover and its subsequent splitting headache. The claw-footed tub was large and shaped like a swan (his grandmother's touch). The faucets were, if not gold, then some remarkable imitation of gold. He sat in the steamy tub for nearly half an hour, unsure as to whether he could ever face Wentworth again.

The memory of the look on her face, a mixture of wincing and sneering and lower lip protrusion, her eyelids trying to close but something in her horror not allowing them to do so, her absolute shock that Justin Gravesend's grandson should sleep without a generous nightshirt—who knows what had gone through her small brain at that moment?

She had turned away quickly to look out the window overlooking the front drive, and would not turn around again. As he bathed, for all he knew, she remained there, looking out that window.

The thought of Wentworth's shock kept him in good humor through the rest of the day.

Bathed, shaved, and dressed in a baggy pair of woolen slacks held up by suspenders and a rumpled white shirt with the collar half free from its buttons, Ethan managed to scare Wentworth less an hour later when he went down to give her a more formal greeting.

He spent the better part of an hour wandering the house, looking at the many paintings along the walls—from images of Joan of Arc to what might've been Anne Boleyn (had she been fair and bearing a remarkable resemblance to St. Joan) to great portraits of his grandfather as a middle-aged man and his grandmother as a young woman. The house had everything he remembered and had loved in childhood. This included his favorite rocking horse, which seemed to be in working condition even though he would have destroyed it had he sat in its back and rocked away the idle hours between naps and snacks and games; and then he saw in the upstairs parlor, the portrait he had always considered the "child in the wall."

4

It was a painting of a toddler in some kind of medieval costume. Ethan's father had told him it was his grandfather's insanity, this obsession with Old World fakery. But as a little boy, Ethan had seen the picture as a mirror into another world. He had imagined his own adventures behind the wall with the child depicted in that frame. And then he remembered the turret room and the window that was now bricked over.

He walked to the west wing, crossing the long corridor his mother had dubbed the Pont d'Avignon, and ascended the curved stairs. Ethan felt the autumn chill here—this part of the house was the coldest. He set his hand lightly along the wall as he went and felt a moist frost on the stone. When he arrived at the arched door to the turret, it was locked. He reached into his trouser pocket, withdrawing the master key—which was supposed to unlock every door in Harrow—but it did not fit in the small keyhole.

Not being one to take "no" from an inanimate object, he began pushing his shoulder into the door; finally ramming it until he was sure he'd dislocated a bone or two. Then he tried fiddling with the knob to try and dislodge the lock.

The door and lock held.

5

"A key?" Wentworth repeated his question without a blink. "To the tower?"

"It's locked," Ethan said. Twice.

"I wouldn't know about that," she said, her voice becoming innocent and nearly girlish. "But that Maggie, she's sticky with keys. She'd know, I'm sure."

"You mean, you don't have all the keys to the kingdom, Mrs. Wentworth?"

Ethan had caught her in the garden, where she had been busy shooing off the feral cats with a stiff broom. "They're the vermin of the world," she said. "And I don't care a fig if they eat mice. I can't stand them."

He persuaded Wentworth to sit with him on one of the stone benches and talk for a minute or two. She had seemed happy to relieve the burden of her feet, and he asked her first about the keys, and then about Maggie.

"I met her out here last night," he said, sensing that Wentworth would bristle at this bit of information.

"By moonlight, no doubt. That one is like these cats, sir," she said, her voice full of authority.

He could tell that she had a flood of stories about Maggie Barrow and her wildness and her scandalous behavior, but he managed to quiet her fairly quickly by saying, "I liked her. She seemed a decent sort, even if she was raiding the shallots."

"Well," Wentworth finally said after a minute or two of agitated silence. Her voice seemed to shrink into a whisper. "I suppose she's the sort that men like."

"And what exactly do you mean—" Ethan began to say: *by that bit of slander,* but let it fade.

He apparently had not lately thrown a virgin to the volcano goddess, because in short order his grandfather's housekeeper erupted in a lava flow of red, fiery vitriol.

"Fallen woman," "bad sort," "devil's harlot," "Irish wanton," "dangerous and unstable," and many other phrases came from the woman's lips. Toads of foulness seemed to leap forth from Wentworth's tongue.

47

Ethan sat there, not knowing whether to laugh or spit. He wanted to tell her that, yes, in fact, she was making Maggie Barrow seem like the most interesting woman in the universe to him at that moment, but part of his being burned with anger at this small-minded biddy and her overly imaginative mind.

When she quieted again—the lava had cooled, the volcano that was Wentworth had gone empty—she said, "And you shouldn't wander here at night."

He nodded. "It's my home now."

"It's still his home," Wentworth said, sighing. She had spewed her venom, and now she was satisfied. "He can't leave it."

Ethan let this go. He looked at her, her round form, her world that was all roundness and curves and beveled views, and realized that despite that, she was all sharp edges. A knife masquerading as a spoon.

Finally, he said, as tenderly as he could, "If you dare speak of Maggie Barrow in that tone again in my presence, Wentworth, you will not only never set foot again in this house, but I will hound you to the end of your days so that no household ever allows you in again."

He looked over at the statue of the beautiful angel, and for a moment he was distracted—her face seemed as one he had once seen. He wasn't sure where or when, but he was convinced he had met that woman depicted in the stone figure. Ethan was about to say something to Wentworth about it, but had the distinct feeling that she was staring at him as if he had just thrust her hands in boiling oil.

48

He glanced at her and saw that his sense of this was fairly close to the truth.

She trembled with some unspoken rage. He reached over and touched the back of her left hand. He said, "Why don't you take the rest of the day off, Wentworth. I can manage from here."

"Yes, sir," she said, her volcanic spirit returning. She stood, stiff as a pitchfork, the scent of kitchen-sweat wafting around her like honey from a greasy beehive. "Mind if I offer one word, sir?"

He shrugged. He had been too harsh with her, and he regretted it. She was getting on in years. She had recently lost the man Ethan had no doubt she had loved and cared for—his grandfather.

She might even be out of a job soon—he was sure she feared this the most. He was something of a milque-toast when it came to women, particularly motherly types. In fact, when Madeleine had begun reading the funny papers, which he had loved, she started calling him Caspar Milquetoast for the cartoon character whenever he gave in to her—and she was right.

So while he was angry with Wentworth for her tirade against a most-likely innocent Maggie Barrow, Ethan felt awful for causing this elderly woman a moment's difficulty. Perhaps this all came from his early training as a nurse to his mother (Freud's theories were beginning to take hold in those years), who was ill so much; perhaps, as his father had once suggested, he wasn't enough of a man to stand up to what his father often called "the fairer sex who can't be depended upon for anything."

49

But then, Ethan's father was a bit of a bastard. Not in the literal sense, but he was the kind of man that men who belonged to clubs admired and to whom women were attracted for all the unhealthy reasons. And still, Ethan loved the memory of his father and mother, and if any can tell why it is we love those who often are the worst sorts for us, you will become the most famous human being in history. But Mrs. Wentworth—before she stomped off to go to her place in the village—her voice not without a tremble, but still very much full of disgust, let loose again:

"Your grandfather was a difficult man and a demanding one. While you may not like my words for the Barrow girl, you will soon see just what she is made of. Men may like women like that, but I can tell you, she is an affront to those of us who live by decent and respectable standards. And she's not a God-fearing woman, neither. Several of the village believe she's a . . ."

"She's a what?" he asked.

"She's a witch," Wentworth said.

6

For an early supper before dark, Ethan walked the quarter mile to the village and settled in for a meal at a local café called The Dog & Rabbit. On his way, he felt the stares and heard the whispers of that peculiar breed of Watch Pointian who were beginning to look less peculiar to him by the minute.

Shopkeepers in doorways actually nodded and said

good afternoon to him as if he were an old friend. A girl of sixteen asked him why he drove such an old jalopy if he was so rich like his crazy grandfather (so, obviously, in the past twenty-four hours, Ethan Gravesend had drawn some small notice on arrival—perhaps Wentworth or Maggie had already begun gossiping).

The pub—or café as it was discreetly called, although it very much looked like a small tavern with tables and a long bar that the inhabitants of the place called "the counter"—was full of local rowdies and old men, all pretending that there was no beer to be had on the premises.

Taking a stool at the counter, Ethan watched the interchange that soon took on the unreality of a play in a theater, a drama being performed for some invisible audience.

A man in his mid-forties, wearing a woolen cap meant for a much younger man, lit two cigarettes. One was for himself, one for the owner of the place (a stout and red-cheeked fellow, bald of head and big of smile), who took it and smoked a minute.

The owner then said, in an overly loud voice, "Well, Jimmy, looks like I need to go to the basement for some more tomatoes," and "Jimmy" replied, "Aw, Bill, you don't need no more tomatoes, not again?" to which "Bill" said, "We can't make a good sauce without the tomatoes, now, can we Jimmy?" and after a few more shows of tomato necessity, Bill and Jimmy nodded to each other.

Jimmy left the café. He returned a few minutes later with a crate covered with a blanket. He set this on a table. Then Bill swaggered over and sat down. Other customers gathered around Bill as well. Soon, everyone had coffee mugs of what could only be tomato sauce.

But a woman remarked, "This is the best batch of sassyfrass yet!"

"It is superb tea," a man added.

Ethan, curiosity getting the better of him in addition to his thirst, went over and was allowed—for an exchange of coins—a mug filled to the brim with some very fine brew. It was an ale that was dark amber and reminded him—with the first sip—of fresh river water with a bite.

The play that had been enacted would have been laughed at in New York City, where speakeasies were everywhere, and even little old ladies knew where a good bottle of hooch could be had.

But here in Watch Point he was to learn that this was a curious little drama that Bill and Jimmy reenacted more than twice a day. It was for the benefit of the local constable, a wizened little man named Pocket. He had no other name but Pocket, and it was said with a bit of a sarcastic twist to it whenever villagers mentioned the name.

Pocket, it appeared, would arrive unannounced at various establishments to make sure that Temperance and Prohibition was being followed to the letter of the law—and, either he was too dumb to notice the strong odor of ale in The Dog & Rabbit, or he preferred simply to be part of the drama and play the part of the Fool.

Between a cigarette or two, Ethan downed a few

mugs of what he soon learned to call sassyfrass tea (a code phrase, naturally, and pronounced precisely that way, with the *y* of irony planted within). He followed the quaffs with a dish they called the Henry Hudson Special. This consisted of a fat sizzling sausage with mashed potatoes reeking of butter and rosemary, and corn. Soon, sausage and ale within his belly, Ethan became as friendly as the next man at the bar, talking with strangers about tomatoes and sassyfrass tea and why Jimmy hadn't yet returned from another trip to the basement. Ethan had thought the people of the village odd all his life to that point, no doubt encouraged by his parents' prejudices about the village itself. But he began to feel a little more comfortable—the sassyfrass tea helped—and he warmed to the residents, even as the temperature began dropping and the sky clouded over. He had enjoyed the show that Bill and Jimmy had performed.

When Pocket had come in—looking older than even the hills—a policeman without a badge and only a whistle and a bludgeon to prove his profession—Ethan felt happily guilty, sipping the frothy tea and grinning along with the other patrons.

They were just like anyone, and what Ethan had mistaken for sealskin clothes (no doubt first imagined as a child), were merely raincoats and mackintoshes and fisherman's garb—for he soon discovered that it rained a lot in Watch Point. It rained a lot there on summer afternoons when he had visited as a young boy; it was, perhaps, the rainiest place on all the Hudson River. Part of him even wondered if the clouds themselves didn't just hang over the village, or if, in fact, Poughkeepsie and Cold Spring also got regular downpours.

Ethan was drenched, in fact, on the walk home.

7

Walking up the unpaved road to the stone wall was made ten times more difficult in a heavy downpour.

Ethan kept to the ferny edges of the drive so as not to sink into the quagmire of mud and muck. For the briefest moment, he was sure he caught sight of a small fawn among some trees. He chose to follow it rather than trudge through the thickening brown slush at his feet. The woods—which began to the south of Harrow and circled in a half moon around the property—were bursting with the sunlit amber and deep red of autumn, whose last canopies of about-to-fall leaves protected the somewhat dry ground.

Ethan navigated through the thin trees, watching for the fawn. As he drew closer to what had seemed a young deer, he saw it was some sort of—elf? He knew how foolish this was—this could not be an elf, but he was sure he was looking at a sprite of some sort, clad in a tawny coat and a cap of . . .

It was a child, of course. A little boy. His hat made of folded newspapers brought together in a triangle on his head. Ethan entertained the notion that this was himself as a child, running among the trees and flying across puddles and into mud. He'd had—as a child—imaginary friends in these woods and thickets

54

and the wonderful secret hideaways of his grandfather's magical house. It felt good to remember it.

The child had boots much too large for his feet. The word that came to Ethan's mind was "scruffy." The boy was scruffy and filthy with mud, and he looked as if he'd stolen his clothes from a much older boy. The boy didn't seem to notice Ethan, but something else disturbed him, and the boy began running as if his life depended on it. He fled through the dripping woods, across a puddle that had grown into a pond during the downpour. As he ran on, his paper hat flew off his head; Ethan went to grab it up for him.

It was beautifully constructed from the *Watch Point Register*, and the child had written the name "Alf" across it. Ethan followed him across the muddy lawn between stands of trees. The boy reached the edge of an ivy-smothered wall, its stones torn down at various points, and he leapt nimbly over it. Ethan called after him, "Your hat! You dropped it," but the child kept running.

The boy ran straight through an opening in a hedge to the caretaker's house.

8

The caretaker's cottage had been occupied by Oliver Palliser. Neither Oliver nor Palliser were part of his real name—a local Episcopalian priest had apparently baptized him before his age of reason, and had passed on the name of the family who had taken Palliser in as a baby. The groundskeeper had run from them at the age of fifteen, and had worked for Justin Gravesend since that day.

Oliver Palliser was part Mahanowack Indian. When Ethan had been a boy, Palliser had stayed as far away from him as he could without ever being completely out of sight. Justin Gravesend had told Ethan on many occasions that Palliser was the most trustworthy man in the world, and that his real name sounded something like "Candlemasseve" which made the young Ethan laugh because it brought to his childish mind images of candles in churches with Adam and Eve. The name meant "Hawk with Two Souls," a Mahanowack-Algonquian name, and had been his first—and real—name. Since Ethan also had two names, he didn't think that this was extraordinary—he was, after all, both Esteban and Ethan, himself.

Ethan, in all those years, had never thought of the groundskeeper as Oliver, but that is how most knew him. The man had lived on the grounds of Harrow for many years. He no longer lived there. Ethan had been informed of this in a letter from the lawyer who had handled the inheritance. "Mr. Palliser has, of his own volition, moved on and vacated the property in question," the attorney had written. "He left no indication of where he has gone, but there is a small token from your grandfather, left to Mr. Palliser, with some papers. Should he return or make himself known to you, contact my office at once so that we might send him the materials in question."

Oliver Palliser's name was still engraved at the threshold of the caretaker's house. In nearly every respect, he had owned it, and my grandfather had had it built specifically for him.

9

It was not quite five o'clock, and sometime in the past ten minutes the dark had begun sinking into the pouring sky like black ink across a gray-washed watercolor. The swampy smell of too much rain and the river smell of fish and rotting trees came up. Ethan could not wait to get inside the cottage to get out from under the endless water that seemed to bear down upon him.

Inside the cottage, it was silent, except for the sound of rain on the rooftop. "Hallo," he said in the echoing corridor. The cottage was dusty; it looked like it hadn't been lived in—ever. He stood in the open doorway and craved a cigarette, but as he drew a pouch of tobacco from his pocket, he found that it was soaked.

"Hallo," Ethan called out again. Again, the silence within, the crack of thunder and rain without. The house was dark. He began to sense something within it. A bad feeling. What he had learned to call a "badsmell," though it was no smell at all. It was more a sense. Dropping the paper hat in the doorway, Ethan stepped back into the rain, out of the cottage.

He ran back up the drive to Harrow, to brood and reflect, and to wonder where his life would go from here.

10

Stepping over the threshold into Harrow, Ethan saw a brief flash of smoke along the stairs.

Something was on fire. With all the candles constantly burning, he was sure something had caught fire while he was out.

He dashed for the staircase, drawing off his wet jacket to douse any flames. As he took the first step up, Ethan saw, not smoke or fire, but what seemed like a frost in the air, or thickened chalk dust hanging in an unnatural stillness.

In the next second, it was no longer there, and in its stead was a young child—not the boy he had seen running among the trees, but another.

A strange child. A little girl. She looked at him for a moment as if she recognized his face. She had some kindness and giggly look in her eyes, as if she had just seen a bunny or had hidden her mother's slipper as a game. She opened her mouth wide and a sound came from her throat the like of which he had never before heard—

The frost returned to the air. Ethan felt himself freezing. This place was full of badsmell, too. The foyer filled with the stink of something rotting—of meat left out in some terrible sun—passing through the icy breath along the staircase. The storm outside began howling, or perhaps the child herself howled.

From the corner of his eyes, Ethan saw what seemed to be a snow-whiteness gathering, moving toward the girl. He began to feel afraid for her. He tried to reach her, but the whiteness spread swiftly—not a mist, not a cloud, but it was as if some invisible hand were erasing the world in front of his eyes, leaving it pure white. The whiteness traveled toward her, and as it touched her, she, too, began to erase from before him—

And someone whispered in his ear, "Welcome home." The badsmell grew smothering, and it brought back something, something he had wanted to forget in all those years, something he had found once at Harrow but could not identify, something full of the badsmell, a place within the house, reeking with badsmell, and as a child he had written it in chalk on the walls, *badsmellbadsmellbadsmellbadsmell*, until his father had tugged him back and then the memory was gone.

And whispering to him now, some little girl, whispering something that felt obscene although it was nothing more than those two words, badsmell, repeated in quick succession as if this were some game.

The front door to Harrow slammed shut.

The lock turned—all locks clattered in turning in Harrow at once—all doors, locking—all windows, closing—all candles, snuffing.

A lullaby began playing from some upstairs chamber.

Darkness embraced him.

Chapter Three

1

Here's the thing about darkness:
  It turns the mind inward.

2

The music of the lullaby ended; the darkness grew.

As Ethan stood at the locked door within Harrow, feeling the chill of winter's breath, he knew that there was something within himself that had already frozen.

Some shadow within his flesh was locked away, just as the house's locks had suddenly turned in on themselves.

It was a momentary flash of insight.

What came to him—as a trickle of fear spread into a glacial movement in his blood—was the image of his mother in her wheelchair. She sat at the top of the stairs in the house on the Cape. The voice of the doctor in some distant room, calling her back to him, but not as a doctor would—as someone else, some other person who would call a woman back from a staircase.

For a moment, he had seen his young mother begin to rise from the wheelchair, and then hesitate when she saw her son with his toy at the bottom of the staircase.

In that flash of remembrance in the uneasy darkness of Harrow Ethan felt as if he had been haunted since the day he was born.

His own breathing brought him back to the shadows of Harrow.

The shutters had closed on the windows in the foyer. The battering of the storm outside the walls ceased. Everything was night within.

The inhuman squeal of the little girl on the stairs abated, yet he could still hear the words in his head:

Badsmellbadsmellbadsmell.

He heard a thumping sound, as of a ticking clock. He stood as still as he could. Afraid to move. He imagined the touch of insects along his ankles, the gentle tickling strokes of tiny spiders along his hands.

A smell came up—not of anything foul, but of a rich cherry wood, as if it were burning in the fireplace, and then a damp odor, but not the dampness of the rain, but as if there were some drain, clogged with standing water.

Imagining things.

He was tired. Maybe it was the ale he'd had. Maybe it was the threat of some madness, the same madness that his father was sure had been Justin Gravesend's madness.

The thumping grew louder.

62

It's my own heart. It's the sounds within my body, he realized too soon. He could hear the swoosh of blood as his temples throbbed. His stomach began making noises. The loudness of them—within his body—grew deafening as any storm.

Minutes passed as he stood there. The panting of some great wolf became the sound of his throat. He swallowed nervously, and it was as if buckets of water had been poured along a tin roof.

It's in my body. Whatever it is that was here. It's inside me. I can feel it.

It was warmer than he had expected—the feeling that something had entered him, was perhaps even looking out through his eyes, was counting his heartbeats, feeling his breath, tasting the fear within him.

And then, it all went silent again.

It was as if someone had taken some kind of radio and pressed it inside his body, amplifying the sounds, and then pulled the radio microphone out again, switching it off.

Something was coming down the stairs. It slapped the carpeted steps like a ball, bouncing against each one, then continued its noisy descent.

His eyes adjusted a bit to the dark. He saw the edges of things—the light beneath doorways, the paper cuts of lightning through the slats in the shutters, and some kind of low ambience to the house itself. He could only distinguish the shadows of sculpture and furniture.

But the ball—for that is surely what it must have been—kept bouncing down toward him, toward the bottom of the stairs. The sound echoed through the hall.

And then, another break into silence.

He again heard the crack of thunder outside Harrow, beyond the shuttered windows.

It's over. The thought came to him.

Whatever this was, it's over now. His own thoughts seemed to whisper outside of his body.

I am alone.

It's gone.

The thought came: *She's gone. She was here, whoever she is. She was here at the stairs, and she's gone.*

He stood there in the darkness. Relief and warmth flooded through his being. He felt as a man who had been pushed to the edge of some precipice, and now could step back from it.

He had not moved from the bottom of the staircase the entire time.

Perhaps only ten minutes had passed.

Something reasonable and logical within him told him that this was some brief collapse of reality projected outward. The candles had gone out because a draft from the storm had swept through the house. This was possible.

Wentworth had no doubt shuttered the house, knowing of the oncoming storm.

Perhaps even Maggie Barrow had doused the candles at some point. Maggie might even be in the kitchen for all he knew, cleaning the range or upstairs, dusting the bedrooms.

You're exhausted. You've had a hellish year. Your circumstances have changed.

Everything has changed. Family memories are coming back. Things you've forgotten. Things you

*wanted to keep buried within your childhood. This is
why you thought you saw this.*

He thought of calling out to Maggie *(she might be
here, and she might be upstairs working on some
room, and she might laugh at you for being scared of
the storm and the dark, and this would feel good)*, but
some instinct kept him silent.

After a brief moment of getting used to the sounds
of the rain outside and the silence within Harrow,
Ethan coughed.

As if an alarm had been set off, suddenly the locks
in the doors clicked, and the front door flew open. All
the shutters opened at once and began beating against
the windows. The doors all around the house opened
and closed against the doorframes. The sound of the
beating doors and shutters was unbearable, and he
wanted to scream.

*Don't scream. It wants you to scream. It wants to
see you be scared. Don't let it see you be scared.*

In a flash of lightning, he saw the little girl, standing so near him she could touch him.

3

Her eyes were bloodshot and wild. Her hair, a tangle
of mud and weed. Some torn and filthy cloth wrapped
around her small body. She lifted her face to his, and
parted her cracked lips.

A howl came from her throat.

Her breath froze midair, a cold wind in a cave, and
she reached out to touch him, but when she did—

4

It was over.

He felt a brief nausea; his eyes burned as if sand had been pressed into them; his tongue was dry; and his hands itched as if with the pinpricks of falling asleep.

The light came up on the wall sconces; the lamps seemed to find their small blue flames again. The door behind him remained open as it had been when he had crossed the threshold, letting rain pour in, as it must have for several minutes, because the front entryway was covered with water.

He wasn't sure—and he never would be sure, he told himself—but it seemed as if some kind of shifting had gone on.

It was like a magic trick he had once seen on the streets of Manhattan, some kind of shell game. A coin had been put beneath one shell and appeared, after some manipulations on the part of a magician, under another shell. It was as if a sleight of hand had been introduced into his consciousness.

He'd felt the shift, from the feeling of the little girl standing near enough to touch him, to this moment of evening and rain and the open door behind him.

As if the house itself were a magician, moving the shells.

5

"Perhaps you imagined it," Maggie Barrow said when he told her.

But that wasn't until later the next day.

6

Ethan had opted to spend the night at a local inn, rather than sleep in the curtained bed at Harrow.

He was, after all, as he told himself, rich now, and could afford the best room at the local place. The inn was not fancy, nor was it expensive, but he got what was called the Honeymoon Room "with two hot water bottles" for less than the price of dinner in Manhattan. The following morning was less than luxurious, with a breakfast that was mostly burnt. After coffee and eggs that tasted like they'd been mixed together, he realized that he was too old to be worried about some hallucination—some imagining—that might've been brought on by Watch Point's famous sassyfrass tea, after all.

As the hours passed, he became less and less sure that he'd seen what he had thought he'd experienced. He'd spent the morning hiking along the hills above the river, and then returned to find Wentworth in a mood once again.

She did not want to hear about what he had gone through the previous night. She did not want to discuss anything about any possible strangeness in the house. She was halfway between heartbroken and furious, and she managed to stop up his mouth with her own tirade about how the dishes had all broken in the china cabinets.

"The good china dishes, the china that my Badger brought back with him on his trips. The china," she added, her eyes narrowing, "that he meant for me to have, if only he'd lived long enough."

Wentworth words pelted him like stones, and she could not be calmed in any respect. She kept having fits about the dishes, and about the beautiful crystal glasses that had been haphazardly piled "like wood for the fireplace!"

"My god," Ethan had said to the empty kitchen after Wentworth had stormed out of the house, nearly in tears for her broken china. "My world is now reduced to Wentworth."

But then, there was Maggie. She was a little less concerned with the china than with the idea of a ghost.

"But it's crazy," he said, nearly wringing his hands, pacing back and forth on the Persian rug.

Maggie busily washed out the great fireplace in the study. She had passed him a rag. ("If you're going to jabber at me while I'm cleaning, you may as well be of some use," she'd told him.) She wore a long dark work dress, covered by an apron much too large for her. Her red hair fell thickly along her shoulders, curling like tongues of fire, he thought.

"You should always wear it down," he said, forgetting that he had said it aloud for a moment. "Your hair, I mean. It's . . . nice."

"If I were smart," she replied, "I'd chop it all off and sell it as a wig and quit this job once and for all. Now tell me again. You saw our ghost, and she did what?"

"She howled. She said things. It's a jumble. I can't remember how it went," he said, nearly stammering. Then he added, "Our ghost?"

Maggie sat back, her apron blackened with soot. "You're not crazy, if that's what you're thinking. People have seen spirits here before. Harrow's haunted. Everyone in the village knows it."

7

Ethan asked her what must've felt like ten thousand questions, although only one really stuck out for him later: He was not the first to see spirits within the house his grandfather built? There was a history of people finding psychic disturbances there? How was he to know this? His father had never told him. While alive, his grandfather had never hinted at that sort of thing. Ethan didn't even believe in ghosts. Even "seeing" was not believing for him. Still, he listened to what Maggie told him, her Irish brogue dimming every now and then where the English side of her family had taken hold.

"The little girl," she said. "She might be little Matilde, your grandparents' daughter who had died while young. She was buried out in the crypt along Bald Hill, and it was said—by the few who had seen her, including that wild man Palliser—"

"The caretaker," Ethan confirmed.

Maggie barely missed a beat. "That she returned to the house now and then to look for her parents. It's really rather a sweet story."

Ethan found this thought less disturbing as Maggie

talked on and on about what the villagers said of Harrow, and of Justin Gravesend.

"People in the village said your grandfather was evil. Well," Maggie snorted derisively. "He was not evil, like they said. He had a lot of love within him. He had secrets, as well. Even Mrs. Wentworth warned me not to work for him, for he had shipments for years from foreign ports—India, Africa, and even Jerusalem."

"Jerusalem?" Ethan asked.

She nodded, laughing. "I never saw any of this. It was merely what I was told. All I've seen are the wash pots and the kitchen for the most part. I've never even seen our ghost."

"You keep referring to it as 'our ghost,'" he said. "As if it's a joke. Do you believe in ghosts?"

She became quite serious on this point. "I do. I believe in spirits." And then she began laughing until her face was red.

"What's so funny?"

"Nothing, nothing," she said. "It's just something someone dear to me told me once."

"My grandfather?"

"All right. It was about how all the servants working here have been scared off over the years. All except me and old Wentworth. He said it was because Wentworth was greedy and wanted treasure."

"And to what do you owe your longevity?"

"I'm an outcast," she said, half smiling. "I've got nothing to lose." Then she picked up her mop bucket and went toward the door to the kitchen. She truly looked fetching with the *clop clop clop* of her work shoes and the way she moved—like she didn't give a damn if a man stared at her or not. "I've only been working here for a year. I haven't met the ghost yet."

8

"And the key, Maggie?" he asked her just before she was to leave for the afternoon. She had taken her apron and skirt and thrust them into her wholly unattractive black stockings (wrapped about wholly attractive calves), and kept scrubbing the upstairs bath because she claimed that "someone's left a ring of filth in it from his bath."

"The key, Maggie," he repeated.

"What key?" she snapped. "And I told you—I'm not Maggie to you, sir. I am Mrs. Barrow, and I expect to be treated with some respect even if I do wash your dirty linens." The sweat on her brow made her pale skin shine, and she looked nearly ferocious with her lips curled. "If you're going to interrogate me, then here—" she passed me yet another wet rag—"wash the basin."

"That basin?"

"The sink," she said, as if he were the dumbest man she had ever met.

Ethan looked at the rag with its drippings of soap rinsing across his fingers, and then looked at the sink. He shrugged.

Since he was so used to cleaning his own bathroom at the dingy little apartment down in the city, he had been feeling nearly embarrassed to watch Maggie on her knees, half bent over the tub, scraping away at dirt he'd left in it from the day before.

71

"Keys, is it? The Keys to the Kingdom of Harrow, one would suppose." She noticed his lackluster washing around the sink, and she let out a gentle laugh. "I suppose that passes for washing in the smart set."

Once Ethan had begun scrubbing a little harder with the mixture of soap she'd brought from the cellar, she muttered something as if it were like spitting poison.

"Didn't catch that," he said.

This time, she nearly roared. "You're talking about Wentworth if you're talking stolen keys."

"She said you were the one sticky with keys," he blurted, and then wished he could force the words right back into his mouth again.

Maggie dropped her rag in the tub. She reared back on her haunches, and then stood, almost reaching his chest. She pointed a finger at the top button of his shirt. He could almost see steam come from her nose and ears. "Sticky with keys. Ha! She's the one who can't seem to keep keys off her fingers. She has all of 'em. She's supposed to turn them over to you. Why, that lyin' old . . . old . . ."

Then, she fell silent. Shaking her head, she let out another laugh. "I can't say's I blame her. She thinks she owns the place after the way he treated her."

"I wondered why she seems so . . . annoyed with me all the time." Maggie nodded, putting her hands on her hips. "She was called his Little Wife, you know. People called Wentworth his Little Wife and she'd blush when they did. It wasn't because of anything he did. It was Wentworth. She stole money sometimes from him, and she always had the keys to things. She acted like he was going to get down on his knees and propose to her any minute. He didn't trust her much, but he let the little thievings go on. I'm not sure why. When I was new here, I told him I saw her taking some money from his dresser, and he told me that that was fine. I never took a thing from the dear old man, but Wentworth had sticky fingers for everything." Then Maggie took a long hard look at him, one eye squinting as if she wanted to get into his brain. "What key is it you're precisely after?"

"The room in the west wing," Ethan said. "The tower. There's a window there. There used to be a window there," he corrected himself.

"Oh," she said. "Well."

Then, Maggie Barrow smiled, and he almost saw something like a devilish twinkle in her eyes.

9

"Come on," she said to him.

Ethan followed her, feeling far too much like a sheepdog tracking a much-smarter lamb. Passing through one of the secondary routes to the west wing (through the empty ghost towns of the servants' quarters, which were vast, as Justin Gravesend no doubt planned on having ten or so servants live and work at Harrow), they ended up at the arched door that led to the turret.

"Ever been up there?" he asked.

She shook her head. "I'm not the curious type." Maggie reached into a pocket of her apron and withdrew a long hat pin. "My uncle Francis was a good man for the most part, but he tended to lose his key when coming home late at night. He taught me a little trick he had, and being the obedient niece I was, I've never forgotten it. Where he got a lady's hat pin every night, I couldn't say." She twisted the pin slightly, and thrust it into the keyhole.

Ethan began asking her some irrelevant question just to fill the silence. She shushed him and bent down to press her ear against the keyhole.

Then, that wicked grin returning to her face, she straightened up. "Eureka," she said, and opened the door to a narrow staircase.

10

The steps were wooden, and creaked each time Ethan shifted his weight to climb. Maggie had procured a small lamp. She walked ahead of him, taking the stairs nearly two at a time.

"I can't believe I've never gotten in here before. Wentworth has always kept me in the east wing or downstairs," she said, her eagerness spilling over in her voice. "I love little mysteries."

In the light of the lamp she carried, Maggie looked like a glowing faerie, her red hair nearly ablaze with the light, and he was reminded of his first impression of her: The Lady of Shallots, the Faerie Queen of Harrow. When she reached the top step, she gave a little shriek of delight. "You should see it, good lord!"

Running up the steps behind her, he glanced over

her shoulder and felt a certain familiarity with the room.

It was mostly dark, but the lamplight glanced off the rows of candlesticks and two low tables, upon which a large painting was propped. The picture was of some saint.

As Maggie went around the spider-webbed room (pressing the strands of webs away from her face) she lit the candles. The light came up in the room slowly, and for a moment, it seemed that the candlelight would flicker down to nothing.

Ethan whispered, "He blocked it."

Then, the flames along the candles burned brighter, turning the small antechamber into a flickering dawn.

"What's that smell?" Maggie asked, wrinkling her face.

"Some kind of sulfur?" he guessed aloud.

He went to examine the painting of the saint. It was like none of the other icons his grandfather had owned. She was definitely holy, with her halo and her prayerful, somewhat mournful look. She had long golden braids, and her aspect was one of a beautiful peasant girl from centuries past. Joan of Arc as the Maid of Orleans? But the face was the same as the woman in the St. Joan portrait in the hallway, and it was nearly like the woman in the painting at the top of the stairs in the front hall of the house.

"It smells like dead rats," Maggie said. "Those cats had better not have some sneaky way of getting up here and leaving all their victims."

Ethan drew the painting down, and set it against the wall. The door behind where the painting had

75

rested was made of thick wood, and studded with nails and spikes.

"See? He blocked it. The door to the room," Ethan said. "Here, help me with this."

11

The door on the other side of the painting was also locked, and no amount of playing with the keyhole would open it.

"They've put glue in this, or clay, something to gummy it up," Maggie said, withdrawing a now nearly useless bent pin. The door's hinges were fastened with epoxy, and were also unmanageable. Large nails had been driven into the door, and bent rods—like brackets—had been stapled from the frame to the door itself.

"Someone genuinely did not want us to get in," Maggie said. "Do you think it's Wentworth hiding stolen goods?"

Finally, Ethan said, half joking, "What we need is a pickaxe."

"You really do want to get in that room, don't you?" Maggie asked, her hands on her hips as if she were about to launch into a speech about how crazy he was. But she looked at him with something that might've been admiration.

Ethan nodded. "As badly as my grandfather apparently wanted to keep me out."

"Well," Maggie said, setting her lamp down on a table. "I just happen to know where Mr. Gravesend always kept his pickaxes."

12

It was seven at night, and they emerged from the flickering room to a house that was half dark.

As they went together down the corridor of the west wing, Maggie made him promise not to be mad.

"Mad?" Ethan asked, and then grew suspicious. "What would I have to be angry about?"

She cocked her head to the side and looked at him as if seeing him for the first time. "You're a most unusual man, Mr. Gravesend." She turned about and continued down the steps to the next landing.

"Thank you," he said. "I suppose."

He had to move fast to keep up with her as she practically bounded down the stairs to the foyer in a decidedly unladylike fashion, and when he caught up with her, she began to look rather grave.

"All right, sir," she said. "I'll tell you the truth."

"You're a ghost, too." He laughed.

"No," she said, so seriously that he felt as if his heart were going to stop. "But here's the truth of things: I am not a married woman."

"Oh."

"There is no Mr. Barrow," she added.

"You're a widow."

"Well," she began, "in some ways, I suppose I am."

"What are you getting at?"

"Sir, be patient with me," she said, but he had to be patient all the way to the caretaker's cottage, where, she told him, there were axes of all kinds as well as hammers and saws and everything that could bring a door down.

Waiting there at the doorway to the room in the cottage that was filled with the hardware, Ethan saw the little boy again. The one who had just the day before worn a paper hat and had run through the mud to escape him. The child wore a pair of brown trousers cut all wrong for his height and weight, and an oversize white shirt with blotches of what was either tomato juice or blood. Ethan assumed the former. The boy stared wide-eyed at Ethan. Ethan had the peculiar sense that the boy felt he was in some kind of terrible trouble.

"Mr. Gravesend," Maggie said. "Meet Alfred. My son."

13

"I believe Alf and I have already met," Ethan said, offering his hand to the boy.

"He's an Alfred," Maggie said.

"Yes, Mrs. Barrow," Ethan agreed, adding the emphasis to the Mrs.

"Good to meet you, sir," Alf said, stepping forward like a puppy who had been caught piddling on the carpet.

"Alfred," Maggie said, shooting a glance between her son and Ethan. "You weren't playing ghost yesterday were you?"

"No," Alf said. "I was just playing in the woods. I didn't think . . ."

"I used to play in those woods when I was your

age," Ethan said, smiling. He took the boy's hand and shook it gently. "You got your hat back?"

Alf nodded, his eyes never leaving Ethan. "Thank you. Sir. Very much."

"He's shy." Ethan glanced at Maggie.

"My Alfred? Hardly," Maggie said.

"Alf, would you like to come help us break down a door?" Ethan clapped his hands together as if it was the most interesting scheme in the world.

14

It all was done with few words among them—what needed to be said was in the air and in a gentle telepathy that Ethan now felt. Some barrier had been broken. Ethan understood it in a glance, and he saw it in the little boy, too.

Maggie had been abandoned by someone, had raised her son on her own, and Justin Gravesend had, in most respects, taken care of her for the past year. She and her son had occupied the upstairs rooms at the empty caretaker's house; Wentworth had been ignorant of this because she had never bothered to go to the cottage, and Maggie had never volunteered it for fear of Wentworth's moralizing.

"She thinks you're a witch. Did you know that?" he asked, trudging the last steps with the heavy axe; Alf ran up ahead and proclaimed the room full of candles as the most mysterious and wondrous place he had ever seen.

"She thinks I'm the apocalypse," Maggie said.

Alf cried out that it smelled like an outhouse, only he used a less savory term, and his mother promptly raised a great hue and cry.

Ethan went in and swung the pickaxe at the door.

15

An hour later, the door was a brittle pile of splintered wood, and Alf began laughing. "You look funny!" he said, pointing at Ethan, his face thick with sweat.

Ethan set the pickaxe down, shaking his head.

Maggie put her hand lightly on his shoulder. "Now why would your grandfather do that?"

"I don't know," he said.

Behind the door: another wall of stone and brick.

16

"It's like he was locking something in there," Ethan said, and then wished he hadn't even thought it.

The smell was stronger here, with the door smashed away.

The badsmell was in his nostrils.

Don't think about it. Don't think of the little girl on the stairs, or the way something got beneath your skin and felt you—felt your pulse and your blood and your heart.

It was imaginary.

80

There's nothing bad behind the wall, he thought. *You're not alone. Others are here with you. It will be some foolish thing. Some room that Justin wanted to preserve. Nothing more.*

He hefted the pickaxe up again and motioned for Maggie and Alf to move away from him.

Then he swung the axe hard into the wall. Once. Twice. He kept swinging, determined to open the room that his grandfather had not wanted him to find.

Or perhaps, the thought snaked through his brain, *this was the very room he meant for you to discover.*

17

When it was over, Ethan sat down in the rubble.

He felt waves of nausea as dust and that awful smell overcame him.

Maggie brought her lamp forward, and said, "What could possibly be in here that smells like that?" She began coughing.

"It's a dead cat," Alf volunteered. "I'm sure of it. I smelled one in the field once. It was awful."

Ethan reached into his breast pocket and brought out a handkerchief, which he passed to Maggie. She covered her mouth with it. She took a step forward into the room. Ethan was about to tell her not to go any farther. He was sure it was not going to be good. He was sure there would be something there, in that dark room.

Some secret thing.

Meant only for you.
A gift from Grandpa.

"It might be bats," Alf whispered. "They live in places like this, I think."

Ethan didn't want to say it aloud, but it was obvious to him. From the look on Maggie's face, it must have been obvious to her, as well. Someone had died in this room.

Someone had walled the room shut.

Someone had nailed the door shut against the wall.

Someone had locked the entrance to the room, and then . . .

Maggie whispered "What's that? On the wall?" She stepped into the room, around the rubble, holding the lamp up, its flame casting a kaleidoscope of whites and blues along the stones.

Ethan arose, dusting himself off, and grabbed a candle. He motioned for Alf to remain behind.

Ethan stepped into the room with Maggie.

In the light, they could make out the scratch marks along the walls, as if a wild animal had been trapped inside.

A human handprint, burned into the brick.

Chapter Four

1

After a few moments of staring and waiting within the room, Maggie said, "It's gone."

Ethan felt distracted by a sense of something completely benign in the room. He heard Maggie's voice as if from a great distance, beneath water. It was as if he were swimming beneath the calm surface of a lake, and somewhere above, Maggie was looking down at him and saying something to him.

"What about you?" Maggie asked her son.

"Nothing," Alf said. "The stink's gone out."

Ethan felt the distance of some watery expanse. For just a second, he closed his eyes. The sense that came up to him, not like a dream at all but like the pinprick of reality, was that he had known he would be standing here, like this. Before. Years ago. Somehow he had known it, once upon a time, when he had been a little boy in the statue garden, looking up at his grandfather standing at the window that was no more.

2

He could recapture that moment: He was eight, he realized, and the world seemed fuzzy, as if he'd eaten something too sweet, or had too much tea. His stomach felt funny. He almost felt as if he would fall down.

The angel in the garden was with him. Her skin was so white it was like bone. He knew someone was at the window of the tower room. The scent of lilac and honeysuckle was in the air, and the yellowjackets of summer swarmed somewhere nearby, their buzzing growing ever louder, and she said (who was she? the angel?), *They live down below, and they come up now, they come up to find you, but do not be afraid.*

He glanced up to see his grandfather, not waving, but shouting and raising his fist—his grandfather was angry at him, but he didn't know why—and the fuzzy feeling kept swirling around him, and he heard her say (was it his mother? the angel?) *Esteban,* she whispered, *they've come to get your sweetness. All your sweetness, all the honey within you, all that you possess, they've come for it.*

You must never let them in, but they will try and get a taste if they can.

His grandfather had left the window, which was stained glass in the shape of a flower. Ethan had felt he could smell the flower in the glass, and that he could almost reach it, all the way from below in the garden. Moments later the old man had bounded out the doors by the conservatory.

Ethan had heard the humming grow louder along his

body. He felt an energy in the sticky heat. He felt something along his neck and arms and circling his ankles.

The thought had come to him: The universe is powered by some engine, and I am at the heart of it, right now. I am where the engine of the universe hums.

His grandfather had shouted to him, waving his arms, but Ethan had just stood there, and—*remembering himself as a little boy standing in the ivy, looking down at his bare feet and seeing the yellowjackets moving like brilliant fireflies around his legs, swarming across his throat, and then a darkness came as they covered his face and eyes. . . .*

3

Ethan, in Harrow, twenty-nine years old, opened his eyes a moment later.

Disorientation took the form of seeing a beautiful woman with red hair scolding a little boy with a shaggy mane, and then the words on the wall, flickering in the candlelight.

Help. Other words—whole sentences were written in white chalk around the room.

Ethan thought: I am here. I am not there. Not a little boy. That is the past. Somewhere in the past. Gone.

"Are you all there?" Maggie asked, too sympathetically.

"Do I look awful?" Ethan asked.

"Like you swallowed a dead rat," Alf chimed in, proud of himself.

Alf was probably the least daunted by the Secret Chamber, which is what he'd dubbed the room once they'd brought more candles and lamps in the place.

He scrambled about the rubble, holding a drippy candle in front of the bricks, and would pronounce, "There's some more words here, look," and then curse as if he had been raised in a brothel.

Maggie would scold him, but she, too, would let out with some brief blasphemy when she saw the fragments of words along the wall. She laughed at one. "It's a joke, this part, see?" and she'd drag Ethan over and hold her lamp up, shining its blue light along the stones.

"When the seventh seal is broken," she began, and then tried to find where the sentence continued.

"It's not a joke," Ethan said. "It's biblical. Seven angels, seven seals."

"Seals?" Alf asked, turning around for a second. "Like in the circus?"

"Seals like sealing wax," his mother said. "The kind you got into last summer and got all sticky with Wentworth's keys."

She's sticky with keys. Ethan remembered Wentworth's words.

Then, a passage from *Alice's Adventures in Wonderland* came to him, the Walrus and the Carpenter: ships and sails and sealing wax and cabbages and kings, and why the sea is boiling hot, or whether pigs have wings.

"What's this?" Alf asked, and then read aloud, as

best he could, " 'Four grey walls, and four grey towers overlook a space of flowers.' It's a rhyme."

"That's a poem," Ethan said. "Part of a poem, anyway." Then he began reciting what he remembered of it. " 'Four gray walls, and four gray towers, overlook a space of flowers, and the silent isle imbowers the Lady of Shalott.' It was my grandfather's favorite poem. Tennyson," he added, noticing the blank stare that Maggie offered.

In the lamplight, despite the strangeness of the find and the day spent hacking at brick and mortar, he had the sudden urge to lean over and kiss her. It was the oddest revelation, and it seemed both terribly out of place and very appropriate. Maggie Barrow was completely kissable, and it made him feel like a schoolboy with a crush.

And then, something in the flickering candlelight transformed her face in shadow into Madeleine's, and he felt somewhat reproached by the thought of his ex-wife.

"What's the matter?" Maggie asked.

"Nothing," Ethan said.

"You looked at me queerly enough," she muttered.

"Did I?" he said, as if he could not think up anything better.

"Look!" Alf cried, his voice echoing in the chamber, while he stumbled into a dark corner of the turret room. "Over here, I found something! Something big!"

And that's when they found the remains of a human body in a recessed corner of the room.

5

Finding a body came with its own set of problems—
particularly a corpse that had been rotting for several
years by the look of it (so saith Maggie, not showing
on her face half the horror that Ethan felt must have
been on his).

Maggie pulled Alf back, completely against his will,
practically lifting him by the elbows.

Ethan convinced Maggie—who then went to look
at the corpse with better lamplight—that they should
all just go downstairs and telephone for the police
like sane people. Alf proclaimed his hunger halfway
down the banister to the first floor; Maggie made
some grumblings about a woman's work never being
done; Ethan volunteered to make sandwiches; but
Maggie pushed him away, told him to "make your
blasted call to the coppers," and so, another remarkable evening in Harrow began.

Ethan rang up the local constable, the man named
Pocket; Maggie went to put some soup on the stove
("And clean up a terrible mess in the kitchen of
teapots that had their own tempests," which she
blamed entirely on Wentworth), while Ethan went to
wait for the officer of the law.

The weather had, as Ethan had come to expect in
his brief time at Harrow, turned sour. Rain clouds
seemed to have blackened out what there was of
moon and stars. But still, the sky at nightfall had a
glow to it, as if the threat of rain were its own kind of
flickering candlelight.

A chilly wind whistled down the valley, stirring up

leaves that magically seemed to turn from gold to brown by the time they hit the driveway of Harrow.

6

Ethan sat on the front steps and had a smoke, fretting more than slightly over the discovery of the body in the upstairs room; and yet, something within him felt free as well. It was as if he had discovered something that he knew would be there all along. Perhaps not a body, but a secret.

Something that had its own reflection in his childhood. Something that had not been right, that he had sensed from the moment he set foot in Harrow.

It's what I imagined with that ghost of the little girl. She wanted me to find the room, to find the body. My mind made her up because somehow I knew things were not as they should be. That was what that had been—a premonition.

He understood about premonitions and instincts. He had them sometimes, but not often. That's what the hallucination of the ghost had been. He was sure now.

Maggie called out from the kitchen that it was a mess but that she'd have some good soup for dinner; Alf came running out to the front steps to entertain him with some riddle or joke.

"And so." Alf concluded his third funny story that Ethan couldn't quite grasp. "That's when the horse turned to the ape and shouted, 'I'm a horse, you dog, not a giraffe!'" and then Alf held his stomach while he brayed his laughter. Ethan grinned politely and tried to laugh along. Every time he looked at Alf, with his mussed hair and face that was both like his mother's and not like her face at all. He thought of the body in the room. His mind kept returning to seeing it there. As if this person had just fallen asleep and had not ever awakened again.

Badsmell.

He tried not to think of what it had looked like. Or how long that body must have remained in the room. Or the scratches on the walls that the body had made when it was not just a body, but a living, breathing human being.

Or the badsmell.

He watched Alf's antics in some kind of wonder: The boy could discover a corpse and within the hour, tell jokes involving talking animals. "What's the name of your wife?" Alf asked, finally.

"My wife? Who said I was married?"

"You know who," Alf whispered, winking.

"Oh, her." Ethan winked. "Well, I'm not married anymore. But her name is Madeleine."

"I bet she was mad," Alf said. "Mad as in Madeleine."

"Alf as in Alfred," Ethan responded.

"Eeth as in Ethan." Alf was not one to give up the chance at the last word. "Eeth and teeth go together. Nothing goes with Alf. I've tried it."

"That's because everything that's spelled like Alf is said a different way. Like half and calf."

"Is that true?" Alf asked.

"Every word of it. From half to calf," Ethan said.

"It's not fair, is it?" Alf said, as if this were perfectly logical. "Now, you."

"Me, what?"

Alf crossed his arms over his chest. "You need to tell me a joke."

"All right. Here's one." Ethan held up his left hand, wiggling his pinky. "Do you know why polite people never ever use this finger when they pick up a cup of tea?"

"No," Alf said, scratching his head in confusion. "Why?"

"Because," Ethan said, pausing dramatically and wiggling his pinky faster. "It's mine."

For some reason, Alf thought this was the funniest joke he had ever heard, and after he laughed as if being tickled to death, he raced inside to tell his mother the funniest story ever told about the human pinky. Then, he raced back outside to tell yet another joke.

Then, he asked, "When you die, do you stay in your body?"

"I guess you go to heaven," Ethan said.

"Even if someone locked you in a room so your ghost can't get out?" Alf asked, and then looked a little sad. "Like you know who."

"Well," Ethan said. "I think locked doors can't keep you from going to heaven if that's where you're meant to go."

7

Alf had grown tired of the jokes and was hungrier than ever; he went back inside to bother his mother some more before dinnertime. Ethan went and stood in the drive, watching the early darkness for what seemed like hours (although, in fact, only thirty minutes had passed since he'd called the constable) until the squeak of a bicycle could be heard.

Remind me never to find a corpse again, he thought. *The police will take forever to show up.*

Emerging from the shadows along the drive, Pocket cut a fairly merry figure on an ill-fitting bicycle that had seen better days. Pocket was a small man of large proportion. Ethan guessed that he was in his fifties, but was not sure which side of fifty he was on—for there was something nearly decrepit about the constable, and at the same time, he had a curious energy.

Pocket wore an enormous coat that seemed to be more of a cape. It flapped in the sweeping wind, and his hat was not the flat-style hat of an officer of the law, but more in line with a homberg of recent vintage, scrunched down over his head.

He looked, in many ways, like a villain himself, right out of pulp novels, for there was something too melodramatic in the way he outfitted himself.

As soon as he was off the bicycle, he let the vehicle fall to the ground as if he didn't care about it; and he did not take his hat off until Maggie suggested he do so in the dining room "to set a good example for my son." Pocket's cheeks were bright red, and his manner both brusque and nearly suspicious—for having brought him out on such an errand at the dinner hour for possibly nothing. "Things have been imagined here in the past," he said, somewhat cryptically.

Ethan watched the constable's eyes for any trace of irony.

What he saw instead was nervousness in the form of a tic in the man's left eye, and a bit of a stammer when he mentioned the corpse.

The first thing that Ethan thought was that the local constable was slightly horrified that he might have to investigate a murder.

8

"You believe this person was murdered," Pocket said, his fingers thrumming the nightstick he held in his right hand as if the stick helped him think better. Then, Pocket launched into his understanding of what was upstairs. Next, he began asking question after question of Ethan, but refused to go up and look at the body.

"It's a girl," Alf volunteered.

"Alfred, don't interrupt. And it was a woman," Maggie corrected, bringing around a tureen of thick chicken and vegetable soup to the dining room table where the two men and the boy sat. The tea was nearly finished, and Alf told her that he didn't want any more milk "because I'm not a baby."

Once the soup bowls were filled, Maggie took a seat beside Ethan, touching the edge of his elbow beneath the table, giving it a slight squeeze. "She's a woman of about twenty-eight. I would guess."

Ethan glanced at her in slight amazement. "How could you tell?"

Pocket watched them both intensely, but said very little.

"Her shoes. Her dress. No one older than twenty-eight would've worn it," Maggie said, as if this were the most obvious fact in the world. "You two gentlemen are telling me you don't notice these things? Now she might've been older if she were a madwoman. But that's an enormous 'if.' She died in winter, as well. And she didn't expect to be in that room, waiting to die. I can tell you that. She wasn't dressed for it." She then went on to discuss the styles of women over thirty versus those under, and why the woman had not yet removed her shoes before she died.

"All right, why?" Ethan asked, fascinated.

"She didn't think that she would really die. She thought that someone was going to rescue her. She wanted to be ready."

"The lady might've been poisoned," Alf said, and then immediately looked back down at his soup bowl.

"Well," Pocket finally said, his white, furry caterpillar eyebrows flexing a bit. "If she were murdered, she would not have had time to take off her shoes."

Ethan slammed his fist against the table, nearly upsetting the soup. "Of course." He glanced at Maggie. "She wasn't murdered like that."

"For the love of—" Maggie said. "You men. It's staring you in the face, but you can't see it. She wrote on the walls."

"She had time," Ethan said. "She had time. She died in there. She must've had a source of light—otherwise, how could she write on the walls?"

"Walled in," Maggie said. "By someone she trusted."

"By who?" Pocket asked wearily. "And when? From what you've told me, she died years ago."

He's treating this as if it were a parlor game, Ethan thought. *He doesn't really want to believe there's a dead woman's body upstairs in that room. He doesn't want to have to begin this—whatever procedure he'll need to begin, whatever headaches the discovery of that body will bring with it. He doesn't want this to be happening.*

Pocket, Ethan guessed, *had probably never had to deal with a murder in his village.*

"The west wing has always been cut off," Maggie said. "Ever since I've been here. Wentworth once told me she couldn't remember a time when it was open."

"Constable," Alf piped up, stirring his soup lazily. "When someone gets walled in to a room like that, wouldn't people hear them scream?"

"Alfred!" his mother snapped, and the boy immediately looked down at his soup bowl.

"It was my grandfather," Ethan said, knowing that this was what no one was willing to say. "He murdered this woman. My grandfather murdered a woman in this house by walling her in. Alive."

"I can't believe that," Maggie said. "I don't believe it. I knew him too well."

"You knew him barely," Ethan said.

"There was a woman who went missing from the village in 1915," Pocket said without emotion. He reached up to his face and pressed his fingers against his nose, sniffing, as if he'd recently washed them and wanted to smell the traces of soap. "Her name was Rory Scopes."

95

"Do you think it's her?"

"I knew your grandfather for many years, Mr. Gravesend. I can tell you one thing for certain. He was not a man to senselessly kill a woman in his own home. And then leave her there." Pocket made a slight sound of annoyance. "We won't know much of anything until we examine the body."

"If we knew when the room was walled up . . ." Maggie began.

"I knew," Pocket said, as if this were common knowledge. "I asked him about it, when I saw him putting the bricks in the window ledge. It was in 1919 or 1920. He didn't like the view. That's what he said. Then. He said he didn't like the view. The window broke, he said. And he didn't like the view. I'm sure it's no surprise to you, Mr. Gravesend. Justin was a true eccentric. I respected him a great deal, despite all the stories. All the rubbish piled on by a village of small minds. God love them, but they're a small-minded lot. He didn't murder anyone. I'm nearly convinced of that from just knowing him."

"You have other officers," Ethan said. "On the way?"

"From Parham, yes, there will be an investigation," Pocket said, wearily. "But I wanted to make sure that this is a murder. That there is a body. That there is, as it were, something to investigate. And what I now discover," he added, and then paused. "What I now discover is that there is a body. It is indeed a murder of some type, and now we must see if this is the missing Miss Scopes. Or someone else entirely. Now, could you, sir, lead me upstairs to where the body rests? That is, if you're finished with your soup?"

Chapter Five

1

Pocket slowly took the stairs to the first landing, leaving Ethan, already halfway up the staircase above him, glancing down from the railing. "The body's been there some time I imagine," Pocket said. "She doesn't need me running up to her, having heart failure."

"Of course," Ethan said, wishing he had more cigarettes to smoke. He'd left them downstairs at the table.

"It's very dark in the room," he said, apropos of nothing.

"Yes, yes, I'm certain of that," Pocket said, grunting as he began the next set of stairs. "Justin certainly enjoyed his little maze."

"Constable?"

"This house. His maze. He told me once that the way a maze worked is it got your mind turning inward. He wanted the house to be a maze. And it certainly feels like one. I've gotten lost here more than once at one of his masques." Pocket may have been in good enough shape to bicycle through the village, but he apparently had not climbed a stair in twenty years. It was as if he were climbing the Matterhorn.

"Masques?" Ethan asked.

"Parties. Entertainments. He always had gatherings during certain times of the year."

"I never imagined him as a party-giver," Ethan said, trudging up the final set of steps to the long corridor between the east and west wings.

"Smoke, Mr. Gravesend?" Pocket offered a cigar when they reached the landing at the bottom of the stairs that rose to the west wing tower. Pocket seemed completely uninterested in exploring the tower. Instead, he went to one of the benches that lined the corridor and sat down. "It's an excellent cigar. The tobacco is from the Vuelta Abajo district on the island of Cuba. I've never gone far afield from Watch Point, but that is one place I would dearly love to visit someday. The cigar is a special thing, sir. A special thing. The tobacco leaf must be cured just so, and these cigars . . . a friend who traveled to exotic climes used to send them to me each year at Christmas. These cigars, sir. Why, notice the wrapping—the leaf is pure maduro. It gives it that mahogany color. And sweet, sir. So very sweet."

"I think," Ethan said, "we should perhaps be going up."

"What's a smoke going to hurt? A fine cigar. Two men who have some serious business ahead of them, sir? Perhaps a smoke and a little conversation." Pocket said this with a grave air, and held out one of the cigars for Ethan. "There are a few finer points of the past you may need to know."

Ethan went over, took the cigar, and reached into his breast pocket for his lighter—which he'd also left downstairs with his beloved cigarettes.

"I always have a tinder box on hand for just such occasions." Pocket grinned, his crooked row of nearly all imperfect teeth seeming almost canine in the lamp light. "But first, sit yourself here. And take in the aroma before we light this ambrosia. A cigar is something to be savored, but these . . . Why, did you know that men would smoke these while drinking brandy or a favorite port? But what a waste, sir, what a waste. For these are like brandy unto themselves. The horrible demon drink would ruin these."

Ethan sat, staring at the cigar in his hand. He glanced over to the doorway that led up to the turret. Then back to Pocket. "Is Pocket your full name?"

"Grayson Pocket," the constable said, rolling the cigar between his fingers. "Born in Poughkeepsie of a Dutch mother and a Welsh father, and the name Pocket was not his own, but one he bought. His Welsh name was nigh unpronounceable and he wanted to be part of this world and not of the one he'd left. Names have their own magic, don't they, sir? They have their own spell. Grayson was too dour a name for me. Son of Gray, eh? Not likely. I became known as Pocket, or Pock, as a boy, and then grew further into the name when I began my servitude to the law," Pocket said.

For a moment, he reminded Ethan of the Walrus from Lewis Carroll's "The Walrus and the Carpenter." Pocket seemed the Walrus, and the cigar seemed his tusk as he thrust it between his lips. The constable struck a match, and lit it, rolling the cigar slowly with his left hand while he held the burning match with his right.

"Hand-rolled, sir," Pocket said. He demonstrated the proper technique so that Ethan could light his own cigar without destroying its flavor. "Sip it like port. Do not gulp. This is an experience to be enjoyed."

"I'm quite fond of cigarettes," Ethan said, coughing for a moment because he had, indeed, gulped.

"Foul nasty things," Pocket said with no small amount of disgust as he held his beloved cigar between his lips. "Cigarettes should be outlawed. They are for the uncivilized."

And then, as if this were part of the same conversation, he said, "You do know who this woman is, don't you?"

2

Pocket Tells A Story Between Puffs of a Cigar

I was twenty-four when I first came to Watch Point to work in the local office. It wasn't as it is now—I don't mean Watch Point, although that is certainly true, sir. What I mean to say is the practice of policing areas like this one was not then what it is today. In those days, the villagers who got into any trouble at all tended not to do much beyond brawl and cause the noise or mayhem toward which the very young tend to be drawn. I would find the Colloquian brothers setting fire to the old barn behind the Westerly's place. Or I would be called in to settle disputes between husbands and their wives, either of which might have gone astray or thrown something at the other. Now and then, a pistol was waved in the village, but no one ever was hurt here.

Certainly, I am not a fool. I knew that the larger towns nearby had their share of genuine criminal activity, and I knew some of it would by necessity spill over to our hamlet. I worked for a constable then who was near his retirement age, and I discovered fairly quickly that he had more than once taken what we would then call "little gifts of gratitude" from shopkeepers and private individuals who wanted some transgression overlooked. Please don't look at me so disapprovingly. When you are an officer of the law, you must of necessity also be a father-confessor and one who understands other people as if they were books meant to be opened and thumbed through for further understanding of—well, to extend this thought—their plots, as it were. So, I watched this senior officer take bits of cash and the occasional Christmas goose among other sundries. As I see you are now, I was truly appalled and disturbed by this behavior. But he sat me down and he told me this. And I will never forget what he said.

That man said, "Pocky," as I was then known, "you are still a boy. You do not understand what men must endure. These are good people. In this village, few have been bad. There are cities and places where truly bad men exist.

Douglas Clegg

They do terrible things. They are inhuman, in some respects. But here in Watch Point I have seen no terrible things. I have seen nothing that was not entirely human. So I shave."

And I said, "You shave?"

"Yes, I shave every day to remove what I think of them. I judge them anew each and every day. I do not hold grudges. I do not hold them responsible for fates that are beyond their control."

"But the law," I said, feeling every bit as indignant as if I were the son of the Almighty.

"I see no one in Watch Point who wrote the law," says he. "I see no one here who goes to the legislature and tells the truth about what human beings must endure in this life in order to survive and prosper." Then, he pointed at me as if he were my judge. "You see the law as immutable. You see it as an eternal truth. But I tell you, Pocky," he said, just like that. "I tell you, there is no law that protects good people. The law protects those bad people in the cities and in the other towns. There is no law for those here. But I am their law. I am their law and their conscience and as they go to their priests and their God to unburden themselves, so they come to me. But should I step upon them, should I press out the law as it is written from their hands and hearts, I would have lost my authority."

He says something just like that.

That was many years ago. I do forget some things at times. But I never forget what he told me or the way he said it. Or how I took it. I understood why he tolerated the little bribes and the transgressions. Because these are good people, sir. Bad people do not live in Watch Point. You may argue the finer points of this with me. You may call me simple. You may tell me that I can't see beyond my own nose. You may even tell me all the things I told myself then. I told myself that no one man could judge who was good or who was bad, and this, I thought, was the reason for the law. Justice should be blind, sir, I thought. Justice should be meted out to all men, no matter if I deemed them good or bad. But one thing I know from my years here: Good people do things sometimes that seem bad. But within their hearts and souls, it is as good as can be understood by anyone. The only problem I see is this: The law does not deal in human souls and human hearts. The law deals in the shallows of life. Did he do this? Did he not do this? Does that woman have the stolen money in her hands, or does she not? It is like a photographer taking pictures. If photographs were the only truth in life, then we would, most of us, be considered a hideous lot, and we would, most of us, never fall in love, nor understand how to love beyond the picture.

I will give you an example with which you are quite familiar, I believe, sir. Just the other evening, I saw you at the local pub, did I not? You were there with the others in town, pretending that it was a place of food and coffee, with not a whiff of ale about.

Douglas Clegg

Yet each night during the week, I go there to dine, as I have for the past twenty years. And each night, since strong drink has been declared unlawful, the stage has been set for what I think of as the ritual of the sacred sassyfrass. I know what our villagers drink there. I can smell it on their breath. I can see it in the cup. But I've seen other villages and cities where the local constable raises his club and breaks glasses rather than allow himself to tolerate a speakeasy.

Yet in those places, speakeasies flourish. They are unstoppable.

Here in Watch Point, the local tavern is the only place where villagers have their illicit fun. And because the ritual continues there nightly, and I am almost always witness to it, it never gets out of hand. Neither do the bootleggers from up the river come here often. I suspect that our Jimmy Winthrop in the village makes the ale himself in the great barrels he keeps in his cellar. Were I to stop this sassyfrass ceremony, I would first have to spit in the eye of nearly every man and woman in Watch Point. Next, I would need to try and keep good people from doing something good people have done for thousands of years: forget themselves with the aid of something I may not approve of, but I can't dismiss out of hand. No, not just because somewhere a law was passed. Somewhere someone with special interests decided that a rule should be made that covered all people in all places.

You perhaps know Adela Wentworth. Of

104

course you do. She has been a common thief in our village since she was in her teens, apparently. She picks up things, and when caught, often says she found them. Is she wrong to do this? Well, of course she is. If she were even aware of her own proclivity toward this, she would perhaps be a bad person. But Adela, dear sad soul, is not bad at all. She is lonely. She is neglected by even her neighbors. The kind of love that exists spiritually between man and woman never came her way, no matter how much she prayed for it. My predecessor in this job told me that she began pocketing rock candy in the local confectionary when she was a young girl, and this pattern continued until she was once seen taking a woman's shoes from her front porch where they'd been left to dry after a storm had gone past.

Yet Adela is not bad. She is not a criminal. She is a human being with a soul and a heart. The world crushed something within her. She takes things now and again because it makes her feel as if she's part of the village. Part of the world she lives within. I understand her. And I generally feel for her, and let it go. I suppose believing this depends, sir, upon whether you believe the world is a benevolent place or a hostile one.

I believe it is a hostile and brutal place. Our modern world allows us to forget this. We have radio now, and newspapers that tell us what the world is about, and somehow make it all sound as if it is taken care of. A benevolent place.

But I see the jungle still, sir. I see the jungle

and the wasteland both. And these people, in this small patch of land at the edge of the Hudson River, are within the domain I have sworn to care for, as I would care for a garden, or children who have been shipwrecked on some distant shore.

I confide this to you, sir. I do not mean to spread gossip of Adela Wentworth. I do not mean to imply that I take bribes, either, as the former constable did.

I am telling you this to prepare you for something more.

And so, the reason I sat you here, and share cigars with you, sir, is because once upon a time, I sat here with your grandfather and shared just such a cigar.

3

Ethan felt as if he'd held his breath through the entire tale that Pocket had spun. He had barely touched the cigar that remained perched between the fingers of his upturned hand. "My grandfather murdered this woman upstairs," he said, as if this were the sum total to which Pocket had been alluding.

"I told you downstairs, your grandfather never murdered anyone. But once, many years ago, when you were still a boy, and I was still a young man, as you are now, Justin Gravesend turned to me and offered me a puzzle to solve."

And then, Pocket continued his story.

4

Pocket Continues His Tale of the Past

Your grandfather was never what one could call "jolly." In fact, the name suited him: Justin Gravesend. He was interested in being just. He was grave. Have you noticed that about names? They often contain the seeds of an interior life. Your name, Ethan. Ethan Gravesend. Ethan puts me in mind of ether. I am called Pocket, and of course I keep things in my pocket most of the time. I have always been somewhat secretive, knowing what I understand about life in this village. You are really the first to hear of any of this.

I trust that you will not allow what I tell you to go further?

So Justin sat here with me, and we shared just such a cigar. It may have been my first cigar, as far as I can recall. It was the most exquisite one, no doubt, for I try to recapture that moment of the first smoke of a fine cigar now and again, and it only returns to me in memory.

Justin said to me, "Officer Pocket, do you like this cigar?"

"Very much," says I. And I did.

"Then I will always make sure you have it. I have people in places who can send these."

Well, thought I, this is a fine mess, Pocky. The man building this castle has already offered me a gift without me first knowing what crime he's committed against the almighty law.

But I was soon to find out.

We began talking of the village, and Justin spoke with great affection of his wife, your grandmother. He loved her dearly, although no one will believe it. I saw it within him. It was there in his heart. But she did not return the affection, and so they lived most of their lives apart after your father was born.

Your grandfather then began speaking—with great pride—of his engineering and construction of Harrow. How he had taken the house that had existed and was in the process of transforming it. Certainly, there was a house here before Justin and Genevieve arrived to buy the property. It was simply called The Cliffs, although there were no cliffs to be seen. It was not a grand estate, but a simple house of several rooms, built originally as a farmhouse in the 1700s and then added upon for its various owners. Finally, your grandfather bought the land, named it Harrow, and obliterated all traces of the old house. He built Harrow up from the foundations, and covered over the ponds that spotted the property. It was rocky soil and streams once, and then he began creating this . . . well, this monstrosity for lack of a better term. I certainly mean no disrespect, sir.

And over the course of years, it grew. He had engineers in to oversee things, and architects. That abbey, brought over in chunks of stone, brought up on barges along the river, some of it hauled by rail. It was a miracle to watch it go up.

And then, as your grandfather told me the history of his building to that point, he mentioned something of his sadness, too. For while the creation of the house was something he felt compelled to do, he had very much lost his family in the process.

"Begging your pardon, sir," says I. "But why build a home just to lose a family?"

And then, I saw it in his eyes.

Some would call it madness. You know the village was calling this place "Gravesend's Madhouse" by then. They thought he had lost his mind and was merely building all of it just to make his own tomb.

But it was not madness to me. I told you, there are no bad people in our village. And your grandfather was not mad. Not in the sense that was meant.

He was on fire, that's what he was. He was a good man on fire. And he said to me, "What I am about to tell you, Officer, you must not repeat to another living soul."

I remembered my superior, the constable whom I would one day replace, and his thoughts on human beings, and my own thoughts on the hostile world. But as Justin told his story to me, I knew that the world was worse than merely a jungle. Merely a place of idiot hostility.

The world was a place of the greatest terror within the smallest moment.

I will hazard a guess as to who that woman in the room upstairs is.

The corpse that I have not yet examined, but which I no doubt shall identify just by the room where she has been laid to rest.

She is not Rory Scopes. I said that for the benefit of Mrs. Barrow and her son. It is easy to think of an unknown missing woman as a possible murder victim without it leaving a residue to bring on nightmares or worse in impressionable minds. We all read the tabloids. There are murders everywhere, men and women who seem as if they've been made up because we have no connection to them.

Mrs. Barrow and her son do not yet need to hear the truth.

No one but you and I should of necessity know this truth now. It is the truth within the human heart, sir. Within the human soul. No one but you and I need to know what Harrow meant to your grandfather. Or what has gone on in this house since your grandfather began building it. Or why your grandmother could not bear to live in this place, and chose instead to raise her son in another place, away from Harrow. Or why your grandfather could not leave this house for long without going mad himself. Of course, the woman in the room upstairs—the dead woman who may have lain there for at least five years, perhaps longer—might be anyone.

But my guess, sir, is that the body in that room is a woman named Matilde Gravesend. I believe she was your father's sister. Your aunt.

No one had seen her since she was a little girl. He had kept it that way. She died, didn't she? That's what was said. She'd died of some ailment while too young. The influenza epidemic swept through, and then an outbreak of measles and other sicknesses from which many children died. That's when she died, so it was said. There's even a grave for her in the family vault. Have you visited it yet since you've returned? Even your father believed her dead, many years gone by. Perhaps even your grandmother wanted to believe it. That may be why she stayed away all those years.

But your grandfather was a good man, sir. Your grandfather was a good man set upon by the ravening wolves of a hostile world. And I know beyond the shadow of a doubt that no one murdered that woman. I was there when she died. In that room. That very room. Well, I can't say I was there, exactly. I watched her, though. I saw things. I know.

This is where the puzzle of the house came into things, sir. Your grandfather conceived of this place as a puzzle within a puzzle. You remember I mentioned that? Or have I yet? Ah, but this cigar has been smooth.

You're looking a little pale, sir. Would you like to hear more, or is that enough for you now?

Pocket's voice grew soft. "That's too much of a shock for you, sir."

"No." Ethan stumbled across the words he wished to say, but "No" was the only one that seemed to come out.

"I had seen Matilde somewhat when she was young. Before she died. Before your grandfather made his confession to me. Before I put the puzzle together."

And then, he said, "We live our lives as ordinary men, don't we?"

6

Pocket Speaks of Dark Deeds

We live our lives as ordinary men, don't we? We watch train wrecks, hear of murders in distant places, understand the notion of insanity, but we never think of these things in terms of possessing them. I can't tell you everything I know, for not all of it would make sense. It doesn't really make sense to me. Matilde was a beautiful child. She was five years old when I first saw her. Her mother would bring her and your father, who was then nearly eleven, into the village. The major construction on Harrow had not really begun. Do you know what it was like then? It already had begun to get the look of a castle. A stronghold against the world.

Your grandfather had done much of the construction on the main house. He brought in stones from distant places, and the wood was carved by the best craftsmen of the time. . . . I recognized early that your grandmother, whom everyone then called Jenny, did not find Watch Point or Harrow to her liking.

But she adored your grandfather, and she made the best of it, at least for a brief period of time. She went back and forth from her other house, and tended to arrive at Harrow for summers and part of the fall. Matilde, owing to childhood illness, rarely left the house.

Your grandfather originally had an entire area of the house just for his daughter and her needs. She had nurses watching her day and night. She had trouble breathing and seemed to go in and out of fevers constantly.

With epidemics running through the cities, and even along the shore, it was thought that Harrow was the best place for her, particularly while she was so young and fragile. The Gravesends brought doctors in to examine her. A specialist from New York arrived and stayed several months, living at the house. He was an unusual doctor with an unusual practice. He spent most of his days pushing Matilde's wheelchair around the grounds when the weather was good. She could walk some days, but others, she would become dizzy and need the chair. I asked him once about her condition.

You see, I was at the house quite a bit. I was

somewhat smitten with one of Matilde's nurses, a young woman named Irene who had come down from Boston to work in the house. She was a handsome woman, very strong and very upright.

She did not like me hanging out at her place of employment, but would often meet me after work to go for an evening stroll.

I was little more than an errand boy to the constable, and I had far too much time on my hands.

So once, when Irene was upstairs with one of the other nurses, fumigating Matilde's room as was the custom, I sat with the little girl and this specialist. What he told me made me wonder at why Matilde was not in an asylum of some sort.

Yes, even a girl of five. Those things were done then. They may still be done. Locking up children who are beyond our understanding. Separating the sick from the healthy, like that.

This specialist said that she had exhibited signs of somnambulism.

Sleepwalking? said I.

Apparently she did things while walking in just such a state. She was, he felt, in grave danger if she remained at the house.

But such a little child, I said. Surely, this is some infant disease that will pass as she grows older.

He looked at me with extreme gravity, and told me that in all the books he had read of the mind and its forces, Matilde Gravesend was unique.

114

He told me that, having studied at Prague and then in New York, he had seen hysterical children and behavior that was both abhorrent and abnormal.

But he had never witnessed what this girl— little more than a baby—had done.

I pressed him for details, but he was secretive. He did say that she was dangerous to herself and to others, and that she would be best confined to what was then called Northcastle, up the river near Albany, or down at some asylum near Baltimore, where she would get the best care. I shuddered, thinking about this, how this sad and beautiful child might be shut away with the insane and the disturbed. No one left those places in those days. No one. I could guess what her fate would be, should this specialist decide that she best be placed at Northcastle.

I asked Irene, the girl I loved, about Northcastle that very night. She evaded my questions, until finally, she had to admit that it was essentially a dungeon for the insane. "There is no one there who has not been violent, no one there who behaves decently, and not a soul who resides within the walls of Northcastle who survives many years there."

Ailments would sweep through the halls of the asylum, and many would die. Those who did not die from epidemic often killed themselves or were killed by their mad brethren. When I told her what the specialist had mentioned to me, Irene was horrified.

At first.

Then, she told me something that caused me to rethink my sympathy for the child. Matilde, it seemed, had tried to murder her brother—your father—a few months before. Your father, shy, lonely boy that he was, kept to his room most summers, reading. He rarely went out to the gardens and was almost never seen in the village. One afternoon, he'd fallen asleep in the study.

As he later told the nurses, he awoke to see his sister standing over him, a large stone in her small hands.

It was aimed for his face.

He moved swiftly, and narrowly avoided having his head bashed in.

Irene told me that the stone was too heavy for any of them to pick up alone.

It had come from the construction, and Matilde had carried it from the garden into the house. She had lifted it above her head with no help from anyone.

She exhibited great strength.

And she told me of the field mice and how they'd been found, torn as if by a cat. At first, they thought it was a cat—the feral cats have always lived in these fields alongside the house. But then one night when the straps from Matilde's bed had torn loose, Irene herself awoke to see the little girl doing something that does not bear repeating. Something that Irene told me I must never tell anyone, for she herself could not fathom it and might lose her job over gossiping about the

Gravesends. But when Matilde finished her blasphemy, she turned, grinning, to Irene.

Between her teeth, a small mouse.

I was chastened in my opinion of the little girl then.

Yes, she was beautiful and sweet and pitiful in her own way, when I saw her in her chair among the flowers.

These stories were almost too much to be believed. Yet I understood that the diseased mind might take on aspects that none of us could predict. Justin Gravesend, one evening, seeing me waiting for Irene to take leave of the house for the night, called me to him. We sat and had some port, and he asked my opinion on some matters. First, he talked of the house, incessantly. Harrow. His true love, I thought then. The house and his plans for it.

After much port and more talk of building and designing, he confessed to the terror that was his daughter.

He loved her, you see.

He loved her more than he loved his son; I am sure of that. The boy, your father, was ignored by his father for much of his young life.

Justin became consumed with Matilde, with her needs.

He told me about how he had done terrible things when he was young. Things that had now come back to roost. He swore me to absolute secrecy. I promised that as long as he lived, anything he told me was safe within my soul.

He began to chatter about his wife and how she had never touched Matilde, not from the day she was born. How he'd had to do the caring for the child, but he was ill-equipped for the task.

He supposed that this might've accounted for the fact that Matilde never had cried as a baby, at least not from hunger or need. She had been silent, and, he felt, she had watched him.

Once, he caught his wife slapping the baby, and had to pull her away. His wife had screamed that there was something unnatural about the child. His wife then had turned on Justin, and had shrieked that it was because of him, because of what he had done, that their daughter had turned out to be so unnatural.

He wept bitter tears recounting this to me. He had been drinking all day, I could tell by his breath. But I knew he needed to let these things out, and, truthfully, my curiosity had become intense.

Finally, he told me that he used to watch her, when she was a baby, in her sleep.

I asked him, "Because she did not cry?"

He shook his head. "She did things," he told me, "that babies should not do."

I asked him, "What sorts of things?"

And then he regaled me with words that had no meaning to me. They were a jumble. He could apparently not sort out what he meant to say, and what came from his lips seemed utter nonsense. I would not have been the first man to doubt his sanity, but I felt very strongly that he was a good and kind man, and loved his child dearly.

Clumsily, I told him that the very ill often behaved irrationally. My great-aunt had wasted away with consumption for years, and she often said vile blasphemies.

"She knows what she's doing," he said. "Of course, it sounds insane to anyone who has not known her since her birth. Of course, it must seem monstrous for me to have done these things. Of course, we seem like a terrible family to anyone who has not lived through what we have. I blame myself," your grandfather said. "I was too interested in things best left alone as a young man. I wanted the wealth of the world," he said. "I suppose," he told me in that most private and terrible of moments, "that I sold my soul to the devil as much as any Faust ever did. And now, my daughter pays for it with her sanity."

I laughed at this, of course. Made light of it. The heaviness of his voice, the gravity of every word, seemed too serious. The pact with the devil joke was ludicrous. I tried to point out the reality: that he was despairing because he had an ill child.

"I have heard of doctors in Germany who—" I began, but he interrupted me with hollow laughter.

"You have heard of fools!" he said. "They would hurt my child, give her diseases and yel-

low fever to cure her of this madness. They would kill her with their cures!"

And then, he whispered something thrice, a word, an invocation.

I said to him, "What prayer is that?"

And he smiled briefly. "I am going to make sure my child is safe from this world."

And that, sir, is when my Irene came down the stairs, and we left the house.

Irene and I quarreled soon after and broke off our friendship. She eventually left Watch Point to work closer to the city.

It was the last time I came to the house until Matilde had died. At least, they said she had died. I saw her in her small casket, and yes, her body was cold, and the doctors had been summoned.

The specialist from New York had arrived, and with him, a strange physician I had not met before. He was what they used to call a mesmerist, and even when she was dead, he passed magnets of some kind over her body. He seemed nearly a priest.

Oh yes, and Father Gleason was there, for Matilde had been baptized in St. Christopher's in Parham before her death. Yet, by then, even your grandmother would not come to the funeral. It was thought best that few arrive, for the little girl had been ravaged by fevers and all manners of illness that in those days . . . well, the fear of contagion was too much. I was told to keep a handkerchief over my mouth and nose *at all times, so as not to breathe the air of the small room where her body lay.*

I helped carry the small casket, through a gloomy day of overcast skies and later, a terrible rain. We laid her to rest in the vault.

I thought that was all there was to it.

Harrow was growing by this time. It was as if an acorn had taken root and had grown in a few years to a vast oak with full branches. In the village, they called it the Madhouse. Your grandfather had lavished his fortune on it as a way of hiding from the grief that his daughter had brought to his life.

Your father and grandmother rarely visited after that. Even when they did, they never stayed overnight at Harrow, but would go to one of the inns by the highway.

Of course, I thought it was finished.

Matilde, poor child, was dead and buried after all.

But years later, when he first offered me the cigar, he finally broke down and confessed the secret that had been eating away at him for those many years.

The mesmerist had put Matilde under using his magnet, and one of the treatments the specialist had given the little girl was an injection of some terrible fever. Under the magnetism used, she did not feel the pain of the illness. She had been exposed to some hideous disease—in order to cure her. The shock of the disease would bring her back to the world. That's what

*he told me. Even that had not worked, and
then, something more terrible had occurred.*

*Something that sounds as if it came from a
medieval text.*

*They performed the rite of exorcism over that
beautiful little girl, while she struggled in fever. I
asked him why an exorcism, and he was evasive.*

*All I could learn from him about it was that his
daughter had no sense of who she was. Finally, it
was too much for her small body. Her breath
gave out, but the priest told them that at least she
had found salvation at the last. Your grandfather
wept as he spoke of her death. He said the priest
was shocked that she had died, as were the spe-
cialists he had brought in. None pretended this
was a victory over the sad life of a little girl.*

*"But then," your grandfather said to me, his
eyes growing ever wider, "two nights after we put
her in the vault, I went to sit in the crypt with her,
to talk to the stone that held her. And as I stayed
there late into the night, praying and talking and
saying words that had no meaning, I began to
hear a scratching from beneath the stone cover."*

7

"Dear God," was all Ethan could muster, and he set
down his cigar. The corridor had become overly
smoky, and he went to open one of the small arched
windows. "Dear God."

He didn't say anything else for a long while. He

glanced outside, at the dark world and the firefly glitter of lights in the village; beyond the village, the river of night.

After what seemed like several minutes, Pocket said, "Your grandfather built Harrow to keep her safe from the world. That night, in the crypt, with his bare hands, he pulled back the stone. That night, he brought her back with him to Harrow. They had buried her alive, but he had rescued her. He had not lost her, after all."

Ethan watched the distant lights, taking in deep breaths of air. "This explains some things."

"Does it?"

"Yes, for me it does." But even then, Ethan could not say what it explained, other than the mysteries that seemed to swirl around him as a child when he visited Harrow. "Not anything concrete. Just the things I felt in this house. When I was a boy. Why my father hated my grandfather so much."

"Do not misjudge your grandfather," Pocket said. "He was a good man. He did what he thought best. He had no one to guide him in this. He could trust no one. It was a different world then. It is hard to imagine it, the place this world was, back when I was a very young man. How you would keep a secret like this your entire life rather than let anyone know it. How the scandal would kill. How the opinions of others might destroy. How you could not imagine your own child in the viper's nest of a place like Northcastle. In some ways, it was better that folk thought her dead. Better that your grandmother and your father thought her dead, as well. I suppose I am the only man who knows this. I suppose your father never

123

knew. I can only guess that your grandmother never ventured into Harrow very much after that."

"But I was here," Ethan said, turning. "As a boy. I was here."

"She was here, too, sir," Pocket said. "But he built within the house itself a hidden world. And he sealed her there. He cared for her there. Until the night she died. In that room. Upstairs."

8

Pocket stood slowly, setting the last of his cigar—snipped at the end—into his breast pocket. "I suppose we should go up now," he said. "If you'd rather remain behind . . ."

"No, I'll come." Ethan felt his blood pounding in his ears, and the curious nausea returned to him. He wanted to sit back down. He didn't want the thoughts or images in his head. Not the pictures that were forming of Matilde in her small casket. Of the vault out in the crypt. Of the mesmerist passing magnets over her body, or the priest reciting Latin at the foot of her bed . . .

What in God's name had he inherited?

A small voice seemed to answer:

Madness.

Ethan went ahead, up the narrow stairs to the small room. Once Pocket had negotiated the stairs, Ethan pointed out the portrait of the saint. "Do you recognize that?"

"The painting?" Pocket asked.

"Is it her?" Ethan asked. "Matilde?"

"Of course not," Pocket said. "It's just a painting, sir. I presume the body's in there?" He took a step across the rubble, grabbing up one of the long candles. "Do you have a better light?"

"I'm afraid not."

"Well, this'll do for now. Bring two in. I want a good view of this." Then, Pocket caught his breath for a moment.

"Something wrong?"

"When one finds a body in a room, something is generally wrong, Mr. Gravesend," Pocket said rather testily. Then, he calmed. "It's the scent. I haven't smelled it in years. Not in years."

Ethan wasn't completely sure, but it seemed as if the constable had a tear in his eye. The man was an enigma. A large cape-wearing enigma, and Ethan was too confused to get trapped in the puzzle.

Pocket said, "It's not her smell. It's not even the smell of a corpse, sir. It's a scent that was always here. Always in these rooms. I'm surprised you don't recognize it." He added, nearly a whisper, "The day she died, I smelled it. The day I helped put these bricks in place. And it's still here."

Then, he took his jacket off and went over and laid

it across the body, swiping at the thick cobwebs that grasped at the corpse.

"I suppose we shall have to put her in the vault for good, now," Pocket said, regretfully. He crouched beside the body, smoothing his jacket along its contours.

But Ethan barely heard him. He held the two candles up, closer to the far wall. He stepped forward, wondering if he were only imagining things.

"It changed," he blurted, and wished he had just kept his mouth shut.

"Sir?" Pocket glanced around.

"The words. In chalk. It didn't say this before."

There, on the wall, another verse from Tennyson's "The Lady of Shalott":

Out flew the web and floated wide;
The mirror cracked from side to side;
"The curse is come upon me," cried The Lady of
   Shalott.

Just as Ethan had read the last line written in the smudged chalk, someone far below them screamed loud enough to wake the dead.

He recognized the voice a second later.

It was Alf.

Chapter Six

1

"Alf," Ethan gasped. He turned away from the wall, and dashed out of the room as fast as he could go. Constable Pocket called after him, but the screams continued; Ethan could not slow down to wait for the older man. Anything could be happening to the kid. Although some part of him said that Alf had probably just stubbed his toe or had spilled hot soup in his lap, some instinct kicked in. Something worse was happening. Ethan was sure of it.

He felt as if the stairs and landings were going up instead of down, and nearly tripped as he rounded one of the banisters, but he managed to make it all the way down to the first floor. He followed what had become high-pitched squeals toward the kitchen, his heart racing the whole way.

2

Ethan threw back the door, and heard a strange noise, as if a storm blew through Harrow. A heat—like the breath of a wild beast times a thousand—burst from the room.

The kitchen was a madhouse.

What seemed to be ice had formed on the ceiling, but was quickly melting into raindrops that fell to the floor; while a frenetic, almost lightning-like fire burned out of control up the sides of the walls. The window shutters were battering as if in constant wind, and for a split second, Ethan thought he had just stepped into a dream.

3

A sweet, terrible stink came at him, and he felt for a second as if he'd just thrust his face into the torn belly of some great beast. He recoiled at the odor. It was the badsmell again, and it was overpowering. He covered his mouth and nose with his shirtsleeve, coughing. The trap from the stove was open, and fire belched from the belly of the machine; black smoke poured from it; the fireplace also blazed with yellow-orange tongues of flames; and there, among the brilliant burning and smoke, stood Alf, shivering, broken glass and bits of china around his feet. "Alf? Are you all right?" Ethan asked, taking a step forward. "Alf?" The boy's body was covered in a shiny coat of sweat; his clothes, soaked through. He looked forlorn and terrified. He had scratches on his face, as if from his own hands. "Get it off me," he whispered. "Please. Get it off me. They're all over. They're gonna bite. They want me." His voice so small, so terrified.

"Where's your mother?" Ethan asked, striding forward, toward the boy.

Something in Alf's demeanor led him to believe that the boy would run like a frightened fawn if there were any sudden movements. He tried to be calm as he went, but the fire was going to be out of control soon, and he had to first get the boy out of the kitchen and then deal with the flames. Ethan glanced at the fire as it licked the edges of the kitchen, and saw the places were it had already burned parts of the wall. "Alf? Alf!"

Alf's eyes rolled up in his head. Ethan was sure the child was going to faint. A shivering took over his entire body, followed quickly by something that seemed like a convulsion or seizure. Ethan heard a crackling as of thunder, but from within the room. Something else was there. He could feel it. A heaviness in the room, as if the barometric pressure had dropped suddenly, or as if they were underwater. . . .

Then Ethan knew. Knew from the time he'd seen the little girl on the stairs, felt her coming toward him, into him.

It was the little girl. He was sure of it. She was somehow here.

Present. In the kitchen.

Alf held up his hands, his fingers extended. Small tufts of flame burst from the ends of his fingers, as if they were candles. And then, around his head, a glowing fire.

A scraping sound—Ethan glanced at the walls, now

129

blackened by the flames. Strange markings and symbols scrawled across them as if done by an invisible hand. The markings blurred and became tiny spiders, crawling along the burning walls.

Ethan knew he must act swiftly, but a terror had entered his heart.

Something wanted him to watch this. To watch and remain still.

Something held him there, something beyond fear. It was like he was mesmerized, watching the boy with the hands of fire.

Have to break through this. Have to get him out. Have to save him, the thoughts battered within Ethan's brain.

"Leave him alone!" Ethan shouted. He felt some crazy laughter come from deep inside him—something was there, something within him, too. Something held him back.

No. Get out of me. Get out, he thought, and knew it was madness to think it.

Blisters formed on the boy's face—Ethan ran for him without thinking of his own safety, fearful that the boy would burn to death in the growing furnace blast of heat. He heard the sound of glass shattering as he came nearer to Alf.

For a second, the room seemed a complete furnace, and he thought he saw others there—shadows in the fire, at least three of them, standing in the blaze along the walls. Yet he was not burning, and neither were the figures that blurred along the fire.

Alf's eyes had returned to normal, but were glassy as he stared at Ethan.

Finally, a voice came from the little boy's mouth. A voice that could not have been his.

"Help the Lady of Shalott," a man said. Although Ethan knew the voice came from Alf, it seemed to echo all around him. It was a bestial, horrible voice, and one that was neither loud nor soft.

And then a woman's voice came from Alf, "You can't help her. No one can. She is one of us. She is one of us."

And then the voice was a boy's, another boy, not Alf, but a boy with a strange accent. "Seven was too many, too many, too many for the chapel. Seven. Seven. Seven. The cross of the chapel took the ritual and he brought it to himself."

Another voice emerged, overlapping with the first. "And moving through a mirror clear that hangs before her all the year, shadows of the world appear." A whisper grew louder, "Shadows of the world appear, shadows of the world appear," and even within these whispers, Ethan heard what sounded like a monk chanting in Latin, and then a language he had never before heard, like the wind and the sound of wild tongues.

A man's voice began singing a strange nursery rhyme, "Mary Anne, Annie, and Elizabeth you know, they are all such pretty maids in a row. Catherine and Mary Jane would like to join the dance, Annie and Fairy Fay they all want some romance, and my knife's so nice and sharp, I think I'll get a chance, will you won't you will you won't you, won't you join the dance?"

Ethan felt spellbound as he stood there, and no longer noticed the heat or the flames. He was aware that glass burst somewhere nearby and he could hear it shattering against the walls; somewhere behind him he could hear the sound of a woman weeping.

But the voices within the child were like a puzzle, and they seemed to move into his mind and take root. "Mary Anne, said Catherine, will you wait upon the lane, your heart belongs to someone else, and you are soaked with rain. Catherine, said Mary Anne, you're in some sort of trance, will you won't you will you won't you, won't you join the dance? We are waiting on the shingle, will you won't you join the dance?"

The boy rose slowly from the floor, his arms spread, the tongues of fire spurting from his fingertips, his eyes bloodshot, and his mouth sagging open while the multitude of voices poured from him.

He floated there, less than a foot above the ground.

Plaster from the ceiling began falling like snow all around them. The voices were clashing together until it was all unintelligible and began to sound like the lowing of bulls and the squealing of pigs.

Above the roar that Ethan could not block from his head, he saw the angel from the statue garden, just the vision of a woman standing beside Alf, and he felt a strange comfort despite the terror that froze his heart.

Then the vision of the angel became the fire, and Ethan felt his senses returning. Quickly, he grabbed Alf, who fell into his arms. Ethan lost his balance, and, still holding Alf, fell backward to the kitchen floor. He felt glass beneath his shirt and sat up quickly, clutching the boy close.

"It's all right. It's all right," he said, relieved. "I've got you. I've got you."

It stopped.

The fire was gone, the wall unburned, the plaster intact, and the only sign of struggle was the broken glass all around the floor.

Ethan looked at the boy's face. The scratches were clearly visible.

His lips were parched, and the stench remained, an indescribable smell that was both sweet and rotten. A memory of a smell: fallen apples in November, the last of the yellowjackets that had survived summer; yellowjackets, fallen and twitching, around the brown rotting apples.

A terrible silence ensued, just as the silence had been when Ethan had seen the little girl in the front hallway.

Ethan felt something heave within him, and a shuddering began. Tears blurred his vision; he rocked back and forth, holding the boy; he felt an overwhelming sadness and loss with Alf's small body against his shoulder and chest. It felt as if Alf were his own flesh and blood. He felt something pass from his hands, something like an iciness. He held Alf close.

Ethan felt confused by the emotion that had come over him so suddenly. Not the fear or terror he'd just felt, but a curious calm mixed with sadness. The poor child. The poor child. What had happened?

What could have happened here? What's in this house? What spirits occupy this space? What nightmare did my grandfather create within these walls?

And then, in his gut, he knew why he had the sadness.

He looked at the boy again, at his eyes, at his sagging jaw.

Alf was dead?

Dead. Lifeless.

No, he thought. *No, you're not. I know you're not.*

Ethan brought the boy's face up close to his. *No, you're not dead.*

You can't be dead. You won't be dead.

Then Alf opened his eyes, but his jaw remained slack. Ethan wiped at the tears across his own face. A melting joy returned to him, as he saw the life in Alf's eyes and the blush return to the little boy's face. Ethan cradled him, supporting his head in his hands.

Alf closed his mouth slowly, as if it hurt, and then opened it again. He said, in a growling whisper, a voice that was distinctly female but also low and heavy. For a second Ethan was put in mind of a nun. *"Stet Fortuna Domus. Stet Fortuna Domus. Stet Fortuna Domus."*

From behind him, Ethan heard Pocket say, "Good Lord. Good Lord."

Then, Pocket blurted, "Where's his mother?"

Alf shivered. He whispered something. Ethan leaned nearer to him—turning his ear to the boy's lips.

"Alf?" Ethan asked.

The boy whispered, his voice weak, "The house ate her."

Part Two

May the House's Fortune Stand

"In another moment Alice was through the glass, and had jumped lightly down into the Looking-glass room."
—Lewis Carroll, *Through the Looking-Glass and What Alice Found There*

Chapter Seven

1

Now I will step back in here, for it seems that the time has come to tell you more about myself.

These are not things that I knew before my time at Harrow—after my grandfather's death. In fact, the night that Alf cried out his obscenities and nursery rhymes in the inferno of a kitchen, some door within myself had become undone, off its hinges. Something within me opened.

But seeing him there, pitching in a fever of some mysterious influence, I remembered myself as a boy, after I'd been nearly stung to death by yellowjackets in my grandfather's garden. You know I was born Esteban Gravesend, and I soon acquired the name of Ethan. You also know that I came to inherit my grandfather's estate. From what I've remembered here, you know how serious I have been about the haunting at Harrow. It was—and is—very real.

It was like breath on a windowpane on a steamy

day. It was like the smell of smoke after a candle has been snuffed. It was there, always, even when the manifestations did not take over a little boy named Alfred Barrow. Even the previous twilight when I felt the little girl approach me, a ghost come to investigate the intruder to her domain.

I mentioned, in my telling of my life, that when I was a boy visiting my grandfather at his estate, I had a singular feeling that something warm surrounded me. In the garden among the statues.

Something that hummed with its own life swirling about me as I stood there, looking up at my grandfather who waved frantically to me from the window.

Of course, I had stepped into a nest of yellowjackets, but there was more—for I felt her presence, a woman who I had begun to feel was my guardian angel, right then, as a child.

I was not protected from the bites of the yellowjackets, and when I next awoke, I was in the bedroom in the east wing of Harrow that had been dedicated to my brief and all-too-infrequent visits.

2

It was a room that was lush, from the velvet of the heavy curtains at the window, to the thick bed on which I slept nightly—piled three mattresses high. The room was papered in gold. I felt as if I were the Sun King at times, sleeping in the glories of a lost empire. A chiffonier—what my nursemaid Mrs. McCutcheon (who never came to Harrow on these trips) called a chiffarobe—stood in one corner with its tall, curved mirror and a bowl and pitcher for water.

My grandfather still believed in chamber pots in every room, and the one beside my bed was big enough for me to sit down in and pretend I was in a boat; I never used it for its intended purpose, and I'm not sure that I knew what it was used for at all, since I had no problem walking down the hall to the water closet.

The room was my world of dreams.

My rocking horse stood in the corner, a gift from my grandfather years earlier, and on the wall, portraits of various children. One of them was me as a baby, one was probably my father, although I did not know which one, and one was my grandfather as a baby; there were others. Recuperating from the stings, I lay in a feverish state for a full day, during which time a nurse came to my side to keep watch over me.

She was a less than handsome woman even by the standards of Watch Point—her hips were broad and accommodating, her breasts boxy and well formed, and her uniform starched and stiff. She looked as if she'd been cut from local quarries and filled with cement. She was a substitute mother for those few days as I recovered from the stings. She placed plasters and salves on me and brought me soups and the dreaded steamed cabbage, which, she told me, would heal me as well as any medicine.

I did not like her at all, nor did I fancy the food she brought—I began to think of her as a witch trying to poison me. This grew into a mania that prevented me from devouring some perfectly good meals by the second day of my fevered incarceration.

I pretended to eat, but slipped the food instead to my right, beneath my pillow. It piled up into an awful stink there, which I further corrupted by pushing it beneath the first and second mattress when my witch-nurse wasn't looking. She must have had no sense of smell, for the pungent odor of quickly rotting cabbage grew, and she never seemed to notice.

She told me her name was Hildy, and that she was from Beacon, but had moved up to Watch Point when she met her husband. She told me too much about her marriage—about how her husband worked with the railroad, but was studying one day to work in bonds down in the city. She began to feel like a very lonely sad woman to me, and by the second night, I had developed sympathy for her. I told her that when her husband was very rich in New York, he ought to buy her a cottage by the sea like the one I lived in. She enjoyed this kind of fantasy, and that evening made plans for her future as the wife of a rich man.

Hildy began recounting her tales of Harrow, as she called them. She thought of it as a very spiritual place, and it was then that I noticed her ever-present rosary and the cross around her neck. She told me that she felt she had seen one of the saints one night when she was working many years before in the house that she was told by the saint to serve the Lord through her service to Harrow. She even laughed about this, for, she told me, she only half believed in the vision.

"My faith is unwavering," she said, pawing at my forehead with a cool cloth, "but my eyesight is another story."

She asked me if I had any playmates, and I told her that I didn't, although I had once had a pet rabbit with whom I spoke. "And I think I saw an angel."

"Sometimes God shows us His face in our minds. In fever," she added, nodding to herself. "Shall I get you some more mustard for your chest?"

"No," I moaned, not wanting the poultice or the plaster or whatever infernal and stinky concoction she would create in that hellish nurse kitchen of hers. I grew curious, watching her. She had not blinked at my mention of my angel. She was an odd woman. Not like my mother who told me that angels were part of the Bible and not life. Curiosity got the better of me. "Tell me about angels," I said.

"We all have a guardian angel," she said. "When I was a child, I had a special candle that I lit for my guardian angel. I would ask the angel to take care of me and my mother." She brought her hand up to the side of my face. "Those hornets made a meal of you, Ethan."

But I wanted to talk about angels. "She's pretty and warm and she protects me," I told her.

"That's the job of angels," Hildy sighed, and later, when she nodded off in the rocking chair, I thought about my angel and why she hadn't protected me from the bites. She wasn't a very good guardian angel, even though I had felt cared for when the yellowjackets surrounded me. I felt cared for and guarded. And bitten half to death.

143

3

That night, I lay back in that treasure box of a bed and began creating imaginary playmates for myself out of thin air. First, I thought of a giraffe with two heads who spoke a quaint version of French—what little I knew of the language—and then I imagined a jaguar from South American jungles speaking perfect English to me.

I grew thirsty, and was about to call out to Hildy, but she snored so loudly and had worked so hard to force-feed me her awful cabbage and broth, that I let her rest. My fever was not burning quite so strongly. I marshaled what energy I could. I fumbled with my nightshirt, drawing my shivery, scrawny legs over to the floor.

Catching my balance, I grabbed one of the bed-posts, and nearly crawled over to the big pitcher and bowl.

Once I reached the chiffonier, I lifted the pitcher up to my face to drink directly from it. As I did so, I caught a glimpse of my own reflection in the mirror.

I was parched and burning up again. I had half a mind to pour the entire pitcher over my head in order to cool my blood. The candles in the wall sconces lent a hazy glow to the shadowy room (and my even more shadowy vision) like streetlights through heavy fog.

I saw my face, waxy and yellow in the candlelight.

My eyes were sunken, my hair greasy and pressed flat against my face, although some of it stuck out at the top of my scalp. My face was puffy from the bites, and my left eye still looked swollen shut, although I could see fairly well through it.

I could neither laugh nor shudder at this vision of myself. I felt sorry for it and at the same time, I felt that I looked like someone other than myself. This wasn't me, after all. It was some other boy who had stepped into a nest of flying monsters, and he looked funny and pathetic.

Then I noticed a movement back by the lamp near my bed. Just a blur. My vision followed the movement in the mirror.

What was it? I found that I could not take my eyes away from the mirror. It was the old sort, with an oval and beveled glass, which distorted the edges of what it reflected.

Was it a sparrow trapped in the room? What moved so frantically at my bed?

I could see Hildy in the chair, her head lolling back a bit against the blanket she'd propped as a pillow. I told myself that I was just imagining things. I was fine. There was no one and nothing else in the room.

I saw the blurred thing again, only this time, it was in bed, and I realized, suddenly, that there were two indentations in the bed—mine, that I had just left—and this blurred thing, this smudge of something, next to where I'd been sleeping off my fever.

I quickly glanced back, nearly toppling over in the process, to see what was on the bed, but the bed was empty. Then I checked the mirror.

A little girl sat in the bed. A little girl with a round face and long dark curls, and eyes that seemed impossibly small. I watched her in the mirror to see if I really saw her. I kept repeating something to myself—perhaps even aloud—something about the girl not being real, that she was imaginary just like the jaguar and the two-headed giraffe. But she sat there, her head resting on one of the pillows. Not watching me. Not watching anyone. It was as if it were her bed, and she lived in the mirror all the time.

When I turned around, she was right behind me. Her hollow eyes. The look of yearning and pain within her flesh.

In the blink of an eye, it was not a little girl at all.

4

Now, after the memory returned to me, I can look back on what I saw, and know that it was probably induced by the venom of those insects within me.

But then, all I knew was fear, and the heat beneath my skin that seemed to steam as I saw it. It was, very simply, a wisp of smoke hanging in the air. Smoke and a voice, which said in a man's voice, "Esteban, you belong to us."

I dropped the pitcher to the floor. It shattered at my feet, and the smoke dissipated.

I felt the full force of fever hit.

Hildy jumped from the rocking chair and grabbed me up in her heavy arms. She brought me back to the bed, scolding me for getting out of it. I spent the rest of the night huddled in a corner of the bed, staring at the pillow, my teeth chattering from fear and fever.

A slight indentation remained along one of the pillows in my bed, as if the little girl still lay there beside me. I even imagined that I could hear her breathing.

My fever burned, and what parts of my body that were not swollen were on fire. Every ounce of my being ached and felt as if the bones wanted to tear from my flesh.

Yet, after an hour or two of this, I became very detached from my body, and felt as if I were watching this little boy toss and turn in yellowjacket-inspired fever.

I saw the nurse, with her round fish eyes and her cold Watch Point manner as she hesitated to put the cool, damp hand towel on the boy's forehead.

I watched myself—the boy—open his eyes briefly, looking as if he were fighting to wake from a dream. And knowing that somewhere in the room, the little girl waited for me. I didn't know why, or what she wanted, or who she was.

All I knew was that I didn't want her to come near me again. That was the memory I had suppressed. The same one that returned to me, like the remembered odor of hot cocoa on a winter's day of childhood, like a pleasant memory, nearly, because it brought with it a feeling a familiarity and comfort even with the nightmare aspect.

And now, I will return you to Ethan and Constable Pocket and young Alf, as they are still in the kitchen, recovering from the beginning of a night of mystery.

Even now I can watch myself, the man called Ethan, and even now I wish to caution him:

Everything is not as it seems.

147

Chapter Eight

1

Ethan felt his heart race, as he stood, still clutching Alf.

The boy's eyes had closed, and he had gone silent. Ethan heard his gentle, steady breaths.

He was in a deep sleep. Ethan glanced about the kitchen. A strange silence continued, as if all sound in the world had ended.

"It's like a game," he said finally, a thought that had come from nowhere. He wasn't sure why he had said it. His voice echoed along the tile floor of the kitchen. He looked at the great Easter range that had seconds ago been an inferno.

Behind him the constable stood, looking every inch the man who had just been thrown from the train wreck of a dream. "Let's take the boy somewhere where he can rest," Pocket said.

2

Ethan had grabbed a silk throw from the large over-stuffed chair in the parlor and wrapped Alf up in it.

The boy showed signs of exhaustion with a sweat so heavy it soaked through his trousers and shirt. His eyes remained closed. He was at peace in some dream. Pocket helped raise the boy to the loveseat. Ethan set a pillow beneath Alf's head.

The child looked so peaceful, it was as if nothing had happened.

"I'm sure she's somewhere nearby," Pocket said.

"It's too much," Ethan said, looking at the sleeping child, and then to Pocket. "What in God's name was that? It's not a hallucination. It's not a dream. It's real. Whatever that was. Whatever was . . . inside him . . . was real."

Pocket went to the lamps and turned them up—the shadows had overtaken the room, and the sudden burst of lamplight created a warmth in the parlor.

Ethan sat down in the overstuffed chair.

"He said the house ate her."

"I'm sure she's somewhere nearby," Pocket repeated, as if this were a chant to comfort himself.

"Do you think he's all right?"

"I couldn't say, sir." Pocket went to the window, where rain and wind battered the pane. He drew the sash. The heavy curtain fell across it. "It's a terrible night, just terrible."

"She must be in the house somewhere," Ethan said, and felt mindless even suggesting it. He had only just remembered something from his own childhood—the little girl in his sick bed, the voice of the smoke telling him that he was one of them. "I believe," he said, as if struggling with these thoughts.

"Believe?" Pocket asked.

"In ghosts," Ethan said.

3

Ethan returned to the kitchen, hoping to find some evidence of Maggie Barrow, but there was none at the small door that led out back to the Holy Land, nor along the great fireplace.

Outside in the garden, he called to her as lightning battered the sky, illuminating the trees and abbey like the bombs of the war; rain came down in great slashes, and he was soaked to the skin when he finally went back inside, muddy with defeat.

Next, he began going hall to hall, and floor to floor. He had been calling for Maggie for nearly an hour, wandering corridors, room to room, hoping to see some sign of her, but there was nothing.

Every door seemed to be locked, although a quick try with the master keys managed to open all of them.

The rooms were empty, or filled with dustcovers, or simply packed with dusty furnishings.

When he reached the tower room, he had a sense of dread. He didn't want to see the dead woman again—Matilde—and in some small way, he didn't want to go up there by himself.

4

Show some courage. It's a corpse. It's nothing more. It's just a corpse. It's a dead body that has probably been there for at least a year. It's someone who is no longer in that body. She's long dead. You could call down to Pocket, but he needs to stay with Alf. You don't need to go up there. Why are you going up there? Why are you afraid?

His thoughts circled in his mind, and then he just blocked them. He was going up there. He had to check every part of the house.

5

Ethan went back up those stairs, past the small outer room, and, holding up his lamp, stepped inside the turret room.

He felt a strange tingling as soon as he was within the walls. He saw the writing in chalk.

It said, "Feed Harrow." Beneath this, "Help the Lady of Shalott."

Ethan closed his eyes for a moment. *Don't let it get to you. Don't let whatever this is get inside you. They want to get inside you, and you aren't going to let them.* He felt the small hairs on the back of his neck rise. His spine seemed to crackle with electricity.

A light static wind came from nowhere.

He looked at the place where the woman's body should've been.

6

Perhaps the worst thing, something within him whispered, *isn't that you think you're going insane the way your grandfather must have been insane. And it isn't that she's not lying there, this dead woman named Matilde. And it isn't that you're feeling the knots in your stomach or the nausea or the dizziness in your head or the tightening in your fists or the sense that every hair on your body is standing on end. It's that you know that somehow you are part of this.*

From behind him, he heard a hissing noise like steam, and something slithered along the dark floor, something moved toward him, crawling, some creature on the floor sliding toward him from a dark recess of the room.

"Esteban, come to me, my darling, my precious, my only one." Ethan felt a hand grab his ankle.

7

Ethan turned cold as he looked down into the shadows to see what creature held him.

It was Maggie.

8

She had on some elemental level become more beautiful in the flickering light of the room. Her hair was swept back, a red so fiery as if to give off its own flame.

153

Her face was chalk white and shiny, nearly reflective, like a mirror lit with a brilliant lamp, her eyes crimson red stones. Her clothes had been shredded around her so that he glimpsed her bare shoulders and back as she lay there, moving like a snake as she held tightly to his ankle. Her tongue, long and lascivious—and yes, he thought, serpentlike—darted along the edges of her thick bee-stung lips as she whispered obscenities to "my Esteban, my dearest, my precious one, my most loved."

She rose in a shocking way, her hips and buttocks rising, her dress torn in strips about her thighs so as to reveal her tender and beautiful flesh.

She moved like a cat in heat, her hindquarters first, and then she pressed her free hand to the floor, her breasts, barely covered with her torn blouse, nearly visible to him.

She was suddenly a demon—a sexual, supernatural being within the flesh of Maggie Barrow, and rather than feel the animal fire that this creature no doubt meant to inspire, Ethan felt a tremendous sadness for Maggie to be so humiliated by the demon that possessed her body. Her fingernails dug into the flesh around his left calf, drawing blood.

"Maggie," he gasped. "Stop. Let go."

She leaned into him, nuzzling his calf. "Oh Esteban, you have returned at last to your home, to the ones who love you."

"Matilde," Ethan finally managed to say, and his whole being trembled. "Matilde, leave me. Leave this place. Leave Maggie."

"Who's Matilde? Who's Matilde?" Maggie looked up at him, a wicked smile upon her face, her head nodding back and forth as she spoke with the voice of a deranged teenager.

As if she were somehow a spray of liquid, Maggie seemed to grow from a crouching position.

Her flesh flowed upward, and she stood before him, the image of Maggie as she had been before—the pure Maggie, the sweet face, the hair falling along her shoulders, her aspect neat and presentable.

Even her eyes were back to normal.

Tears streamed down her face. She moved her lips as if trying to speak, but no words came out. And then, her eyes went wide. Her arms went to her sides as if she were being bound by unseen rope.

She opened her mouth to scream, but again, all was silence. Then, something pulled her—something drew her so quickly it was as if she'd been jerked back. Something drew her against the far wall—swiftly. And then every lamp and candle extinguished, including the one in Ethan's hand.

He dropped it to the floor, but did not hear the glass break. Ethan stood in the darkness and began hearing the voices.

9

At first they were faint, and then they began to get loud enough to understand. They seemed of indeterminate sex—one moment, Ethan felt sure they were women's voices, then children's, and then men's.

"You were supposed to wait. He could've waited."

"I am so hungry."

"Please, just a spoonful?"

"A taste?"

"The child was mine. The child was mine. I could've tasted his blood."

"Mirror cracked. Mirror cracked. Side to side."

"He's scared now. Watch him. He'll come to us soon."

"I want to play. I'm tired of this game," a little girl said, almost haughtily. "I want to play my game."

"Don't let her have her way. Wicked, wicked child," someone—an elderly woman?—said. "She'll bring them out again and then there's no way to put them back."

"I am starved. Give me some life. I want it now. I want the taste. She doesn't need to live."

"The other one is coming. I can hear her. That devil. That devil!"

A man bellowed, "GET OUT OF MY HOUSE!" again and again, and the voices all began chattering.

Ethan felt frozen to the spot.

The entire room was dark, and even the candles in the outer room had been snuffed. He was afraid to move. He felt his throat go dry. He wanted to call out, but he didn't know to whom he would call.

Maggie?

Pocket?

God?

There is no God, he thought.

There is no God. No one is going to come help you. No one is going to rescue you. You must do this yourself.

Or die.

And then, he felt it as he stood there.

Despite his trembling, despite his abject fear, he had a sense of something beyond the room, beyond the house.

Was it God? He hated to even think it, but it felt as if there were something within him—some inspiration—that was not part of his physical being. A sense of not being alone against this.

A sense that he was here for a reason.

He stood in this dark room for a reason greater than mere survival. He knew it. He felt it.

There had to be more to this life than standing in the darkness with the terror he felt.

The dread.

There had to be something more.

He stood there, and managed to clasp his hands together. He knew no prayer to offer. He knew no magical words of religion.

All he knew was that if there were a God listening, to just be there. To just be there with him.

On one hand, he felt as if he were fooling himself. On the other, just the thought of God—the thought of some being taking care of this, watching this, protecting him in some indefinable way—comforted him.

And then it was gone, and he felt a growing panic in the dark. Fear split his being. He thought his mind might be playing tricks—casting shadows within the dark. Ethan began to feel his mind unraveling, showing memories like moving pictures, all the way back to his childhood, all the way back to lying in his bed as a toddler, and even further, he was there in a nearly dark room as a woman screamed and beat against a wall with her fists while two men and a woman stood over her.

The inky darkness within his mind returned, and suddenly the keening wails of a baby burst all around him, echoing. The badsmell began—wafting toward him, as if by memory alone.

Someone whispered, "Esteban, come to me, come within these walls."

A woman said, "You can't take him from me," and then began screaming. "Esteban! Esteban!"

A man began shouting, "GET OUT OF MY HOUSE! GET HIM OUT OF MY HOUSE! HE'S ONE OF THEM! HE'S ONE OF THEM!"

And then, another voice came from the woman, a child's voice, "Let me play now. I need to play. Give me my little playmate."

He felt a child's hand slide across the thumb and forefinger of his right hand, which now trembled along with the rest of his body.

"Come with me," the little girl said, her only image darkness.

10

The darkness took on a shape and a texture—it was like a smooth alabaster surface, and its coldness became numbing. Then he felt spots of heat pass along his neck and shoulders, and something brushed along his ankles. He was led down a winding staircase, which he took slowly and carefully, step by step.

He went along in the dark, the hand of the child clutching his, drawing him forward.

Someone said, "Let me taste him."

"No," said the child, her fingers tightening around his. "He belongs to me."

She squeezed his fingers harder, and he tried to draw back from her grasp but could not. Then, a sudden flare of light came up. Ethan stood there, alone, clutching no one's hand within his.

He was in the turret room.

Constable Pocket stood in front of him with a lamp. "I thought you might've come back up here."

As if expecting just such a jolt—for Ethan had been positive that he'd been going down a staircase with the little girl—Ethan nodded. "There are hundreds of manifestations in this house, Pocket."

"No," the other man shook his head. "I think there may be just one. One disguised as many."

11

Shaken but relieved and both trembling and laughing to himself, Ethan went with the constable back down the stairs.

"The house has Maggie. I saw her. I saw what it wanted me to see of her," Ethan said.

"Perhaps," Pocket said. "Perhaps what you saw—"

"I saw too much," Ethan added. "I heard voices. I felt them. I saw things. I saw."

"There are illusions here," Pocket said. "I knew it when she was a girl, Mr. Gravesend. Matilde could throw her voice. That was the beginning of it. And then, perhaps after her father had brought her from the tomb, the voices had become more than voices. Perhaps she . . ." He paused as they reached the landing of the first floor. "Alf is no longer himself. He woke up. He just stared at me. Unblinking."

"Catatonic?" Ethan asked.

"I don't know. It began to make me feel uncomfortable, his staring. As if he could see through to my soul." Pocket withdrew a beloved cigar, and thrust it, unlit, into his mouth. He spoke around it. "There's nothing scarier than a child who looks through you. Tell me, sir, have you ever done anything truly monstrous in your life?"

Ethan didn't respond right away. Then, he said, haltingly, "I don't think so. No."

"Not the small monstrosities of ordinary life," Pocket said. "But the grand ones. I did something monstrous once. I helped wall your aunt into the house. I helped your grandfather keep his secret. I knew about the others."

"Others?" Ethan asked.

"The ones she murdered. The gathering that your grandfather had invited into the house. The psychics."

12

"Murdered?"

"Yes," Pocket said.

"What do you mean? What precisely do you mean?"

"I didn't witness it, of course. I don't even know

for sure. I just suspect. I suspect, and I . . ."

"You're sworn to uphold the law and you never investigated murders at—"

"You don't even know," Pocket said, with such authority that Ethan took a breath and stepped away from him. "Insanity, sir. Your family. Your aunt. She manifested things. She was not always herself. She was splintered in some way. Mentally. I suppose with what she'd gone through as a child, it might be expected. But it was not your grandfather's fault if she killed, is it? He kept her safe here. He kept her safe. But the others. Those others. They came to take something from her. To get inside her. And they did. I suppose. They got inside her. And she," he added, "got inside them."

13

They went to check on Alf, who had fallen back to sleep, curled up in a ball like a kitten.

Pocket began jabbering about knowing things, but not knowing them, feeling them, sensing them, of people who came and went in the house. ("Famous people. People with names like Lizzie Borden and Aleister Crowley and other names, and the gossip in the village became unmanageable. Isis was famous, too. She was known around the world. Crowned heads and all that kind of thing. She could talk to the dead. She could predict the future. She was considered to be the whore of Babylon when she'd arrive in her fancy roadster. . . . I finally had to say something to your grandfather. I finally had to mention the scandal he was bringing down upon us, but by then, by then . . .")

Pocket had just reached the study and, as if not having thought much about it, picked up the telephone and pressed it to his ear.

"It's dead. Of course," Pocket said, setting down the receiver.

The air seemed charged in some way that Ethan could not have described—and he felt that Pocket must have sensed it, too. It was like a drop in barometric pressure in this room.

The thought came to him: *Something is here. In here. With Alf.*

Pocket hesitated, as if he were about to say something of some gravity.

Then, "He still used the old kind. That's so much like him. And yet so modern of him, too. The most modern thing in this house is his telephone."

"The line would be dead with this storm," Ethan said, but felt as if he were just assuaging his own fears. Despite the crashes of thunder outside and the hard rain that had battered at the windows as they'd descended staircase after staircase, this room was peculiarly silent.

He wanted to say something about it, but thought better of it. *Pocket must feel it, too. We're just talking around what we're feeling here.*

"Blasted storm."

"What time is it?" Ethan asked.

"There's a clock in the hall," Pocket said.

"I know. It stopped sometime earlier. I certainly haven't been winding anything lately. I assumed Wentworth . . ."

"She hasn't kept up," Pocket said, as if this were a given. "I suppose we can thank God she's not here to-night."

"She never stays after dark."

"I can't say as I blame her."

A brief silence ensued; then Ethan said, "Tell me about it. About this gathering."

"A salon," Pocket said, nearly amused with the word. "Are you hungry?"

"Not at all. Just exhausted."

"I could eat a whole sheep right now. A whole sheep spread with mint jelly. I'm that starved."

"All I can think of is Maggie. She's here somewhere."

"Yes, I'm sure of that. There are other ways."

"Ways?"

"Ingress and egress."

"Secret passages?"

"Very much so," Pocket said.

Ethan arched an eyebrow, begging the question.

"Don't look at me like that," Pocket said. "I don't know the ways through the inner part of this house. I just know there are ways." Then, an afterthought: "Perhaps after the storm—at dawn—we can go get help. We'll have a search party."

"A search party in a house?"

Pocket shook his head. "You don't even know."

Ethan felt as if he were being led into a game of Blind Man's Bluff. "Know what?"

Pocket half smiled, shaking his head, but amusement didn't seem to be etched there. It was nearly a half grimace. "Mr. Gravesend with his puzzles. It's a looking-glass house."

"Looking glass?"

"Mirrors. There are mirror rooms for every room in this house. He built it that way. For every bedroom, there is another crawlspace. For every library, there is a room of ancient tomes. For every staircase, there is a descent into the caves that open beneath this house. There are bedrooms that may not be the kind of bedroom with a comfortable bed. There is a foyer, I'm told, that is quite grand. And then, well, I've heard . . ." Pocket's voice trailed off. His mood shifted, and suddenly he brightened. "Here's the thing, sir. Here's the thing." Pocket began fumbling with words as some people fumble for change in their pockets—words like "spiritualists" and "magicians" and "explorers" and "grave robbers" spilled out when his mouth had emptied.

Ethan very much felt like having a good stiff drink, but he still wasn't sure if Pocket's hypocrisy would allow him to openly have one. "Grave robbers?"

"Body snatchers. All. He gathered people around him who had unusual occupations. He was fascinated with the afterlife. He was drawn to the rituals of death. He was said to have books stolen or bought dearly from great collections. Your grandfather. He was a remarkable man. He was a haunted man."

"Look," Ethan said, "all I want is to find Maggie. It won't wait until dawn. It won't wait for a search party. If she's in this house, this looking-glass house, we will find her. You and I both. And I don't want to find out an hour from now that you know something about this house and its passages and you haven't told me."

Chapter Nine

1

But, in fact, nearly an hour had passed, and Ethan had learned very little from Pocket beyond words to the effect that his grandfather had a great deal of fear of what he called "restless spirits," and of the condition that affected his daughter.

They had decided to move Alf to a bed in the caretaker's cottage ("Safer there, I'd think," Ethan said, somewhat warily, wondering whether the constable knew of any hauntings at the smaller house); in the slashing rain, returning to Harrow, Ethan shivered as much from fear as from the cold. Pocket began shouting at him about how insane it was even to live in Harrow and why did he come. Ethan shouted back, equally ferociously, that none of that mattered now; all that mattered was finding Maggie and making sure she was unharmed.

Somehow, as their shouts barely rose above the cracks of thunders and the steady hammering of rain, it was comforting to be free of the house for even a few minutes.

2

Their shouting had turned to whispers and murmurs by the time they were inside again.

Upon entering Harrow, Ethan felt a weight pressed against him—as if the pressure of his mind were closing in around him.

It was almost like the beginning of a deep but unwanted sleep—a feeling of being warmly drugged in some way.

"Do you feel it?"

Pocket nodded. "You feel something?"

Ethan nodded, but the sensation intensified. "It's like . . . like someone is wrapping me in blankets."

Pocket reached over and felt his forehead. "You're running a fever."

"Am I? Am I?" Ethan asked, not sure if he could make sense. Sleep beckoned; that's what it felt like. Sleep within him was drawing him down into some darkness. Then he gasped, "It's Harrow. It's Harrow. I wasn't sleepy five seconds ago. But now . . . ."

Pocket reached over and put his arm across Ethan's shoulders. "She was like that. Here, let me help you sit down."

"She?"

"That woman."

"Matilde?"

"No. The other one. The one he loved. The Lady of Shalott, he called her."

The words seemed to echo his own voice, for Ethan felt he heard himself say, "The Lady of Shallots," and remembered seeing Maggie the first night in the garden, digging up her vegetables from the Holy Land, and calling her that, as a lark, the Lady of Shallots. Words from the poem by Tennyson went through his mind: *Four gray walls, and four gray towers, Overlook a space of flowers, And the silent isle imbowers The Lady of Shalott.*

"Her name was Isis. She was quite beautiful. She was in love with your grandfather. There was no mistaking. I suppose he loved her, too," Pocket said. "I suppose one would have to love a woman to do what he did to her."

"She felt . . . things?"

"Well, she would. She was a medium. A spiritualist, she called herself, but truth was, she had come into his life to destroy him. To draw him back to something that he should have well left. And she felt it here, too. She said it was a special place. She said she had traveled around the world, but had never felt it like she did here. I can't say too much of her. I can't say much. She was who she was. And Harrow destroyed her. It destroyed her. But enough of that. Do you believe in the spirit world, sir?"

Feeling a bit stronger, Ethan coughed and said, "Ever since I was a boy. Returning here has only reconfirmed that. How can I help but believe?" Then he felt cooler. It was gone. It had passed over. Whatever had caressed him in the foyer had vanished. It was as if a chilly draft had entered the house.

He held his hand out, half expecting to feel a form in the air.

Instead, his fingers began tingling with something that at first seemed like iciness, but as he kept his hand steady, he realized that he could create a shape in the air around the feeling of electricity. A cold electricity.

"Here," he whispered, as if afraid of being overheard. "Pocket. Put your hand here. Like this."

Pocket thrust his hand in the air as if he were saluting some foreign dignitary. He gasped, withdrawing his hand.

Then Ethan nodded to him. "Do it again. Feel it. It's amazing."

Pocket pressed both his hands in a cup formation, and held them against the spot near Ethan's hand.

"It's as if there's a window—" Pocket began.

"No, not a draft. I thought that at first. It's like an electrical current. It curves, see? It runs vertically, and it curves. It has a form. It's here, wait."

"Enough, sir. Enough," Pocket said, shivering slightly.

"I wonder . . ." Ethan said, and then thrust his fingers into the cold spot.

The tingling went through his fingers and seemed to travel along his palms to his wrists. It moved like fluid, and his hand began twitching.

It began flowing along his forearms, and something told him not to let it go to his heart, that there was something about it, something within the energy he had tapped into that was not going to let him live, that wanted him dead.

The feeling sped through him, and he quickly pulled his hand back from the spot.

Panic melted. He was fine. It had not gotten to him. The fear had seized him, but he had not let it get into him. His hand felt numb for several seconds. "How do we get to these hidden areas?"

"Perhaps," Pocket began. And then, the telephone rang.

3

Ethan glanced at the constable, who would not look him in the eye. "It was dead."

"Yes, sir. It was."

"Now it's ringing." Ethan grabbed the candlestick telephone, lifting the earpiece, and holding the speaker in front of his lips. "Gravesend," he said.

The sound of whistling wind on the line, and then somewhere a woman began shrieking, but it was so distant as to be barely audible.

It grew louder: "Ethan! Help me! For the love of God, help me, help me, thousands are here. They want to— They have me in here. They want to bury me with them, oh God, help me—"

The wind came up on the line again, and he was sure he heard the sound of gentle laughter. The phone went silent.

Ethan clicked it on and off again, but the line didn't come back up. He set the phone down. "Maggie. I know it was her."

He felt his blood go cold, and he turned to face Pocket. He felt a change within himself. It was not the feeling he'd always had of innocence and world weariness and sadness mixed with a general happiness despite circumstances—in other words, it was not the feeling he had of who Ethan was, of what Ethan had become.

He felt as if he had been turned into an entirely different man. "The devil is in this house," he said, smashing the phone down to the floor. "Whether it is my grandfather or my aunt or this Lady of Shalott, I intend to find its source and destroy it."

He felt as if he had risen above something that had never grown up within himself. He felt as if he had been baptized with fire, and would not ever be the same man again.

4

"She said they were going to bury her with them," Ethan said. "We've wasted time. We have to find her now. Now—while she still has a chance."

Pocket nodded. "Then that's where we start looking."

"Where?"

"The crypt. Where people are buried," Pocket said.

Chapter Ten

1

Pocket donned his great black cape for the journey up to Bald Hill, where the graveyard spread, muddy and gray in the storm, which had only begun to let up a bit.

Ethan managed to grab an umbrella that barely protected him from the downpour as they walked in silence to the mausoleum of the Gravesends.

Bald Hill was a bare patch of sloping land just large enough for the graveyard that had once been an English farmer's family's final resting place, and now held what looked like a small stone structure. On closer inspection, in the great sweeping flashes of lightning that burst like bombs along the hills, it was a shining beacon of a mausoleum—shining because it seemed to reflect the storm like dark glass. There was something both ornate and simple about the building, and Ethan saw his family name carved in stone over the doorway.

Pocket slid in the mud getting to its entrance. He was over eager, Ethan could tell.

But something within Ethan hesitated. He wished to be elsewhere. He wished he could avoid whatever journey he must now go on.

And yet, he had a conflicting thought—beyond his duty, beyond even finding Maggie—that this was the most exciting moment of his life. That somehow, while he'd grown up, visiting Harrow, living with his parents, married to Madeleine (dear sweet Madeleine who had left him so that he'd return to Harrow alone, so that he'd have this adventure at all), it had put something within his soul to sleep—and now, he was waking up. Ethan hated to admit it to himself, but life had seemed a bit dull and gray to him. Suddenly, he felt his own blood surging through him. He felt fear and excitement. He knew that somehow it would all turn out all right. He would find Maggie. The secrets his grandfather had held dearly would be revealed. The night would pass into dawn.

He felt less self-assured when he stepped into the entryway of the stone structure and saw the lights inside.

"It's as if someone has been expecting us," Pocket said, fear evident on his face.

They stood in the chilly entryway, Ethan glancing back into the storm and then down the steps into the crypt. "Before we go there. Before we seek this out . . ." Ethan said, haltingly.

"This haunting," Pocket interrupted. "It's funny, sir. I have a revolver. I have my club. But what we're going to face is immune to this. I saw the séance. I was there, laughing while they held hands. Laughing while they contacted the dead. The artifacts were laid out. Relics of cathedrals. Ancient graves, robbed.

172

She—the woman named Isis Claviger—claimed that a helmet had belonged to a tortured man, a Knight Templar; that a spike belonged to a child murderer from hundreds of years ago; that perhaps even the Holy Grail itself was there, along with other ritual objects that she and your grandfather had collected over the years, all magical in some way. All had significance. And they brought her."

"Matilde?"

"Yes, sir," Pocket said.

Ethan thought, *He's shivering. His teeth are nearly chattering.* "Why? If she had this sickness . . ."

"Sir," Pocket whispered. "She was magical. I saw it with my own eyes. She made things happen. They were contacting the dead, and she was their radio. She brought things out. Some were her, but I saw it. She made those . . . those . . . things . . . come alive. She brought back the dead."

2

Down the stairs of the crypt, words were scrawled along the walls, although all seemed the fevered writing of someone who was insane. At the floor of the crypt, there were three graves with torches brightly burning above each. Pocket continued speaking nervously, and Ethan felt as if he were there in the room, years before, experiencing a séance: "It was a night without a storm, sixteen years ago. She was still young—at least, Matilde had not aged a great deal in those years she'd spent in darkness. She was beautiful, but she had that lost look,

173

as if she already lived too much in another world. Things had been taken from her. Her world had gone from the looking-glass to the prison of this house. Time had, in many ways, stopped for her many years before. She called some name over and over, and was driving your grandfather mad with it. He was mad and desperate, and the years had taken their toll. Your grandfather had kept her life a secret from all but a few. I was one of those. And this circle of his. This group, begun by this woman. But that woman—that Claviger—wanted to use his daughter for this grand experiment in spiritualism. Well, she learned soon enough, didn't she? There were others—perhaps half a dozen—from all over the world, people who called themselves spiritual, but I was sure they were merely charlatans. One man of seventy-two told me he'd been cataloging demons his entire life and believed Isis Claviger could call them up, if anyone could.

"Yes, sir, I kept laughing even through all of this, and I smiled when Isis Claviger showed me what she called the *Egyptian Book of Eternal Darkness*, written, so she claimed, on the skin of the priests of a god. Within the book, sacred words. And Matilde. Looking as confused and frightened as she had ever seemed to me, so skittish that they had to restrain her as if she were an animal, calling out some foreign name as if an imaginary lover would come to her rescue. Justin was nearly in tears with worry for his daughter, but that woman had reassured him—in ways that I can only imagine—that this would cure the girl, once and for all. That this would take her mind and close the doors to the world of the infinite. That's what that woman said.

"But you know, it did just the opposite. They began their circle at the table, and still, I smiled and chuckled, and thought that nothing would come of it other than poor Matilde being further pressed into the cage where her father kept her.

"Justin sat back and nodded as Claviger began her invocation to the dead, to the dead within the bones and rocks and pieces of history she had laid out upon the table.

"And then something was unleashed within Matilde. The voices, yes, the sounds, the cries of tortured children. There were the screams of women and men in agony. We were surrounded. I looked up and saw them there, like the smoke, and the temperature of the room dropped to near freezing. Hundreds of them. Faces within the smoke. Hands that came from nowhere. Mouths that opened and closed as if speaking. A smell as I have only smelled in a medical laboratory came up. An awful, vile odor. Matilde, who had been holding the relics in her hands, began shrieking, calling out a word, over and over as if the word would make it stop. I saw the armies of the dead standing around us. I knew the soul of madness, what was both within Matilde, who had something unimaginable in her mind, and outside her body as well. Something brought forth from the rituals that Claviger intoned, brought forth from the artifacts, and then, the bloodshed . . ."

3

Ethan had already begun investigating the corners of the room, and his grandfather and grandmother's grave as Pocket spoke.

He tried to lift the heavy table of the stone sepulcher, but it would not budge.

He glanced back at Pocket. "Matilde killed them all."

"No," Pocket said. "I don't really know. It seemed logical that she did, at least in terms of what I could not then believe. The candles went out, and all was silence. By the time your grandfather had lit a lamp, it was over. They were gone, all of them, all but Justin and myself. We didn't find them for several days. Horrible deaths, sir. Horrible. Beyond description. She had taken them to her rooms somehow. Between the apparitions we witnessed and the ritual, unspeakable things had been done to them."

"Nothing," Ethan said, "is unspeakable."

"Sir, some things truly are. I will say this about them: None of them died without agony. None of them died without seeing something terrible. They witnessed something so frightening that they must have been paralyzed with fear, sir. They showed no signs of struggle. No fight. Given what was done to them, any human being would've fought back, and probably could've. No, they saw something terrible that night, and they allowed themselves to be used as some kind of toy for whatever had been let out from the power that Matilde had. The power of your aunt and of those items. She had blood all over her body, sir. She was soaked in it. Their blood. And she was drawing strange markings along the walls of her rooms within the house.

"Perhaps the house itself was evil, for your grandfather told me something the next dawn.

"We sat together. No, we huddled together, and he confessed that he had gotten mixed up in a society of some sort when he was younger, and that he had done terrible things, but never knew that his own child would be infested from it. He had constructed the house based on some principles he had learned and some rituals he had performed when he was young and ignorant of the future he had created for himself. He rambled that morning, and I shivered just as I am doing now, sir. Just as this feels like that night again. Just as I know your grandfather built this house and its rooms to reach the other side. And now, after all these years, sir, I do not believe that Matilde was anything more than one who was tortured by her father's own guilt, driven mad by his own twisted desires to use her to reach some unfathomable goal known only to him. Or perhaps, he owed some debt to this society he had once belonged to. But he sacrificed his daughter's happiness to it, I knew this for sure. Still, I pitied him, but more than that, I pitied myself."

More quietly, he added, "I pressed this back in my mind. I refused to acknowledge it. After a while, it became like a dream. Like something that I had merely imagined but that had never happened."

"Why were you there at all?" Ethan asked, the question suddenly springing to his mind as if he'd meant to ask this all along. He looked at the constable, and suddenly saw it there—what he had mis-

Douglas Clegg

taken for fear. It was some kind of relief in the man's face. He had finally unburdened himself of this awful memory.

"I suppose I was the only human being your grandfather felt he could trust through this," Pocket said. "It seems monstrous now. All bad things do after they're done."

"Monsters." Ethan shook his head, wanting to grin, but feeling too grim to smile. "You all were monsters, weren't you? And there are still monsters here."

Ethan had just slipped his finger around the lid of the sepulcher that was meant to contain the remains of his aunt, and something gave.

There was a small trigger, which he pressed down upon, and the stone floor beneath him seemed to shift slightly. "Help me with this," he said. "I think I've found the way in."

4

The two men managed, after much huffing and puffing, to pull the stone table back. Pressing down on the trigger Ethan had found—a spring mechanism to one side of the stones—the floor beneath their feet moved, drawing back a flat wooden door that had previously rested beneath the grave. It felt less like a sepulcher than some kind of altar now.

Ethan took a deep breath. "I guess we need to go down there," he said.

Pocket took one of the torches from the wall and passed it to him.

Ethan stepped down into what he thought would be absolute darkness, but with the torchlight he could see several feet ahead of him as he crouched low, ducking his head as he moved through a narrow tunnel built of stone.

He held the torch ahead of him as he moved crab-like along the path. He brought the torch to the walls around him, and saw that they were loosely built against a cavern wall, which must have been a natural formation beneath the property. Thin streams of water flowed down the sides.

Soon, however, the tunnel opened up into what seemed at first like a room, but was actually a hallway of sorts. The first things he thought of when he saw it were photos he'd looked at in the magazine of the National Geographic Society recently about the ancient cities of Egypt that were being discovered beneath the sand.

It was like walking into a tomb of the Pharaohs.

Pocket, slowly moving behind him, called out, "Have you found anything yet?"

Ethan turned, torch in hand, and saw the man push himself from the narrow, low tunnel into the light of this corridor.

"It's not a mirror of the house," Ethan said. "It's a world. It's a complete world beneath the house."

The first thing Pocket said (after taking a few breaths) when he saw the columns and the hieroglyphs on the yellow stone walls: "It's waiting for us. She's here."

"I know. We'll find her. Maggie is alive. I can feel it," Ethan said.

"It's Matilde. She's here," Pocket said, mostly to himself. "She's been waiting for me."

5

"I feel it, too. She's here," Ethan said.

He felt overcome with a light-headedness, a burst of uncontrollable laughter within him, trying to get out. *I'm going mad,* he thought. *This is the first sign of my madness. No, perhaps the third or fourth, for I've seen more in these past several hours than a man is meant to see in a lifetime.*

Grim thoughts overtook him, images of an insane little girl dancing in a circle in the dark, and the mad giggle that had been within him subsided. The thought of nightmare and the fear of death were too much here. "Matilde is all around us," he said, an afterthought.

"Precisely," Pocket said. "Dear God, look."

He brought his torch along a wall, to the curious markings and symbols. There seemed to be a cross within a circle, surrounded by lines, forming a curious letter *H*. Around this symbol Ethan identified "ankhs"—the Egyptian symbol of eternal life.

"It's them."

"Who?"

"The Chymera Magick. The gathering of spiritualists and mediums. This was their mark."

"Just markings on a wall," Ethan said. "We'll find Maggie. We'll get her out of this place, and then . . ."

"Then?"

"We'll destroy it. This is a place of the dead," Ethan said. "They should remain buried here."

"You can't even begin to understand!" Pocket called after him, his voice echoing. "You were a child when your grandfather created this place. You were a child when she murdered them. You were a child when your grandfather came to me in tears because he needed help!"

Ethan turned back to face him. "Your guilt won't help anything, Pocket. Either keep quiet, or go back to the vault. Maggie may be dead for all we know. Maggie may be hurt. I am not going to leave her to the same fate that befell my aunt. I will not let this house have her."

Chapter Eleven

1

You see—I interrupt my own tale—I knew that I loved Maggie.

Oh, not the way that you imagine love comes with time and trouble and knowing someone. I had known when I met her that I felt love for her. I can still see myself in that chamber of the ancients, torch in my hand, feeling the courage of those who love and have stout hearts and must seek fate.

Part of me knew that Maggie and I were to be intertwined, even when I saw her in the Holy Land; even when she chided me and tossed me a wet rag for cleaning; even when I made little jokes with her son; she and I had that indefinable something, perhaps it was chemistry, that was meant by God and Nature to bind man and woman.

There is so little that human life can accomplish. The only true achievement is the binding of two human hearts in strength and love. I know this now. I did not know it then, but I wanted it. I wanted Maggie alive and with me. I wanted the nightmare to end.

2

I led the way in torchlight and silence. Pocket remained many feet back from me, mumbling to himself nearly incoherently. As I went forth—into what I perceived to be an ancient Egyptian tomb—I felt the majesty of what my grandfather had created here.

This was no mere imitation of history or reassembly of parts as if from a factory. This was the tomb of some pharaoh. Some great kingdom had held this space, thousands of years in the past. Each stone and statue placed in just such an arrangement, each jackal of some pure black rock, carved centuries before, lovingly set here to guard this underground realm.

I glanced up to the ceiling—it, too, was from some ancient city of Egypt and covered with designs and hieroglyphs. I remembered hearing from my grandfather of museums in Europe that held entire temples and wonders of the ancient world within them. This is what he himself had done. He had managed to carve out from the earth a place for his manias, a museum within caverns.

For a moment, I was caught up in the magnificence of it.

The great statues of a pharaoh and his queen dominated a brief staircase into another passageway. A sarcophagus lay at the center of the chamber, a beautiful woman's face over it—Nefertiti perhaps, or

Cleopatra—her headdress in the form of an ibis, her arms folded across one another, wrapped in a cloak of gold. I could not resist—I had to touch the image. I had to look at the sapphire eyes and the lips that nearly seemed to shine in my torch's light.

I tried to lift the lid, but it would not budge—it was sealed tight. That's when I heard a noise, and glanced about in the fog of shadows.

3

I thought I saw the darkness moving—but it was an animal. A cat.

Then I saw another and another—several shadows ran along the passage. The feral cats that were all over the garden above. They ran from the light, and I guessed that I now stood beneath the abbey ruins; and that these cats had means of escape into the upper world. I moved into the passage ahead, which, as I looked about, was built of blocks of stone, put together with the precision of an interlocking puzzle, with more markings carved in and around them.

A catacomb.

Human bone and skulls were set within depressions in the stone. Rather than grow afraid, as one might, I began to experience the wonder of all life. This was like entering a true wonderland, and yes, it was frightening in some ways, and yes, it also gave me comfort. I did not fear bone or skull. I feared what I sought here. My grandfather had been a genius of some sort, albeit a mad one. But his madness had managed to build a world beyond the one of this small Hudson Valley village. He had tamed the earth and its holes and filled them with the beauty of the ancients. I had no doubt that some foreign governments would be fighting for these treasures—had they known about them—for even among the catacombs, there were jewels and diadems and masks of gold and silver as only ancient kings would have in their burial mounds.

Pocket called out to me from the previous chamber, but I continued on—I would find Maggie.

In the next chamber, the ceiling sunk low, and I had the sense that I was nearly beneath—or beside—the house as it grew from these roots into its towers. The line from the poem came to me: "Many tower'd Camelot." That was Harrow: a legendary castle, and I walked the island of Shalott.

Something was in the air here—an incense? A fragrant smoke that held the air captive? It made me feel dreamy, even sleepy. I glanced across the chamber, but it was darker than the last, and all I could make out was a well at its center. I went over to it, and found at its edge, a dagger. I held this up and examined it. It was shiny and black, and put me in mind of a stone like obsidian. I left it there—after all, what weapon could be used against the dead? I could not see far enough in front of me to go on. I glanced back down the narrow, low corridor from which I had just come.

I could just make out the small orb of torch that Pocket held in the distant chamber behind this one.

And then I felt it.

The shiver of dread.

The iciness of something that was there without being seen. Of knowing something without being able to picture it or describe it or even intellectually understand it. It was an animal instinct, one that I suppose we all possess but have buried within ourselves for these thousands of years of human existence. Perhaps our ancestors living naked in the wild knew this. Perhaps when they buried their dead, they had been more sensitive to the ways the essences of spirits lingered and the forces of life that did not dissipate when the bodies of their brethren stopped moving. I felt it, I tell you, and it was as if I were feeling with my eyes a warm wet velvet curtain, and with my flesh the rippling of water all around me, and with my nostrils, the smell of flowers and incense and some drug burning in some cup.

I remembered the laudanum mixture my mother had taken when I was a very little boy, on those days when the pain for her was great, the opium and alcohol mixture that she told me had helped her grandmother, that helped her handle life. This was what I imagined this drug in the air must be—a mist of laudanum sprayed to take away the sense of dread and terror that grew in me.

You see, I had forgotten Maggie. I beheld the grandeur of my grandfather's creation, and I traveled through it like a great adventurer through a foreign land, but I had forgotten why I had come. And I had forgotten that the horror of life was here, inside this place, pushing at both the constable and myself.

4

I saw her, Matilde, the manifestation of evil and of innocence, the child and the woman, but without my eyes, for at the moment when the shivering was most intense, my torch went out completely. I stood in absolute darkness, the yellow-orange point of what could only be Pocket's distant torch providing a single jot of light in what now seemed an endless night.

She was there.

Matilde. I saw her as an outline in darkness: a corona of imagined light splayed around her form.

She was merely form then—shape in darkness, curves and lines and dots of purple-blue sparks that slowly swirled in the black. I imagined her, perhaps, or I had closed my eyes and could only see within my own mind because in the dark that was all that could be.

How could a man see without light? Or with that small point of torchlight at a distance—Pocket was there, somewhere down the corridor behind me, and his light moved, barely a flyspeck now.

But she was the dark. I realized this as if I had known it all along. She was not going to be found in the candlelight of the house. She might travel there; she might even play her games in the house.

But the darkness was her gown. Her voice was soft and warm when she spoke.

"Esteban," she said. "I have waited so long for you to come to me."

I replied to her. I said something aloud that felt true. It was something that I could not know in the light of day. Something that I could not have guessed as a child. Something within my instinct of darkness that had only just begun to emerge within this place, my legacy, my home.

My shivering was ferocious, like a lion tearing at my flesh from within, like an earthquake erupting from my very soul. All that I knew of life was torn asunder then and there; all that I had learned of myself was destroyed; I thought of my father and mother as they had raised me, of my sickly mother with her doctor lover, of my father with his distance from me and the inexplicable way that he could not bring himself to touch me or even hold my hand; and of the warmth of my grandfather's hand as he held my small one in his, absolute love and companionship I felt from that man, and the feeling of having "come home" by just visiting him in the house called Harrow. And seeing him at the window of the tower room, signaling something to me when I was a child. The yellowjackets surrounding me, biting me, but the warmth they held within their bites, the love of what seemed to be a stone angel, the love of some entity of Harrow, the love without barriers or conditions that I had felt in that great and awful moment.

Within my blood I knew.

Within my soul.

She herself was a kind of magic. She was what they had been afraid of, wasn't she? She had ability—true psychic ability. She could throw herself, she was spirit from both within and without flesh, she was trapped within the house as a child, and she was able to move through it like spirit, even when alive. She was Alice, who had been trapped behind the looking-glass. They had once thought her possessed when she was a little girl and had tried to cast demons from her. They had thought her insane and full of voices, but they had not understood.

She was many. Within herself.

It had never mattered—probably least to her—that she had died, walled into the tower room. She had already harnessed the way out of her body years before.

She showed me there in the dark.

Showed me without image.

Showed me without light.

She showed all to me.

I had seen a child ghost when I was small, but she was alive then, wasn't she? Alive and still a child in spirit. She had not physically murdered the gathering of my grandfather's spiritualists. It was the others within her mind, the child who had never been exorcised from her, the girl of sixteen (she whispered in my dark night) who had fallen in love, the shattered young woman of nineteen who had lost two loves in a short period of time and whose splintered mind had splintered even further—

This, the darkness told me, told me through brief visions and flashes of shadows in the dark and through some inborn knowledge of my own. I knew it all then. I knew it from within and without. She had tried to show me when she pushed into my body my second night in Harrow, pushed into me and held there for a second, to show me how it could be done, how spirit could invade matter, how I could see from her eyes and she could see from mine.

Even as a child, with the swirl of yellowjackets embracing me, I could feel her, and she was there, buried alive within the house and still surrounding me, loving me in the way she knew.

Within my mind, the knowledge blossomed in the dark as I watched her manifest into a shiny being of firefly-light in the blackness.

"Esteban. Esteban. The nights I've wept for you. The nights I knew I would never again see you. Esteban. You have your father's eyes. You have your father's eyes." She knew my secret name. My real name. The name that I had been given, according to my parents, from a promise to a midwife. The name my father despised, although I had assumed then that it was because some foreign woman had named his son against his own will.

But now, I knew who had named me.

I said it to her, knowing who she was.

At last.

"Mother," I said. "Matilde."

5

I found the truth of it, not in daylight or in a well-lit room, but in the absolute darkness of the house-within-the-house that my grandfather had built for his daughter.

You may think I am mad for believing this, but it was like the moment when you discover who you are in the world and what you are meant to do on this earthly plane—or the moment when you know you are in love, or the moment when you understand your destiny as marked somehow in some book, or across the heavens, or within your own heart.

I was the son of Matilde Gravesend. I was not Ethan Gravesend, the boy who had grown up in a distant and unfeeling household, the boy who had done everything in his power to make his father pay attention to him.

That boy was never meant to be. He was a figment of my father's imagination. He was the unfulfilled dream of a man who probably could not sire any children, let alone a son.

And my mother—my false mother—she had known. She had understood who I was, had even allowed the name "Esteban" to remain—and had taken to me for want of love, for surely my father had never truly loved her, nor she him.

I had always known of the distance between them, and of my false mother's ailments, all of which seemed neurotic and carelessly constructed on her part.

If she had a defect of the heart, it concerned my father and the life they had created around themselves, and the lies. She had been wheelchair-bound only as a way of avoiding duties—for I had caught her, hadn't I? Along the rocky beach, standing—perhaps even running—toward her lover? I stood in that darkness and remembered it all. It seemed as if it were a dream, and I knew that the life I felt then in the dark of that chamber was more of a life than any I had ever known.

Matilde Gravesend was my true mother.

She had brought me into her womb, here in the subterranean passages of Harrow.

She was my angel.

She was my blanket of yellowjackets. She had let her child-spirit sleep beside me in my illness as a child, not to frighten me, as I had thought—but to tend to me and protect me. She had called me back in some way, as if the umbilical cord between us were a slender strand of spider's silk that had never left my navel, had never been cut between us.

I was Esteban.

And my father?

That was the only mystery left to me, but it was enough that she was there with me and always had been.

Her so-called insanity had been her way of surviving in the monstrous world she had lived in—hidden from the world, brought out for my grandfather's shows and his guilt and whatever else had riddled him.

Yes, I had loved the old man, and yes, I had happy memories from Harrow as a child.

Now, I was nearly thirty years old, and I felt like a child again.

Her warmth surrounded me. The badsmell gushed up my nostrils and choked my throat, but it no longer seemed like a terrible thing. I welcomed it, as I welcomed the feeling of my mother's embrace.

Shutting my eyes, I could see her in the clean light of imagination, as she must've been when she had given birth to me—a teenager, weeping over the child that had been torn from her. She had been little more than a child herself, but in a woman's body, understanding the fate she had been cursed with, the powers of mind and psyche that sprang from her like water from an eternal fountain, understanding the love that she would have locked within herself. The love for her son. Her only son. The jealousy perhaps at her brother and his wife for taking her baby, the anger at her father for drawing the child from her arms, and—the father? Who could my father have been? Who among Harrow was unaccounted for? What lover had come to her in the night and held her and brought the two of them together in love and had made between them a child who was by society a bastard, but by their love sanctified and perfect?

I opened my eyes to the dark.

And then, she was gone. I was alone in the midnight place. A moment of pure silence and the crystal inner vision of saneness and sense overpowered me.

I heard three startling shrieks of a woman from some part of the darkness, and I heard Pocket crying out like a lamb about to be slaughtered by a wolf.

I stepped forward and stumbled across stones in the path. My head hit the side of the wall. An enormous pain exploded where my scalp had scraped rock. I felt a gash open along my ear and touched the stickiness of my own blood. I cursed myself for it and nearly laughed at myself. I laughed, and I laughed, and I felt completely sane there in the darkness.

And then a shot rang out.

A flash nearly blinded me coming from down in the other end of the corridor.

But it was too late, I was helpless—I had begun to

black out, and no matter how I tried to fight it, I felt the sickening dizziness inside.

Just as I reached up to press my fingers to the side of my head to stanch the flow of blood, I heard Maggie's voice screaming for me.

6

My senses shut down, and I lapsed into unconsciousness.

I dreamed what Harrow wished me to dream, what my true mother wished me to dream. I saw her: a young girl trapped within rooms that spread to other rooms.

An entire labyrinth of rooms existing on the other side of mirrors within the house. As she grew into a young woman, she watched from her mirror windows as the world went by. She watched others live their lives while she remained among the ancient walls and altars of the dead.

I awoke, feeling something moving across my face.

7

Insects crawled along my cheek and lips. I wiped at them—beetles? Cockroaches? Some form of subterranean life.

I remembered where I was, and the shock of throbbing pain along the side of my head continued.

I reached up and touched the sticky blood. It was not a deep wound.

195

After several seconds, I found I could sit up. I felt a hand along my elbow, trying to lift me.

I had the distinct impression of a young girl standing there, doing her best to get me to stand. It was her.

It was Matilde.

I felt the warmth and rose-petal scent of her breath, mingled with the smell I had come to think of as bad, but that was rich, like just-turned moist earth. It was the smell of the grave perhaps, but in this context of darkness, it seemed comforting. The badsmell, the stink of death, had become perfume.

I wanted to ask this spirit so many questions, but I felt an urgency in her touch.

I rose with shaking knees, and a lurch in my stomach. Some noise echoed through the corridors—a series of high-pitched screams? A squealing and bleating as of animals being slaughtered?

I could not tell what kind of beasts could be making such a racket.

I remembered Maggie's cries, and my heart beat faster.

And then, a strange luminescent orb that had been at some distance began to grow in size.

It was Pocket's torch, hurrying down the corridor toward me.

8

When Pocket arrived nearer to me, I tried to say something, but the air seemed to have left my lungs and all I could manage was a hiss as I stood up.

196

He stopped, not three feet from me, nearly dropping the torch. And I knew. I felt it.

"You see her," I said.

Pocket said nothing, but continued to stare at me. His eyes went wide, and he had to be watching the shadow of the spirit as it passed into me.

"Tell me you see her," I said. "You see Matilde."

"It's insane," Pocket whispered. "This has all been insanity. Your grandfather raised the devil here. And it's you," he gasped, pointing at the swarm of darkness that was my mother as she curved around my shoulder.

And then, I felt her press against me, just as she had before.

She was trying to possess me. She was trying to invade. I had to resist, but I wanted the closeness. I wanted it, I tell you, because I had never felt close enough to anyone who had ever loved me.

Her invisible hands pressed against my side like some new Eve reopening Adam's wound to return to the ribcage, to push into flesh. I began to see the stone chamber as if it were made of flesh and blood. Beneath the stones, I could nearly see the veins and yellow fat of a living, breathing entity.

For gasping seconds, I entertained the thought that this place had been somehow brought to life through my grandfather's ancient rituals, through entreaties to gods and creatures he could not even know truly existed.

He had, with his daughter and a host of spiritualists, called forth the beating heart of life itself within stone, and that Harrow was alive and frothing with fertile life.

Douglas Clegg

And then I saw her again: the angel from the garden, the one I'd seen as a child.

It was Matilde, it was the face of all that was Harrow, it was the guardian and protector of this place. She was inside me, and she was everywhere. She was the eternal mother, trapped within this stone. She was my flesh and I was her flesh, and she was all. She whispered her love to me within the warmth of yellowjackets and nightmare. I felt her arms go about my waist as she said, "Esteban, Esteban," and it was not some foreign personality, nor was it the trickle of a child's voice. This was the woman who had died in the tower room, thinking of her only son, wanting to bring him back to her womb, this house. I knew in my heart I had failed in my mission. I knew that what I had come here for—to understand my past—and why I was now in the heart of the beast—to find Maggie— was not as it seemed.

Matilde whispered to me: *We have her now. We will have you, too.*

In the breath of my mother, I smelled the the earth and the shallots and the cats and the lizards and beetles—death and life both were mingled. My mother held the doorway open between the finite and the infinite within this looking-glass house that reflected nothing but the shades of those who had once dwelt in the flesh.

I felt my mother's spirit as it possessed me. The ache was delicious. Dare I describe the sensation? For it was not painful, nor was it as uncomfortable as I would have expected.

I felt a tickling along my side as she entered me,

198

and something akin to the feeling of extreme pleasure that one imagines animals feel in rutting—not the happiness or joy of human intercourse, but something altogether more instinctive, a driving force of nature within bestial necessity. I felt shame at the way my flesh seemed to open like the mouth of a river to this current of heat. And I felt the stinging warmth of the yellowjackets as she swam through my blood. It was a rush of barbed sensation.

She had, in essence, slipped me on like a glove.

I began shivering. A chill took over my body. I felt an absolute hatred from her, not the love I had expected, but anger and fury. She was jealous that I had lived my life in the world. My own mother held jealousy for what I had been able to become. I had practically invited her into my body. Had practically wished her to be this close to me, as close as the dead can get to the living. Now that I felt her within me, her heart beating against mine, I didn't feel the reunion of love and caring that I had wished.

Instead, I felt the stings of the yellowjackets. Her love was venom. She began spitting obscenities at Pocket, railing at him for what he had done, she said, to the boy she had loved, screeching like an owl in some kind of pain, and with each cry that arose from my throat, I felt the icy stings followed by the heat of fury. She truly had been mad. Whether she was mad from birth, or whether my grandfather had driven her mad, or whether the house itself was a madness that had seeped into her—it didn't matter now. Evil was evil, and she was part of it. She was the child and the woman and the teenage girl and the creatures of shadow that she had brought into her abode as play-mates for her incarceration.

That was all she wanted.

More spirits.

More souls to feed her furnace.

I felt her mind within my own, battling my memories, biting down on the succulent fruit of my brain as she spread her virus through all that I could remember. I experienced her life as if at the moment of her death in that tower room. I saw the child and the personalities within her, and the walls that had grown up around her, the rooms that her father had built and hidden her within.

At first, they were pure replicas of the other rooms in Harrow, but soon he had brought in the relics and had made rituals, had even sacrificed to ancient gods, all in order to keep her safe but within this labyrinth.

And then, I saw him.

My father. A boy who had just reached manhood, perhaps a few years older than Matilde, his dark hair long and wild, and his manner as unkempt as the dusky clothes he wore. I saw their love, their spring-time love, their love so full of passion and hope, and how he came to her from the crypt and brought her into daylight, where they made love; and where her shame increased when it was discovered that she was with child. My father was a man I had never formally met, but I had seen from a distance when I had been a boy. He had watched me carefully, I knew. He had never spoken to me, and now we would probably never meet.

The legend was that he had run off.

The story was that he was part Mahanowack Indian. Perhaps my grandfather had even killed him, or had him killed, or paid him to leave. Perhaps the house had taken him.

The first caretaker of Harrow, Oliver Palliser, who, like me had another name: Hawk with Two Souls.

They had been young and in love, and even that bit of sunlight had been taken from her. And I witnessed—within her virulent memory—my own birth. I watched her fury and jealousy when I was passed to the parents who had raised me, and I heard my second mother promise that "Esteban" would be my name.

Even that had not appeased my true mother, and she let out a keening wail. I felt my bones ache and grind as if they would, at any moment, break through my skin and tear away from muscle and tendon. I managed to shout—between her curses—"Get her out of me! She's killing me! Shoot me, Pocket!"

9

I couldn't see Pocket at all—my eyes seemed to be covered over with blood. Darkness clouded my vision further. I was trying to get her out of my body. I wanted this awful creature away from me.

She began laughing—or I began laughing—I knew not which. She fought against Pocket with both arms—my arms!—and I tried with all my might to draw back, to let Pocket go, but she was scratching at him.

Her claws raked across his throat. I felt bits of his skin beneath my fingernails.

My mind could not get my body to stop its attack. I felt more helpless than ever before in my life. To be controlled by someone else, to be manipulated by a being that could not be fought, and yet, I knew, must be fought at all costs . . .

All costs.

She was a demon.

She was the devil.

My body had become a wildcat's, tearing at prey.

10

When it was over, I picked up the fallen torch.

She had left me, satisfied in some blood game I could not comprehend.

I felt as if I'd been beaten with a club, and wondered if I would ever leave this place alive. More frighteningly, I felt the pleasure, as if I had just been satisfied by some lustful embrace.

I could not bear to look at Pocket's fallen body. I could not bear to look at what had become of his face. I just knew: Maggie could not be here. She had to get away.

I realized that she had kept screaming—that it had not let up, but had become a subliminal sound, as of running water or the cries of birds.

My mother's spirit had blocked it when she had possessed me.

Maggie's screams had become a hoarse bleating.

She was weakening. I had to find her. I had to find her. If I died so that she might live, that was all right. If I could even save her soul from this madness, it would be enough. *If we must die,* I prayed, knowing that there had to be a merciful and just God even in the bowels of Harrow, *allow us peace. Allow us escape. Allow us heaven.*

Anything that befell me would be all right, so long as Maggie escaped the hell within Harrow.

11

I felt like a trapped animal and heard the whispering of voices all around me.

I rushed from chamber to chamber, hoping to follow the sound of Maggie's cries.

They were weakening, and I prayed again and again to find her and save her before the others could get her. Before my mother would have me do to her what she did to Pocket.

That was my greatest terror now—that my mother would invade my being and wreak further havoc and murder upon Maggie. I knew my mother's jealousy now. I knew her damning love.

I could not let this touch Maggie, who was an innocent. Maggie, whom I loved. Maggie—the woman I would not let this house touch. Not let Matilde Gravesend hold in her bloody embrace.

12

I followed Maggie's screams, which had trickled to a croaking shout, back to the great tomb of Egypt.

I carried my torch along the walls, through the chamber, overturning the Anubis figures, looking in each wall recess for the trap in which she'd been caught. And then, dread flowed within my body as if my blood had turned to ice.

When I worked up the courage, I turned, and looked at the great mummy case with its ancient queen carved on the surface. Maggie had been put inside the sarcophagus.

She was meant to be buried alive there.

13

I leaned the torch against the great statue near the sarcophagus and pulled at the lid. It was sealed shut, but I heard her within. "Help me, oh God, someone," she gasped, her voice muffled.

"I'm here Maggie. I'm here," I said, my fingers raw and bleeding as I fought the edge of the lid, trying to pry it open.

I glanced about for some tool, but there was nothing I could use as a lever. I remembered the obsidian dagger in one of the rooms down the path.

"I need to get something to help," I said.

"No, please, don't leave me," Maggie pleaded from within.

"I have to. I'll be back. You'll see," but even as I

said this, tears streamed down my face as I looked upon the carved figure, imagining Maggie beneath.

"They're inside here. They're already inside here. Crawling on me. Please. Ethan. Don't, Ethan, don't, please," she said. Her voice finally faded, as I wept, as I debated in my head, as I scratched at the lid of the sarcophagus, trying desperately to release her.

I grabbed the torch back up and ran down the corridor, passing through the catacombs to the other room.

The dagger was there. I picked it up and turned back to the corridor I'd just left.

I'd get her out, I knew.

We'd get out of this place and go out into the world again.

It was only a few more seconds to run back down in the shadows.

A few more seconds.

I ran as fast as I could, stumbling along the way, passing Pocket's body, passing the feeling of my mother there, watching me, reaching out to grab me with her fury.

But I had escaped her. I knew I had. She could not have me, and she was not going to keep us in that place.

"We don't belong here!" I shouted. "You were in love once! You know! My father loved you! You loved him! It was wrong to imprison you here! It was wrong to take me away from you! But you don't need us! Let us go, Mother!" I shouted with a belief in the insanity around me, and I felt her linger nearby.

She would leave us alone. I knew she would. She must. She was my mother. She was the spirit of my mother. She had been human once. She had loved. She must understand. . . .

But when I arrived back in that chamber, I had already lost.

14

The mummy case was open.

Matilde lay back within it, her skin pale, her body shivering. Shiny beetles crawled along her arms, and yellowjackets swarmed along her fiery hair. Her eyes had turned up into their sockets so that only the whites of her eyes showed.

My mother was inside her.

"She will always be with us," my mother said, forcing Maggie's lips open like a perverse puppeteer. Her voice was halting, and she stumbled through the words as if Maggie was still there, somewhere, fighting against her. "Your love. Your love. Gone. Esteban. Stay with. With me. Wait with me." Her voice was like the scraping of a rake against stone.

15

Too late for Maggie, I thought.

She's with them. For all I knew, she had been dead from the moment the house had taken her.

For all I knew, I was already damned to Hell with them. Maggie was part of the nightmare, part of Matilde, and part of Harrow.

And then my mother's voice came from her beautiful lips, and the languages poured from her—foreign tongues I had never before heard. And then the nastiest words I had ever imagined, the words that invoke the ugliness of human existence, the words that, like a spell of evil, curse all who hear them.

They were about lust and appetite and the predatory beast of sex, and the voice was like a little girl's, and it was all I could do to not shout for her to stop.

I approached her, kneeling beside the sarcophagus, and pressed my hand over her mouth to shut her up.

16

I wanted to release Maggie from this torment, you see. I wanted her to escape the house that had drawn her down into its bowels. It was my fault. It was all my fault for even allowing her in the house.

Allowing her to be taken by the house and the spirits inside it, the shadows that could not be stopped, the darkness that spread like diseased roots beneath Harrow.

A demon was inside her now—a spirit of darkness possessed her, and that is why I put my hand gently at first over her mouth and nostrils, to stop it, to send—if I had to—the devil himself back to hell and away from the soul of Maggie Barrow, my sweet Maggie Barrow, whom I could not watch suffer so.

To release her.

The demon within her struggled for a time, and its

talons flailed out at me, trying to draw my hands from her face, but I kept them locked over her nose and mouth and wept as the beast struggled and beat ferociously against me—

And still I held fast.

But even with my hand over her mouth, her voice came through, and she was sucking at my palm, trying to draw me into her mouth.

My mother was using my own flesh against me.

My hand began to blister with icy breath.

I didn't know what to do.

She had killed Maggie, and now she was going to keep her imprisoned in this evil place.

I had to do something to get my mother out of her body. To get that evil away from Maggie.

To keep Maggie safe.

Somehow.

To make it right.

To make the ungodly leave the temple of her body. I reached for the dagger with my free hand. I brought it up to her heart.

The yellowjackets had begun to swarm there, along her breast.

They crawled up the dark knife to my fingers and hand and wrist. I pressed down into her heart, to release the diabolical spirit of Matilde Gravesend from this innocent body.

And to free Maggie's soul.

You understand? To free her soul. Just as she went limp, I saw a brilliant flash of light as if there were lightning inside the chamber. The strange thing—after all these years I feel comfortable mentioning this—in that sudden white light, I thought I saw all the others, not just my mother as a child, as a girl, as young woman, but also others, more than the spiritualists who had died, but others, shadows of many others, and I wondered what my grandfather had invoked within these stones. What demons had he raised?

Their shadows burned against the far wall, standing together, watching me. And then the torchlit darkness returned, as if a flickering veil had been drawn over everything. It had happened in seconds, that vision of shadows. But I will never forget it.

Eternity happens in seconds, I thought then.

I think this still. Eternity happens in moments like flashes of lightning.

I felt my mother with her yellowjacket embrace blanket me in a humming warmth. I was sure that I would die.

17.

But I did not. I must've remained there, holding Maggie's body, for hours.

I went mad, I would gather, at least from what I was later told. I went mad, but even in that mindless disorientation, I had managed to crawl through the grasping shadows. I found my way into other rooms, each more forbidding than the last, and I saw monuments to the ancient world, and the shadows that danced even within the dark corridors. I stumbled across stone and rock, and saw statues of ancient gods and goddesses, and the armor of soldiers, and finally, I reached a thin stretch between two walls and found myself feeling for other entryways.

At last, I was in the house within the house, the thin passageways between walls drawing me upward. Harrow had gone quiet, as if I had indeed defeated the spirits of the dead. I saw a mirror that looked out, like a window, onto the bedroom that was once both my nursery, and Matilde's.

The mirror was just large enough for me to squeeze through; I broke it with my fists, and crawled into the room where I had once slept as a child.

The room where her childhood spirit had slept beside me.

After Harrow

As you can see, I told you the story of my life at Harrow as if I were watching myself, and perhaps I told the truth, and perhaps I did not. You will never know, will you? I am, as I told you, nearly one hundred years old, and my mind is intact.

That is more a curse than you can imagine, for I can remember it all clearly, my twenty-ninth year, that one October that changed destiny for me.

I brought Harrow into the light of day in autumn, in the year 1926.

I called Pocket's assistant in the village, who then brought in authorities from other areas to investigate the murders on the estate.

Naturally, I was the first suspect. But I told them about the house, you see.

They understood.

They began to understand about the threshold of the infinite. How the ghost had destroyed both Pocket and Maggie. And how I had to release her soul from that pit so that she might not remain with them in that awful clamoring darkness.

And Maggie?

Yes, Harrow had gotten into her. But that had been her flesh. I released her soul from that prison.

She was found within what could only be described in the Poughkeepsie newspaper as a "cave full of stolen artifacts beneath the house."

I tell you, the house itself has a will, endowed by the magic my grandfather practiced, the ancient and obscure arts that invoked spirits and deities long forgotten.

Many of the authorities seemed to understand this, but they kept it out of the papers.

And still the term "Nightmare House" was attached to Harrow in nearly every newspaper along the Hudson River.

I was imprisoned for a period of time, despite my innocence, and taken eventually to the asylum at Northcastle, the very place where my grandfather had not wanted my mother to end up.

Alf, who had reverted to infantile behavior after Harrow, was sent to live with his aunt in Providence; when he was in his teens he ran away, although no one knew where he had gone.

But even in the madhouse, I knew where Alf would show up. I knew he needed to be near his mother.

During my stay at the asylum, when I underwent the humiliations of various treatments with electricity and radio waves, I was visited by men and women who had known my grandfather, and had known Harrow.

Among these visitors were the notorious, such as Aleister Crowley and Lizbeth Borden, as well as the folk who had happened across Harrow's path in the early part of the century when I'd just been a boy.

Even my ex-wife, Madeleine, came to see me one day.

She was as beautiful as ever, and she said something to me that I think I will never forget.

"You shouldn't be here," she said. "You weren't meant to be here. It must be some mistake. I know you. You could never have done what they claim."

I returned her sad smile with the only words I knew to say, "God will take care of me. Don't worry, Madeleine. There are those who wait in eternity for me. This time will pass. I will die, but the heavens will open and she will be there—Maggie, and my mother, among the angels, swarming me in their arms, swarming around me like yellowjackets, blessing me."

Madeleine began weeping.

"Why are you crying?" I asked.

"Because," she said, tears in her eyes like jewels. "You have your faith again. You believe. You believe in God. You are saved. You believe."

"I do," I said, knowing that it had come at a great price.

My faith had returned to me from a journey through the pit of hell. I had touched the face of the infinite, and I had returned, burned, but with a genuine faith in creation.

My other visitors—Mr. Crowley and Miss Borden—had also witnessed the darkness of the house, and many of them called authorities on my behalf to get me an early release, although, in fact, I'd had no trial.

It was considered scandalous, what had happened to me.

Through both my grandfather's money and my grandfather's many rich friends, who understood the nature of Harrow, as well as the Ladies' League for Justice and Mercy of the Hudson Valley, petitions were circulated, authorities were bought, and public sympathy grew locally for my release from the madhouse.

I knew a greater hand was at work.

I knew that nothing less than the indomitable spirit of my mother herself had somehow determined my destiny.

After several years at Northcastle, I returned to Harrow. I lived in the caretaker's cottage, with my father's name on the threshold: Oliver Palliser.

By then, the deaths at Harrow were old news; the village still whispered, but villages whisper about everyone who has ever transgressed.

I was one among many who had scandal attached to his name, and a true belief was afoot that Harrow was indeed haunted, as many had believed.

Old Wentworth herself had helped end speculation about my guilt or innocence by mentioning the queer things that had gone on there, and by the things she had thought she had heard or seen over the years.

Alf had returned, as I suspected he would.

I allowed him to take up residence in one of the empty upstairs rooms of the caretaker's cottage. He was unable to leave Harrow altogether. He was sullen and prone to moods, and when he spoke to most people, they commented on how odd he seemed.

He told me that his mother had been calling to him

since he'd last seen her, and she had told him to wait here for her, that she would come again for him.

"And she told me to tell you something," he said. "She will wait for you to come to her."

"I know," I said, and did not think it strange, then, to love a woman so strongly whom I had barely known in life.

I waited nightly for her, but neither Alf nor I ventured into the main house at Harrow.

I contacted Alf's aunt, who had all but given up on the boy. Because I did not want him to lack for his schooling or social skills, I hired a tutor at the cottage, and, with my inheritance, had additions built onto the cottage.

Alf's aunt came to live at the cottage—she was a harsh woman, a former schoolmistress, but she was a good influence on Alf overall.

As the years went by and the old reports of the "Nightmare House of Watch Point" faded in memory, Harrow seemed to return to just being a house. None of us ever went inside it mainly from fear, and I kept the doors padlocked and the windows nailed shut.

As I grew older, things changed there, and Alf became Alfred.

After the Second World War, Alfred Barrow returned home to the cottage with big plans. He wanted to turn Harrow into a school.

I let him have his wish, so long as the underground rooms of the house were sealed.

I could not forgot my feelings of horror within Harrow, but I knew that it needed a new life.

It must rise from the ashes of what it had been.

215

We have not seen or heard anything unusual in all those years, and there were times when I wondered if my own mind had played tricks on me, and I had, perhaps, murdered Pocket and Maggie myself, as some have said at the time.

After all, I am telling this story, and no madman who has murdered would ever accept blame for the deaths of two people, would he?

He might spend his life concocting a story of ghosts and demons to draw attention from the blood on his own hands.

He might see himself as a victim of forces greater than merely human, that the gods themselves had used him as a tool, or had manipulated through magic and spiritual agencies the world around him.

I believe the Puritans called this Spectral Evidence when brought to trial.

Would I have had any genuine Spectral Evidence had I been brought to trial for the murders of Pocket and Maggie?

You will never know, will you?

All you will know are these things: I am Esteban Palliser. I was born Esteban Gravesend.

My mother was Matilde Gravesend, and my father was Oliver Palliser, also known as the Hawk with Two Souls.

And I am still, at the end of my life, waiting for Maggie to come for me, to be there when I take my last breath.

She has promised, through her son, that she will wait for me.

I am the caretaker of Harrow, the son of the previous caretaker, the son of the true owner of Harrow.

I live in a different place in Watch Point now, for I am feeble, and even Harrow has changed since I was a young man.

A nurse wheels me places and feeds me, and sometimes Alfred comes to visit when he is able.

As I sit here, a cigarette in my mouth, feeling the last days of life flow through me, I think back to my crimes, and I look across the rooftops of Watch Point to the towers of the school that Alfred Barrow founded many years ago, the way he had the land changed, using money I had given him—for he is like a son to me and the only inheritor of the millions of dollars that have grown from my grandfather's estate over the years.

I can almost hear Maggie's voice calling my true, secret name, and it makes me smile for a minute.

She is still, in my mind's eye, the Lady of Shallots in the Holy Land of my mother's house, surrounded by the wild cats in the garden of night. I wait for another night to come.

A night of darkness, and the feeling of her hand in mine.

You may say that one cannot love the dead.

But I know.

My dreams are there now.

You can go in any room, any secret chamber, and you will find them—shadows of dreams, like smoke from a fire that has only just died.

They are no longer with me—I do not dream.

I live now in stark reality. In light. In a harsh sun.

Did I leave my dreams behind on purpose?

Of course not. They were taken from me, by Harrow.

Harrow is ancient.

Harrow has existed, for all I know, before the world ever was created.

Before the world ever was imagined.

I feel my death coming to me—coming just as Maggie will come to me, like the angel, my mother, comes to me with caresses in the mist of twilight. I was born to the century's end; I will be born within Harrow to the new century's beginning.

Stet Fortuna Domus.

May the House's Fortune Stand.

Purity

For Robert R. McCammon,
for Boy's Life, Usher's Passing, Swan Song,
Stinger, *and* Blue World, *among others—*
and for giving a young writer a few kind words
when no one else would.

"Vast, Polyphemus-like, and loathsome,
it darted like a stupendous monster of nightmares. . . ."
—H.P. Lovecraft, "Dagon"

Prologue: Why I Called You Here

1

There is no madness but the madness of the gods.
  There is no purity but the purity of love.

2

Someone once wrote that "the most merciful thing in the world, I think, is the inability of the human mind to correlate its contents."

This describes my feelings perfectly. I correlate too much of my own mind's contents. It's always troubling.

I don't live in the chronological moment; I doubt you do either. I live all at once in the past with only glimpses of the present. I live mostly on that island, when it comes to me, when I think of my life as it formed.

I live in darkness now, but the dark brings the memories back.

The dark brings it all back.

The dark is all I know.

I call the dark.

It's there that I find the god I met one day when I was just a child. I remember that day; not the days of blood to come.

In the end, we were together.

In the beginning, we were not.

3

Here are the words I will never forget:

"Owen, I'm so sorry. I'm so sorry. I should never have come this summer."

Before that, the gun went off.

Before that, I looked into her eyes.

Before that is when it all began.

Dagon, bring it back to me.

Chapter One: Who I Am

1

These are the things I know:

Outerbridge Island has briny water running beneath its rocks, a subterranean series of narrow channels between the Sound and the Atlantic. You can see the entrances to these channels on the northern side of the island at low tide. These channels feed into the Great Salt Pond on the westerly side of the island before it empties into the sea. It was said that once upon a time, a Dutch trading ship smashed up against the rocks, and local pirates fed upon the treasures found within the hold of the ship. The treasure, it is said, was buried in the narrow caverns. To add to the chill of this tale, it was also said that the pirates fed upon the flesh of the survivors of the wreck for days.

I've actually swum into the caverns at times. I'm slender enough, and in good enough shape to maneuver in the darkness of the water, but I never found treasure, nor did I emerge in the Great Salt Pond by

Douglas Clegg

following the channels within that part of the island. I needed air, after all.

If you want something badly enough, there are ways to get it.

This doesn't mean that they are traditional ways. It doesn't mean that pain is not involved. It doesn't mean that the cost may overwhelm the need. It just means there are ways to get what you really want in this world.

If one has a conscience, one can be driven mad. Therefore, a conscience is a key to madness. Everyone is a potential madman. Everyone. The sweetest boy in the world can be driven to the most irrational of acts. The girl who has the world at her feet, likewise, could be driven to some act of desperation and tragedy.

In many ways, we want the irrational and the tragic and the desperate because they bring meaning and life back into our existences.

Another fact—my mother prizes three things above all others:

The rose garden my father planted for her before I was born. It runs in spirals along the bluffs and the small hillock behind our cottage. There are fourteen varieties of roses, with hues ranging from pale peach to bloodred.

Her koi pond, which is really the Montgomerys' koi pond, but it sits on our side of the property. It is largish for a pond, and narrow, nearly a reflecting pool. It was built deep for the harsh winters—the koi can survive a thick layer of ice as long as they can bury

226

themselves down in the silt. My father covers the pool with a plastic tarp to further protect the fish.

And lastly, my mother prizes the gun.

My maternal grandfather had a small pistol that had been given to him by his mother. It was a small Colt pistol—what my grandfather called a vest pistol, but which I thought of as a Saturday Night Special. It had mother-of-pearl grips, and a clip that could not be removed from it. My grandfather had given my mother the pistol in the early years of her marriage for when my father would beat her. My father never beat my mother, but my grandfather apparently would not believe it. The pistol is useless, I heard my mother once say. Never been fired. I could barely shoot a cat with it, she joked. Someday, she told me, when she was weepy and bitter about life, she would go to Boston and sell it to a collector and take the money and go far, far away. When I first discovered my true god and his nature, I took the pistol.

Final fact:

Faith plays into all this. One must have faith that one can do what one sets out to do. One must have the courage of one's convictions. All the world's history teaches us this.

For me, it is that god I discovered.

I call it Dagon, although its true name is unknown to me. It came from the sea, and I held it captive briefly. I am its priest.

And Dagon, in a twisted and true way, upholds what I stand for.

One must stand for something.

For me, it is the force of love.

The undertow of love.

But that sounds romantic, and I'm not a romantic at all.

I've been called a lot of things since the day I was born; never romantic.

Schemer. Athlete. Brain. Manipulator. User. Common. Handsome. Shallow. Arrogant. Mad. Sociopath. Cold eyed.

All by my mother.

Jenna Montgomery once told me I had the most beautiful eyes she'd ever seen on a boy.

I had to catch my breath when she told me that.

She said it the same day I made the first sacrifice to the god I'd met.

2

Years ago, I came upon the god during a storm of late November, a frozen, bitter storm, in which I had gotten caught down at the caverns, taking a dinghy out to look for the famous buried pirate treasure. I was twelve and lonely, and when I saw the god thrust between a rock and a hard place, as it were, I knew immediately who and what it was, and how I should please it. I read in my father's Bible that Dagon was the god of the Philistines; the Fish-God. I found other books, too, with titles like *The Shadow Over Innsmouth* and *Dagon* that further told of the god and its worshippers and what was needed to feed the god.

Some may say it is just an abominable statue, a

cheap and even grotesque trinket of some distant bazaar, brought by sailors or perhaps even the pirates. It is green with age and made wholly of stone. Its eyes are garnet; its tail and fins carved with some exquisite artistry.

But when I bled a seagull over the cold eyes of the little god, while the storm raged around me, I felt a prayer had been answered.

I breathed easier then.

3

Breathing is essential to survival, and although this seems like a given, we know—scientifically—that it is not. Most of the problems of life are like that: simple, obvious, graspable, yet shrouded in a secret.

If one can breathe well—through any crisis, and exertion—then one will survive.

It is those who stop breathing who have let go of their wills to live.

I am what people in this world call a sociopath, although the idea of killing someone has never interested me. A sociopath is not necessarily a killer, and to assume this is to play a dangerous game. Just as not all famous people are rich, not all sociopaths are Jeffrey Dahmer. If Jeffrey was one at all. You must know this about me if you're going to understand exactly what went on at Outerbridge Island the summer I turned eighteen, the summer before Jenna Montgomery was to leave me forever.

They say that people like me can't experience love,

but I find that ridiculous. I'm fully capable of giving and receiving love, and it is monstrous to suggest otherwise. Even all those years ago I was, and love burned in me just as it did any boy who had fallen.

My mother would take her daily pain pill as I grew up—her pains being life itself and even her child—and tell me that there were two kinds of people in this world, the kind who give and the kind who take, and I knew I was neither, but somewhere in between the rest of the world: I was someone who observed, perhaps too coldly sometimes. I still observe, and observation has brought me to this place again.

Outerbridge Island, with its rocky ledges and glassy sea, the fog that came suddenly, the sun that tore through clouds like a nuclear explosion, the summers that went on for years; the years that passed in a summer.

The storms that came and stayed and never left.

4

Let me turn it all back to the day I was born, since from what I've read about sociopaths, it's fairly genetic. My grandmother was probably the carrier of the gene, since she went crazy and ended up in what they called a nursing home over in Massachusetts, but which I found out—later in life, of course—was an impoverished sanitarium, the sort of place where nightmares are born. My mother told me that it was my grandfather's fault for driving her to do things—again, not kill, for we have never been murderers—

just things that caused people to believe my grand-mother was insane. My mother told me when I was eleven or twelve that I had been a difficult birth and my own umbilical cord practically strangled me as I exited her body. She said I was blue in the face for nearly a minute from lack of oxygen before the doctor got me coughing. I spent the first two weeks of my life in the hospital, for I was a month premature and no one thought I would live.

Sometimes I think this is why I'm a sociopath. I've seen documentaries on PBS about baby monkeys who are separated from their mothers for a short time, and this makes them seem without conscience (if that is truly what a sociopath is, although I don't believe it). My mother said she didn't touch me for the first month; she was terrified I'd die, and because she had already lost one child—two years earlier—in some kind of crib death scenario, she feared holding her first son, me. My father had to do all the touching and picking up, and even—my mother told me—when I had to nurse from her breast, she was too terrified. Instead, my aunt became my wet nurse—she who had, just five months before, given birth to twins and seemed to have milk enough for the entire population of the island. There were times, when I was older, that I wished my aunt had taken me back to her home on the mainland. Times when I hated the island. Hated my mother and father. Hated looking at the Montgomery house—the Montgomery Mansion, the Montgomery palazzo, the Big Place—staring down at us. But I suppose all this anger came about because of those first few days of life.

231

Douglas Clegg

These things aren't spoken of much in families—how we each came to be. My mother suffered through bouts of depression, particularly in the winter, and she would stand in front of her bedroom window, looking out across the Sound, her face a shimmering reflection in the thick glass, and tell me all about myself.

She told me that when I was six weeks old, she realized I had never really cried, at least not the way babies were supposed to. Instead, I would turn red, and my mouth would open, and I'd scream. That's how she'd know I was hungry or needed changing. Because she was so grateful to have a child after she felt God had taken away her first in retribution for youthful transgressions, she tried not to think about what my lack of tears might mean.

As she'd tell this kind of story, I'd shift uncomfortably on her bed, wishing she'd release me from this intimacy—the closeness of her depression, the morbid way her mind would pick over my birth and early years.

"I'm so sorry that you turned out this way," she said once, her hands going up to her face. "I'm happy you're so smart. Not like your father. But this madness that comes over you . . ."

I remained silent, letting her have her feelings. I didn't understand then to what she referred—I was not mad. I took the ferry to go to school over on the mainland and did quite well in school. The ferry took an hour and a half in the winter, and only ran twice a day—for school hours, since Outerbridge had no school of its own. Thus, I spent many nights with my Aunt Susan in Rhode Island, and learned more about

232

my mother's mother than I had ever wanted to know. I also managed—through my cousin Davy—to make friends off-island, friends who believed I was like them. And I had a lot of friends as a child. Although I was not considered handsome at first—at least by my mother who found my hair to be too ominous in some way, my eyes too blue and perhaps too sharp, my manner arrogant (even as an eight-year-old, she'd called me that)—I began learning the secret of athletics early, and applied myself to molding my body the same way I went about molding my mind: I studied and read and found the boys who seemed to know what they were doing, and I gravitated toward them. I learned what they knew by nature. I was uncoordinated in most sports until I realized that, as in all things, it was about breathing.

This is one of the secrets of life: It's all about breathing.

5

Voices in the dark:

"It's all right, I know you. I know what we both want."

"Shut up. Just shut up."

"Come here. Come here. Let me help you. It's all right. It feels good."

"No, not like this. No."

"I've been so lonely."

"Oh."

"Wanting this."

"Oh."
"Since the first time I saw you."
"Oh."

6

Have you ever felt that you would do anything to be with someone?

I almost feel sorry for you, if you haven't.

7

The purity of life is in the secrets—they're simple, they say everything, they are there for anyone. But we must wake up to the purity first in order to understand the secrets.

My pursuit of physical excellence began early. I tackled solitary athletics since this seemed best for my character. They were also cheaper. My family was poor—have I mentioned that? Not poor poor. Not "out in the street with no food" poor, but poor nonetheless. My mother's first husband had been rich, but had been a gambler. My mother—I should call her Boston, for that's what my father called her even though her name was Helen—had been the fifth daughter in a wealthy family who had married well the first time around. But that man—someone I had never in my life heard of beyond knowing he existed—apparently lost all their money, and soon she found my father, a good man one would suppose, who began his work life as a groundskeeper at the Smithsonian Museum in Washington, D.C., but ended up working as a gardener for rich folk. It paid well enough—like I said, we weren't poor poor.

My father probably would've had more money, but he had a sister who was dying—for years—down in Annapolis, Maryland, and he was her only support. So, according to my mother, half of his income went to her. "She has the longest-lived cancer I've ever heard of," she'd say, sometime right in front of him.

Of course, this wasn't all there was to it, but if I tell you all the secrets of the world at once, you'll either be dazzled or overwhelmed, and there's no point in making it all explode right now. You'll want to know why breathing is one of the secrets of life.

All right, do you know how breathing is voluntary? I've heard that people with dementia sometimes end up forgetting how to breathe. That's a terrible way to die, although one would suppose that any method of dying would be awful. Well, breathing is the essential component of accomplishing anything.

I observed this early—I was on the school bus, and I noticed a little girl next to me who was terrified of an upcoming test we were about to take. She would, in fact, stop breathing for seconds at a time. I began to count her breaths, and I saw that for every four I took, she took one. I suggested to her that she try just concentrating on her breathing. After a bit of persuasion, she did. It didn't seem to work. I withdrew my father's pocket watch—the one I'd stolen. (Yes, I stole things regularly around the house. I have reasons, none of which you want to know.) I had learned a bit about hypnosis, so I asked her to stare long and hard at the brass of the watch as the sunlight reflected on it. She asked me if I'd be putting her under. I told her no. This was, after all, just suggestion, nothing more. I would suggest something to her and hope that her mind would accept it. Of course, I was a child. I didn't say it that way. I said it in some little boy way. But eventually, staring at the watch so much that her eyes teared up, I began to help modulate her breathing. By the time we reached school, she wasn't half as upset about the test.

I began asking the other boys—the older ones who were good at baseball and running—what their secrets were. To get their secrets, I entertained them with my modest ventriloquism skills—I could do bird calls and the sounds of crickets and even get a brief sentence out without moving my lips.

Boys like entertainment—so they opened up and told me about athletics and sports. They all said screwy things, but what I noticed were two solid answers: breathing and imagination.

They made sure that they breathed through everything. They also imagined that they would win.

This was a huge revelation to me, since I had never felt that I could win anything. I realized that these other boys were winners in athletics because they believed they were—whether from coaches, friends, family or whomever—and because they did not stop breathing. They used their breathing—without even knowing it—to help keep their bodies working.

All right, that sounds simplistic. I believe that the simplest things can lead to the strongest results.

So I began working on breathing.

This was not merely inhaling and exhaling, but swimming at the beach in the icy spring and holding my breath under water. After all, if I were going to be lord of my own breath, I needed to master everything about it, didn't I? I wasn't sure that I'd ever be a great breath-holder because I never seemed able to go much beyond a minute. I was holding on too much to my fear of dying. This is one of the first lessons about breathing—if you have breath within your lungs, you will not die. Death comes once there is no more breath.

Again, simple. Again, true.

"Owen," my mother said, pinning the laundry up outside the cottage that the Montgomerys housed us in. "What in God's name are you doing?"

I had come up after logging in a minute and a half beneath the water, right at the rocky ledge. I had just leaned over and thrust my face underwater. I was eleven at the time. I tried to explain to her the principle behind my experiment, but she did not seem to understand. However, within a few short months, I had become best friends with the captain of the swim team in seventh grade, and by fall, I was running cross country. I would never be the best—this was not my goal after all. I would be a winner.

In fact, I knew I would close in on this with each sport or endeavor I tried—the other kids were lazy. Life and their families made them that way. I did not intend to let a day go by that I could not claim as my own. I was going to own life in a way that neither of my parents ever had.

Academics slipped in my middle school years—but

not enough for anyone to notice. I read studiously, and never for enjoyment, but to understand systems of thought that the world was trying to push at us. I learned quickly that an A+ in school sometimes meant a D– in life, and that equal effort had to be made to excel in both spheres. Breathing helped. When I felt overwhelmed by it all, I practiced my breathing again. Even in December, when the island was desolate and the water was cold enough to drown, I would leap into the sea and stay beneath the water for as long as I could; I would, if possible, use the Montgomerys' indoor swimming pool for my morning workout which began at six A.M.

8

That was the wonderful thing about the Montgomerys' place:

They were usually gone all winter unless Mr. and Mrs. Montgomery were fighting, or Mr. Montgomery had gone off with one of his mistresses and Mrs. M was so angry she came to the island for a blisteringly cold February. I used to see Mrs. M in those cold Februarys, and I ran errands in town for her because she spent too much time staring at the walls or sitting along the indoor pool while I did laps. She enjoyed letting me swim there, and she sometimes even got in and did laps, too. Once, when I was twelve, Mrs. M told me, "You're turning into quite the handsome boy, Owen Crites." She was in good shape for a woman of forty, and there were times when I was with her that she reminded me so much of Jenna it was almost like having Jenna there with me. When I watched her back, as she got out of the pool, bathing cap on, her narrow waist, the way the water beaded upon her skin—it was like seeing Jenna for a moment. This made me happy. Jenna meant a lot to me.

But the pool—dare I describe it now, how I remember it? It was vast. It was Olympic-size. I could do real laps there as opposed to laps at the beach, which ended with a summer lifeguard blowing a whistle for me to come to shore before I'd gone out twenty yards. The pool was off the southern wing of their estate, and had glass surround it, so that it was as if you were swimming outside, as if on the bluffs over the Sound; you owned the world as you went back and forth, breathing, carefully breathing so as not to wear out too fast.

Because, during those winters when the M's stayed down in Manhattan, my father and mother and I had the run of the house. I could swim naked in the pool and rise to see the reflection of my body in the long mirrors that were in the small locker room off the pool. By my sophomore year in high school, I had created—and mastered—a beautiful, strong body, and what average looks I had were masked by health and physical near perfection. I didn't admire this because I believed in beauty.

Beauty is for the lazy.

I admired it because I knew the world admired it, and I wanted to own the world.

Wrestling was my winter sport at school, and I did not excel at it, but I held my own. The girls loved

Douglas Clegg

me—and the boys, too. I never got too close to them, though, because I had to spend all my concentration on creating who I was. But the girls all cheered for me in the sweaty matches as I brought some great bull of a boy from a competing school down to the red mat. Because the psychological aspect to sports can't be emphasized enough, I would—with each match—create some threat to my opponent. Something I could whisper in his ear.

This took no small planning, as it meant I had to do research on those I wrestled, so I would know just what button to push to take away their psychological edge. Dagon helped me; my god took me to books and ideas and notions, if you will, that showed me just what other boys would be most hurt by. Usually, it involved their sense of sexuality. After all, even I knew that showering with other boys all day, wearing jockstraps, cracking jokes about everything from dicks to pussies, was a veil across homoeroticism among adolescents. And who but wrestlers were closest to puncturing that veil? So, I would whisper to my opponent something about him, something perhaps his closest friend had told me—his closest friend, drunk, being taken out to a parking lot—his closest friend who, with six beers in him, would finally admit to something that my opponent would be happiest to hide for a thousand years.

Sometimes, it was less interesting. My threat might be, "I know your little sister, Trey. I know all about her leg. I would hate for something to happen to her. I would hate for someone to do something to a little girl so sweet."

You may judge me for this if you like. It was a competitive edge, and this is what we, in athletics, were taught: to find our edge.

Skill alone never wins.

I wish it did, but lazy people think that way.

Faith is necessary, too. I had found mine. It had grown within me.

Now, this began rumors about me, but I had built up a loyal following of other boys and girls in school. I became head of the pep squad for the football team—team sports were never my thing, but I knew that I had to somehow attach myself to them. So when kids from other schools began talking about me saying "crazy, psycho" things, I had friends who were willing to lay down and die for me rather than accept those lies. I really liked the kids I went to high school with; I liked the teachers. It was easy for me to like them. I think even being poor helped—teachers saw me as an underdog rising. I would tutor children in the local elementary school some afternoons; I took the coach's daughter to the junior prom, just because I was a nice guy and I felt bad that she wasn't pretty enough to get asked by any of the other guys. I was well-liked, and sometimes, that carries you.

But I haven't mentioned much about Jenna yet, have I? In all this talk of myself, she has not yet entered—not in the way she should've. She was not at my school. She was not within my sphere. She was outer; she was beyond beyond.

How could I take her to the prom when she only arrived at Outerbridge Island in the summers?

I would count the days until Memorial Day weekend, when the Outerbridge Majesty would arrive in Quonnoquet Haven, heavy with tourists and summer people, and there, on the highest deck, I'd see her with my binocs and I would lay back in the muddy grass and look up at the paling sky and think: Please remember what we promised. Remember everything and don't leave anything out.

Remember why I came to you and why you let me and why it would make everything be the way it was supposed to, and why you're the reason for my every breath.

That's what had happened when I was twelve and dedicated my soul to the god of dark places. By the time I was seventeen, I was a dedicated servant to the one I worshipped.

And all I asked of this divinity was:

Give me Jenna.

I found a cat over in town and with just a pen knife, offered its soul to my god.

9

I'll tell you now that it's safe, what really happened the summer that I discovered purity—genuine purity—in the shit of human existence. I can see myself as I was then: handsome, young, even pretty in a way with my thick hair falling to each side of my face, my blue eyes sharp, yes, but expectant. My shirt is an Izod, a preppie affectation—my mother never wanted me to look like the other islanders. She wanted something better for me, as did I. Khakis, no socks, Topsiders or sandals—my face burning from the beginnings of summer sun, my heart racing. It's no longer me as I am, it's that boy, that boy who is almost eighteen, a man at this point, a man who has nearly won in life.

I, he, you, it doesn't matter what I call that boy-man, he just is, I can feel his breath, I can smell the Old Spice on him, I can practically see the cap on his front tooth that cost his father a pretty penny after he fell and chipped it in sixth grade while he was running—I can practically see the fog lift between this day and that one.

He watches for her.

Chapter Two: Memorial Day, Restless Nights, and an Open Window

1

Let me take you there.

Fly like a bird over the crotch of New England—that place where Rhode Island clutches at its small corner between Massachusetts and Connecticut, and out to the Sound, across the scattering of islands and islets and outlands until you see the One Man Rocks, the places where misanthropes going by the name of New Englanders lived two to three per islet—and then, beyond the beyond, as my mother would say, thar she blows—Outerbridge, Outerbridge, Outerbridge. The name conjures up older names, and for me—or for him, for the me who was Owen Crites, the Dutch fighting the Indians, the pirates burying treasure beneath the land, and the people who built the walls. It even conjures all the names it must have had before, when the gods themselves had granted it some secret name. If Owen had known the secret name, he might have had power over it, but as it was, the island was master, and all who occupied its ground, servants.

The island's history began eons ago when some glacial giant swept the rocks and earth into the Atlantic and the world grew up around it. The Pequot and Narragansett Indians held it against the Dutch for as long as they could, and then the Brits wrested it for themselves. The island never provided much in the way of existence for any of its inhabitants; all that's left of the early English settlers were walls made of stone and foundations of cottages that speckle the northern end of Outerbridge (originally called a Dutch name that had sounded to the English like Outerbridge, although there was a movement afoot among the summer residents to restore the old Pequot name for the place). The largest beach, called the Serpentine by the British for its snaky shape, runs the western length. A Victorian Wedding Cake House called the Mohegan, converted in recent years to a twenty-room hotel, sits perched on the main bluff overlooking the most public part of the Serpentine. On each side are the summer homes—the large and the ordinary, and the woods all mixed in and winding through them. More than half the roads on Outerbridge were still dirt; there was no McDonald's, no 7-Eleven, and only two stoplights between the three townships.

Spring shat out of winter in New England—and

along the uneven row of islands called the Avalons
that skirted Connecticut, Rhode Island, and a bare tip
of Massachusetts, it was a heavy crap of rain and then
sun and then rain and finally sun—the merciless summer sun that never left until two weeks after Labor
Day. Outerbridge had it the worst, for the two other
large Avalons—and the smaller rocky ledges called
islets that formed part of the coastal barrier against
the Atlantic—got the good weather first, but no one
much lived there to care.

Outerbridge, the farthest up the coastline was
more narrow than wide—six miles long, two and a
half miles wide—with bluffs to the south and north,
the Great Salt Pond at its center, the Wequetaket
swamps in the lower points to the east; there are 253
summer residents; there are seventy-five in the winter,
most of them over sixty. At the height of winter's cruelty, helicopters come in with supplies. That sounds
outrageous, but it's true, for Outerbridge is farther
from the mainland than even the Vineyard and Nan-
tucket to the north—it is beyond beyond beyond, and
there is no crossing easily. The historic landmarks are
South Light and North Light, the two lighthouses
that still work, sentries at each end of the island; Old
Town, or Old Town Harbor as the old-timers call it, is
at the southern tip; Quonnoquet Haven, with its
bluffs and spectacular view of what they call the Big
Nothing, where even the mainland is unseen in the
distance, lies to the north of the island

This particular day was the glinting kind. Sun
glinted off the Sound, the virgin leaves on the wet
trees, and the bark, too—all of it spattered light re-

fracted through the hangover of a night of rain recently ended. He hated it—he hated the end of winter because it was usually the end of control within his parents house. His mother had been in bed for most of the season, nursing imagined traumas, while his father had spent his hours away from home, either working as a handyman and gardener at the Big House, or in town or down to Old Town Harbor for drinks with his friends.

Owen Crites looked to summer for one thing, and one thing only. It would be the arrival of Jenna Montgomery, and that would mean that his misery, his feeling of loneliness would vanish.

It was a singular obsession of his.

She was purity.

2

"Hi," he said to her when he was six.

"Hi," she replied. But she hadn't needed to. She was six and all ringlets and ribbons and party dress.

"Owen," he said.

"I know. Hank's your daddy."

The fact that she called his father by his first name shocked Owen. No other child called a parent by the first name. It was taboo. And to call his father "Hank" and not "Henry" seemed far too familiar.

"I know where you live," she added, an afterthought.

"Here," he said, meaning her property.

"In my yard," she said. "You have the big goldfish pond."

"Koi," he corrected her.

"And all the roses my mommy loves," she said, and then took him by the hand and brought him into her world—the birthday party, the children from New York, the pony rides on the bluffs, the smoked turkey sandwiches, the games of pin-the-tail, and the dance. He had been woefully underdressed in a torn pair of jeans and a t-shirt. The other boys all wore white shirts and little ties; their hair glistened with gel. The girls were in puffy dresses and glittery shoes. He had no gift for her. It had panicked him midway through the party.

He went and found a gift she had not yet unwrapped, and he threw away the other child's card. On the wrapping paper, he scrawled—Hapy Birthday from Owen. As it turned out, the gift was a small hand puppet, and Owen took it from Jenna and began doing something that he didn't even know he could do.

He threw his voice, so it sounded as if the puppet were speaking without Owen's lips moving.

When it was found out what he had done, he was punished, but even Mrs. M commented to Owen's mother about her son's delightful talent.

But forget that for now, forget it. Years passed; punishment was the result of knowledge. Smart people punished themselves, his older self knew. All people with brains received punishment.

He had only recently turned seventeen.

He knew better than to reveal secrets.

He waited for her, watching the Sound for the ferry on the Thursday before Memorial Day weekend.

3

His eyes turned to slits against the western sun; it was the last ferry of the day, and he couldn't find her or her parents among those on the deck.

Perhaps she wouldn't be coming until after the holiday—it had happened before, but several years back. He didn't want to believe it because he never liked to consider the options that people had. His own life felt without option. He had created within himself the person who could most handle his life. He had worked his body, developed the grace of an athlete, he had tried to keep his face pleasant—and when the anxieties of his family or of studies became unbearable, he would go to the mirror and practice relaxing his facial features until he was sure he looked pleasant again. He did not want to seem anxious, even if he was. He wanted to give nothing away to those around him.

He ran down to the docks to see if she might be somewhere else on the ferry—perhaps she was sick and wanted to stay below. Perhaps she was taking a nap in the backseat of her family's Range Rover. Perhaps, perhaps, he repeated to himself as he sloughed off inertia and jogged down to the paved road near the marina.

The summer people were like ticks—they attached themselves to every aspect of the Haven, they drank all the beer, they ate the best the local cooks had to offer, they had all the accidents—more people would die from boating or swimming mishaps in three months than would die in six years in the other seasons of the island.

They were careless, they were bloodsucking, they were here to forget the venal world from which they came.

They, he thought. They. They debarked the ferry, bicyclists, clownish men and women in golfing outfits, or overly gilded women with poodles and wolfhounds and shih tzus, followed by weary overworked doctor-husbands; the college crowd, too, had begun filling up the local bars and the beach, and all these he hated with a passion. He had spent his life watching them come and be carefree in the summer. He had watched them spend more money some nights than his father could make in a month.

Dagon, he prayed, Dagon, hear me. Cast them down. Raise me up.

He ached for what they had. The lives they had. The freedom from this island. From the world he had mastered.

He read books on Manhattan; he learned about Jenna's family, how her great-great-grandfather had worked on railroads and then had gone on to own them, and how her great-grandfather had lost that fortune; how her grandfather had gotten into radio and television and magazines, owning several, selling them, building up a small but substantial media empire; how her mother had continued that work, married a great media magnate, divorced, married again, had Jenna and remained with Mr. M although the marriage ran hot and cold.

The story of Jenna's family was the story of all the summer people, and though they lived simply on the island for the three months, though they rode cheap bikes around the Great Salt Pond, though they dressed casually even for the one restaurant in Old Town Harbor (the Salty Dog), they were all over-moneyed as his father often said.

His father spoke of money as evil; his mother spoke of it like a lost child.

Owen felt it was something like fire—to be feared and mastered. It was what other people were given.

It's what he would be granted.

And these people tromping off the ferry had it. They lived it. They did not dream of getting off this island. They dreamed of things beyond what Owen could imagine.

4

She never arrived, and he walked the long narrow wooden staircase from the beach up to the bluffs; and then he ran along the fringe of pines to the dirt path that went farther up the rolling cliffs; and he didn't look back down to the water until he was at their property.

At the house, he went and sat in one of the wrought-iron lawn chairs and leaned back to gaze up at the sky.

"Owen?"

He sat up, looking around. He rose from the chair,

practically knocking it over, and there she was—at the third-story attic window.

No, it was Mrs. M. Her auburn hair was swept back from her face, damp from the swimming pool; her robe fastened none too tightly. She possessed the air of having enjoyed life too much that day. "Owen? It's good to see you."

"Yeah, Mrs. M, you too. I didn't think you had got here just yet."

"Oh, my husband still hasn't left his desk yet. I've been here since Wednesday. Good to be back. I despise the city."

"Survive winter okay?"

"Superbly," she said, but in a way that meant its opposite. Mrs. M was a woman full of irony; he had known it for years. Mrs. M embodied the house: beautiful, classic, and rich. "Do you want coffee?" she asked.

5

"I saw you waiting for her," Mrs. M said. They were in the sun room off the kitchen, and Owen had just finished his first cup of cinnamon coffee. He got up to pour himself another, but Mrs. M interceded; she had a fresh cup, with cream, all ready for him. He sat down at the table again. She took the chair across from him. He saw her knee emerge from her robe. The hint of her champagne-glass breasts, small but perfect. Mrs. M was in many ways more beautiful

Douglas Clegg

than her daughter; but still, his heart belonged to
Jenna.

He did what he could to look at her face, but something in her eyes bothered him. He looked, instead, at
her silken arms.

"You're in love with my daughter. No, that's fine.
I've known it since you were both young. Do you
think it will lead anywhere?"

"Lead?" He said the word innocently, but she
must've seen through this. "I don't know."

"Yes, you do. You're smart. I've watched you grow
up. You're smart and handsome and wise. But do you
think that she will have you?"

"I haven't . . . I haven't considered . . ." he stammered.

"You're a remarkable young man," Mrs. M said.
"She doesn't deserve you." Then she put down her
own untouched coffee and stood up from the table.
"She gets in tonight. After midnight."

"How? The ferry—"

"She has her ways," Mrs. M said. She brushed
something from the edge of her eye and combed her
hands through her hair like a mermaid would. "Fancy
a swim?"

"Not today," he said.

"Come on, just a nice long swim. Have you been
practicing all winter?"

He nodded.

"I thought so. You ripple now. You don't move, you
ripple. You're in better shape than he is," Mrs. M
said, and then went to get her bathing suit.

6

Come midnight, he saw the shroud of some sailboat press beneath the lights of the harbor. He sat up on the bluffs and watched as she docked; as the sail came down. No one stepped off the boat at the jetty. Was it her? Was this what Mrs. M had meant?

He fell asleep in the cool wet grass and awoke at dawn.

And he knew.

Jenna Montgomery had found another.

7

"Jimmy," the guy said, his face gleaming, tanned, teeth so much thoroughbred he could've been in Pimlico, his eyes squinty, his nose small, his hair honey-blond from too much sun, and his handshake strong and sure and arrogant. He looked rich without ever having to say it. He smelled rich. He probably tasted rich. "Good to meet you, Crites."

"Owen."

"You're not an Owen or a Crites," Jimmy said. "You're a Mooncalf."

"Mooncalf?" Jenna laughed, looking at Owen and then back at Jimmy. "That sounds ghastly." She wore a bikini, but had a long towel draped about her waist that ran all the way to her ankles. Her hair was wet and shining from a morning swim. For a moment, Owen imagined how it would feel to untie the bikini

255

top and press his face against her breasts. For a moment, the image was in his mind; then, gone.

All Owen could think was: They slept together on the boat. Jenna and this Jimmy character. Jimmy had done it with Jenna.

Done it.

A sacred act if it was love.

A debased ritual if it was lust and emptiness.

Which it had to be.

He tried not to imagine Jimmy drawing her legs apart, or the scent of passion that clung to them, the sweat and fever, as they joined together.

Tried not to imagine the thrusts.

"Mooncalf reminds me of upstate New York, or Pennsylvania," Jenna said with no little disgust. "Cows and chickens. Amish in carriages. Birthings and midwives. Owen can't be a Mooncalf."

Jim snorted. "No, it's a beautiful name. Mooncalf."

Owen remained silent, still numb from meeting the interloper.

"Well, if he's Mooncalf, then what am I?"

"Kitten." Jimmy laughed.

"If I'm Kitten, then you're Cat."

"All right, then I'm Cat. Now, what shall we call this island?"

"Outerbridge," Owen said. "Call it Outerbridge."

"That's not the game." Jimmy grinned, and damn if his smile wasn't dazzling. Anyone would fall in love with this guy—anyone, man, woman, or dog—he was so damn attractive and warm, it made Owen want to walk away and forget about Jenna completely. "The game is everything, Mooncalf. It doesn't matter what things are. You shape them into the way you want them. That's how you gain mastery."

"Mastery's the thing," Owen said, faking a sort of blissful—and very nearly nonchalant—take on all of it.

I'll beat you, he thought as he watched his rival, this apollonian boy with his golden hair and squinty green eyes and the way he had arrogance that was absolutely seductive.

I will beat you, Owen made the oath then and there. He glanced up briefly at the unfettered sun and prayed to God that if nothing else went his way in this life, he would beat down this Jimmy.

Then, Owen reached a hand out and gave Jimmy's shoulder a friendly squeeze. "Just not big on games I guess."

Jenna laughed, "Owen, the game is called Paradise. You rename everything to your liking. Jimmy invented it. Isn't it . . . marvelous?" She pecked the bastard on his ear. Owen noted: The kiss went to his earlobe, and Jimmy barely has an earlobe. His ear was smooth and rounded and touched down right behind one of his several dimples.

Jimmy laughed, shrugging, grabbing her around the waist and pulling her close to him. "Let's call the island Sea Biscuit."

"No," Jenna groaned. "That's terrible. Terrible. Owen, you name it."

"Outerbridge," Owen said.

It was noon, and they were at the jetty. The sailboat bobbed gently with the current, and Owen finally took his baseball cap off.

"There now," Jimmy said, approvingly. "You look

less like a little boy than like a man. The Mooncalf has such pretty hair for a moody guy." He reached over and scruffed his hand through Owen's hair. His fingers felt electric. "I know the name for this island. I know. It's called Bermuda. We're in Bermuda," he laughed, leaning into Jenna, kissing her just behind her ear.

No, Owen thought. You're in the realm of Dagon.

8

A restless night came to him, and then another and another. He lay on his single bed, sheets pulled back, and a fever such as he had never before felt washed over him.

Whosoever has loved the way I love Jenna Montgomery, he whispered to the stars through his bedroom window, has known sacrifice and torture and days and nights of endless wanting, thirst without satisfaction, hunger without morsel. Whosoever has wept within themselves for what they could not reach, could not touch, has felt what I feel.

Whosoever has spent his life working his body, mind, and soul to its absolute limit to be the extreme candidate for the love of a beautiful and angelic girl as I have for her, as I have given myself to the shape that she would long for . . .

That man would not rest were a rival to steal the prize from him.

Dagon, he whispered soundlessly. Dagon. My god. Bring her to me.

Eventually, Owen Crites slept better imagining the world under the sea where the people who were part of the Dagon had dwelt, with their vast and imperious citadels, their large cold eyes and their wet shapeless forms, and he imagined the great sacrifice he would throw to them for their entertainment.

9

"How are you going to waste your last summer?" Owen's mother asked as she switched off the faucet, plunging her hands back into the soapy water. "Now, don't blot, Owen, dry. There's a difference." She passed him the first dish, which he sprayed down and then wiped with the green-and-white hand towel. The kitchen in the caretaker's house was as narrow as one of the closets in the big house. The window looked out on a small sunken garden, behind which the pine trees stuck out like crooked teeth. "Don't blot," his mother repeated.

Owen began stacking the dry plates carefully. "I need a job."

"You work for your father."

"Not this summer," he replied. "Hank'll do without me."

"Hank?" his mother said, nearly laughing. "Hank? Next you'll be calling me Trudy." Then, her mood darkened. "Show some respect."

His mother reached down to pull the plug on the drain. She reached back to her hairpins, pulling them out so that her gray-streaked hair fell along her shoulders. She smoothed it back, and turned to watch him dry the rest of the plates and bowls from supper. "I know what you're thinking."

He glanced at her for the barest moment.

"You're thinking that you'll work down where she goes at night. The restaurant. The dock. You'll be there for the dances. I've seen the boys working at those places. They live here all year 'round. But in the summer, sometimes they get the rich girls. But those girls don't care about them. The boys are just part of summer to those girls. Just like the beach. Just like a walk."

He remained silent and kept his eyes on each bowl as he carefully wiped the towel through them.

"I grew up in her world. I know what she'd have to give up. Don't ask her to do it. Not if you care about her," his mother said. Then she nearly snickered.

"What's funny?" he asked.

"I remember your father at your age, is all. I remember him so well," she said. "He's working on the pump now. The pump and the well. Today he worked on the azaleas and the roses. Tomorrow, he'll probably check the pool. If only I had known then. Owen, you might as well go find that pirate treasure as think that a girl like her will be interested in you beyond these summerish flings."

Owen dropped the towel on top of the cutting board, and turned to walk away.

"I know what you get up to," his mother called to him, but he had already stepped out of the house, letting the screen door swing lazily shut. "You're nearly a man, Owen. You need to grow out of all your imaginings now."

Her voice, behind him, was part of another layer of existence. The smell of fresh grass mingled with the slight scent of the roses, which were just blooming in spirals and curves up on the bluffs.

He walked to the edge of the hill, feeling the late sun stroke him like a warm hand. At the rim of the koi pond, he knelt down and looked at his reflection in the green water. Soon, the patchwork fish came to the surface. He reached his hand into the murkiness, shivering with the chill, and found the god laying where he'd left it, behind the lava rocks.

He felt the edge of the god's face.

10

In a school notebook, Owen wrote:
Things Jenna likes:

1. She loves swing dancing.
2. She likes expensive perfume. The kind older women wear. Not like other girls.
3. She likes sandals.
4. She likes to let a boy open a door for her.
5. She likes clothes from Manhattan.
6. She likes to be complimented on how smart she is.
7. She likes someone who listens to her.
8. She likes holding hands.

Douglas Clegg

Things Jenna hates:

1. She hates heavy-metal rock.
2. She hates boys who look at her breasts.
3. She hates having to wait for anything. Ever.
4. She hates Julia Roberts movies. She reminds me of movie stars, though.
5. She hates when animals get hurt.
6. She hates being treated like a piece of meat.
7. She hates boys who want to go all the way because she told me three years ago that she's going to wait for the right one.
8. She hates having to do things she hates.

11

He waited a week before going back up to the Montgomery place, and even then, it was after eleven, and the house was dark and silent except for the kitchen, where Mrs. M always kept a light on. At first, he intended to stand beneath Jenna's bedroom window and maybe toss a pebble at it to get her attention. He noticed that the window—on the third story—was open, and he decided he'd call to her.

Then he noticed that one of the guest room windows was open, too.

That would be Jimmy's. The bastard.

Owen glanced along the trellis and gutters, and decided he'd try that route first. He climbed the trellis with the agility of a monkey, although it threatened to pull away if he didn't balance his weight just right. It wasn't much different from the rope climb in gym. When he worried that he wouldn't make it to the third story roof, he remembered the breathing trick and began inhaling and exhaling carefully. That was where the balance was: in the breathing. Then, he grabbed the gutter, and scaled the slant of the roof. He crawled along it, slowly, cautiously, and went to look in on Jenna while she slept. He felt himself grow hard, imagining how he could hold her while she slept, imagining how he would smell her hair.

When he looked through the open window, he saw the other boy there, Jimmy, in bed with her, holding her, moving against her.

Owen caught his breath and held it for what felt like the longest time. He could hold his breath under water for a few minutes, and holding it now while he watched Jimmy press himself into her, like a hummingbird jabbing at a flower, but not as pretty, just dark and murky, Jimmy's body rising and falling as he plunged into her, not gently the way she would want it, but like he was a jackal tearing apart some carcass.

Chapter Three: The Morning Swim

1

"The Salty Dog," Owen said, lifting himself from the swimming pool. "Waiting tables. Since Memorial Day weekend. Lifting weights, too."

"That must be delightful," Mrs. M said. She stood near the changing rooms, swathed in a red bathrobe, dark glasses covering her eyes. She looked like a movie star. She had a cigarette in her hand, which she waved dramatically. "I imagine you meet lots of girls and boys your age at that dive."

"Some."

"You're still very young for your age," she said, and then caught her breath for a moment. "I'm sorry. I didn't mean that in a negative way. I meant it as . . . as . . . you're so innocent compared to the boys at that school she goes to. They've already begun those patterns they'll have for life." She exhaled a lungful of smoke. She was like a beautiful dragon, he thought. A jade dragon with sparkling eyes.

Owen drew himself up over the pool's edge. He exhaled deeply coughing.

"My smoking bother you?"

"No," he said, swiveling to sit down more comfortably, his legs still in the water. "Just holding my breath. Trying, anyway."

"Trying to reach some goal? Underwater?" She took her sunglasses off, and dropped them carelessly on the tile.

He nodded. "To beat the *Guinness Book of World Records*. This guy, he held his breath thirteen minutes."

"That's impossible." She walked casually over to him. He could see her sapphire bathing suit top, and her sparrowish breasts cupped within it as her robe fell open. She stepped out of her sandals. For a moment, he thought of what she would look like with her suit ripped from chin to thigh, with him pressing into her—no, not him, Jimmy, the way he had torn into Jenna. Mrs. M, a smile on her face, could not read his thoughts, he hoped. "No one can hold his breath that long," she said. "It must've been a cheat."

"If you believe in something, maybe you can do impossible stuff, Mrs. M."

"That's magical thinking, sweetie. And Mrs. M, good lord," She laughed, dropping her robe completely. She shimmered. "You're a man now. You'll have to start calling people by their first names, Owen. I feel like a schoolmarm when you call me that. Is that what you want me to feel like? A haggish old schoolmarm? I'm forty, not seventy. Catherine. Or Cathy."

"Oh, yeah, okay," he said, grinning. "Cathy."

As she walked along the edge of the pool to the far end, she pulled her hair back and tucked it into her white bathing cap. She lifted her arm in a certain way to him, like a salute. Then, Jenna's mother dove into the pool, graceful as a mermaid. He watched her do laps while he caught his breath.

2

When he went to shower off, Owen saw the other boy's towel hanging from the bathroom stall. Steam began to fill the changing room. He pulled his wet trunks down, and tossed them on a chair. He grabbed one of the long white towels that the Montgomerys' maid kept neatly rolled in the cabinet over the toilet. Then, he walked the narrow hallway to the large shower. All three shower heads were running, and the boy stood there rubbing soap along his arms, his face frothy with white soap foam. Owen ignored him, stepping beneath the farthest shower head, and grabbed a bar of Ivory from the holder.

"Mooncalf," Jimmy said, as the foam rinsed from his face. His hair stuck up high on his head. The smell of Ivory soap was overpowering. "Haven't seen you in awhile."

"I know," Owen said, his voice husky. He didn't feel the way he did in school with the other boys, not with this Jimmy, this eighteen-year-old whom he had watched deflower Jenna. He felt disgusted. "Been busy." He turned his back on Jimmy for the rest of the shower, hoping the other boy would leave to go swim in the pool. But Jimmy toweled off, and began dressing just as Owen turned off the water. He slipped his shorts on, and reached for his t-shirt. "You've been working out a lot. Me, too. I run every morning. I play tennis."

"Swim," Owen said. He walked back to the toilet to take a leak.

"Swim?"

"I swim."

"Ah, a complete sentence out of the Mooncalf," Jimmy chuckled. "That's the first thing I noticed about you, you know."

Owen said nothing; flushed the toilet. Sat down on one of the chairs, and reached for his shirt.

"You talk in bits of sentences. Well, that and your hair."

Owen twisted back to look at him, his t-shirt half over his head. "My hair? What's your problem?"

"You've got pretty hair. It's soft, too. Most guys' hair is like bristles."

"Weirdo," Owen said. Then, "Sleep in the guest room much?" He pulled the shirt down and went to grab his socks. Jimmy followed him, sitting down on a short bench.

"No. That bother you?"

"No. It's weird that her parents don't care."

"They don't. Well, her mother doesn't. Her father's

still down in the city. And I thought you were hot for Jenna. That's the third thing I noticed about you."

"We're friends. That's all."

"Boys can't just be friends with girls."

"Okay," Owen said. He laughed, but it was a fake. It echoed off the turquoise tile and sounded less genuine as it went. He looked at Jimmy, who was watching him with a sort of paternal take—the way Owen's father would look at him when he didn't understand him.

"You know, Mooncalf, you comb your hair to the left a little more—make the part slightly higher—and you'd look top drawer. You really would. Your chin's strong, your body's in excellent shape. You need to get rid of these," Jimmy pointed at Owen's red t-shirt, "and start wearing some oxford cloths, button-downs. With sleeves. Short sleeves are for kids. It would show your best side. And maybe some khakis. When you grin, don't show all your teeth."

"Bite me."

Jimmy laughed, and reached out, pressing his hand against Owen's shoulder in what could only be a casual and friendly—even brotherly—gesture. "Good. Some spirit. I'm just trying to help. You look good, but you look too island. You need a little charm. All guys do. Swimming only goes so far, after all." Jimmy, ever-annoying, kept up the jabber. "I'm not much of a swimmer. I sail, but the idea of water, well, let's just say I do a passable dog paddle. But you've got those biceps. Amazing shoulders for such a Mooncalf runt. Pretty good. How much you bench?"

"Who cares?"

A brief silence.

Then, "I do."

"Well, not all that much," Owen said. "I just stack the weights on and push. I don't notice how much."

"Don't notice? My God, sport, you mean to say your goal isn't the weights?"

Owen shrugged. "I never think about it. I just want to be powerful. I mean strong."

"You said powerful."

"Same thing."

Another brief silence.

"You ever up for tennis?" Jimmy asked.

"Not really."

"I can teach you if you like. It would be fun to do a doubles match one day. Early, before it's too hot. You, me, Jenna, and maybe you could find a friend to bring. We could have a good match. It's always fun to play doubles," Jimmy said. Owen noticed the combination of arrogance and nonchalance, as if none of this mattered. Even this small talk was something to fill some empty space. Jimmy probably screwed Jenna on a nightly basis. But he never thought about Owen, or Owen and Jenna. He probably lived in the moment. Completely.

"Saturday should be fun," Jimmy said, wiping the last of the spray from his shoulders as he pushed his feet into the cheapest sneakers that Owen had ever seen. "You bringing a date?"

Owen glanced up. "Her birthday?"

"Yeah, you know, the whole crowd's coming from the Cape, and then we'll just do tequila shots 'til dawn. You got a girl off-island?"

Owen began to lie, just to fill that emptiness between them. Yes, he had a girl. Yes, he was excited
about Jenna's birthday party, even though he had not
been invited to it. Yes, he was considering his options
as to which colleges he was looking into—Middlebury looked promising, he didn't think he had quite
the grades for Harvard, but his uncle had been a dean
at Middlebury, and yes, they could all go skiing in the
winter up there in some distant holiday. The whole
time, Jimmy reached into his shaving kit; went over to
shave at the mirror, and then applied some kind of lotion to his face. He finished it off with a spritz of the
most obnoxious cologne that Owen had ever smelled.
While they small talked, Owen knew, standing there
in the diminishing steam of the changing room, he
knew.

Owen knew just by standing there with Jimmy in
the shimmering mist.

Jimmy had a weakness.

He began spending time, after that, thinking about
that weakness.

Thinking about how he could get Jenna back.

3

Owen's shift at the Salty Dog began at three and
lasted until eleven, six days a week. He emerged
sweaty and stinking of grease because half his job was
cleaning out the fryers and grease pits at the end of
the night, and when he got off shift in early July, it
was nearly two A.M. He went down to the jetty to

stare out at the early morning mist of the Sound, smoke some cigarettes, and chill.

He didn't turn around when he heard the footsteps coming up behind him.

"Mooncalf."

"Hey, Jimmy."

"Got a cig?"

"Take one." Owen tossed a cigarette back.

"Thanks. I guess you want to be alone."

"Didn't know you smoked."

"I don't. Not when anyone looks, anyway."

"That's nice. Anything else you do when no one's looking?"

"If I told, you'd know my secrets."

"How's Jenna?"

"She's okay. She fell asleep early. I just needed to wander a little. How's the job?"

"Good. You can smell it on me. You wander late. It's almost morning."

"In Manhattan, I wander at all hours. I like this time of night. I kind of miss work. I used to work summers in one of my dad's stores. It was fun sometimes."

"Seems like more fun to run around the island all summer. Like you two."

"It gets old. I take that back. Yeah, it's fun. I guess you want to be left alone."

"You guessed right," Owen said, cricking his neck to the left a bit.

"Your neck hurt?"

"It gets stiff. Leaning over a mop half the time. On my knees cleaning out all kinds of shit."

"Here," Jimmy said, and Owen felt hands at the back of his neck, gently massaging. "Better?"

Owen let him continue. "This fog depresses me."

"I think it's peaceful."

"You would."

"Mooncalf, you hate me, don't you?"

"Not really."

"How does this feel?" Jimmy pressed his thumbs into Owen's shoulders.

"Oh yeah," Owen said. "Right there."

4

Before dawn, he had gone to the pond. He knelt beside it and reached down among the algae and slimy rocks until he found it.

He drew the statue up, and set it on the wet grass.

"I guess you're just made up," he said aloud. "I guess I'm just a screwed-up guy who made you up. Maybe when I was twelve I was warped. But you're just some cheap souvenir someone lost. No one believes in gods."

But still, the itchy thought touched him somewhere between his eyes and scalp—he could practically feel the fire crawling on him.

But if you're not.

If you're real.

I'll do what needs to be done.

5

Mrs. M, in her own words:

Here's what I thought of it all: My daughter Jenna had been trouble from the day she was born. She was pretty and plain at the same time, and I say that as a loving mother. She inherited her father's face, not much of mine, although I guess she got my eyes. Lucky her—my least favorite feature since my own mother always told me I had sad eyes. When Jenna was four years old, she told me that no man was going to do to her what her daddy did to me. Definitely wise beyond her years, but just not special enough to handle what life would deliver to her, that's for damn sure.

It was her trust fund. It made her trouble.

Look, there's something that everyone pussyfoots around but no one ever talks about. That's money. Pure and simple. Money. When a girl has some, she can be elevated to the status of goddess. The most ordinary—even homely—creature can become ravishing with just a portfolio or a trust fund. That island—in summer—is full of trust-fund widows who should by all rights be considered blemishes, but instead are constantly sought out for parties and gatherings and literary events. For Jenna, there's always been money. And I've watched it feed her in a way that can't be healthy; but what could I do? She has access to money. Lots of money. Money clothes her.

She was ruined because of it, basically. She could never learn how to survive. She could never learn how to rely on herself and her own character to get through a difficult or challenging situation.

She could always buy her way out of things.

This isn't true of me. I was raised solidly middle-class. My father had died when I was six, and my mother didn't have too many options, not back then. In many ways, I feel for Owen because of this. His life is a lot like mine was as a child. Yes, there was some inheritance later for me, but when you spend most of your childhood wanting things, you never really get over it.

And money becomes a prison, too. When you know what it's like to live without it, and when it's within your grasp, then you know what it's like not to have it.

So you cling to it. Pure and simple. You hang on for dear life.

I suppose people will say things about my marriage to Frank that reflect this, but my marriage is a different kettle of fish. We've got our way of living, and yes, you can assail it all you want, but it works for us nine times out of ten, and those times when it doesn't quite work, well, we have places to go where he can live his life and I can live mine, and the breather is well-needed. On both our parts.

I'm not the easiest woman in the world to live with.

And he's no saint.

I sat down with my little girl when she was just learning about sex, and I told her that men have different ways of dealing with love, and usually it's through the one part of their body that seems to cause others the most damage. "But it's just his body," I told her. She cried over all this. She cried when she found out her father had another woman. A mistress. But you have to cry at first, don't you? To get all those little fairy tales out of your head about how life gets lived, about how there are a few good men, how some men don't cheat.

And it's not true. All men cheat, and all women marry cheaters, and to not look at that square in the face is like not looking at the good side of marriage, too.

So she cried off and on for a few years, and I held her sometimes; I was cold to her at times—I knew she needed to work out this idea in her mind.

When she fell in love for the first time, she told me that she was grateful for what she'd had to go through with her father. "I don't know why men do what they do," she told me.

"If you did, you'd have solved the greatest mystery of life," I said to her. Or something like that.

But for my money, she should've avoided that Jimmy McTeague. He was bad news. I know every little deb and sorority girl east of the Mississippi thought he was just the end of the world, but they were such goofy little virgins it was hard to have patience with them.

Jimmy McTeague is the devil incarnate. I know that's an over-the-top way of putting it. He wasn't evil, but he was cold. I knew a little about his family, and none of it was very good. His father had some bad business deals going, and even if he had all the stores, Frank told me some things that alarmed me.

With Jimmy, I felt it the first day I met him, which

was sometime before summer. Perhaps some Easter break? She brought him by the house in Greenwich, and the first thing out of his mouth was, "Hello, Catherine. I've heard so much about you, I almost feel like we've had an affair."

He thought that kind of thing was funny, that off-the-cuff jokiness. Within minutes, he'd given me some nickname, which of course he had to repeat five or ten times to truly annoy me, and within an hour of chatting with him, I knew more about that boy than I cared to know.

He is dangerous.

And so yes, I think it all has more to do with Jimmy McTeague than with anybody. At her birthday party in late July, he told me that he thought the world was meant to be owned by people like him.

I believe those were his exact words.

Yes, he had money. Yes, he was extremely good-looking for a boy his age. Extremely. Only a fool wouldn't notice that. But he had no spirit. What he had was pure badness. He was absolutely pure in his badness.

I once had a dog like that. Beautiful. Completely bad.

Jimmy McTeague's like that.

I really began to hate that boy at Jenna's birthday party.

Chapter Four: The Birthday Party

1

In the mirror, Owen combed his hair, parting it a bit higher, not to the middle of his forehead, but certainly an inch higher than his usual. He also brushed it back so it rose a bit higher. The summer blond streaks looked better this way. He rubbed some gel into it and made sure the part was clean. He smiled as naturally as he could. No, that wasn't right. He let his lips pull back slightly. He squinted his eyes the way that Jimmy did. It looked rich to do it. Like the sun was always on his face, even on a cloudy day.

Then he rubbed some of his mother's Neutrogena lotion on his face. It brought a shine to his cheeks and nose. He wasn't sure if he liked it, but it seemed to be what the rich boys had. That shine.

Hanging on the bathroom door: the crisp J. Crew shirt, pale blue, and the tan chinos. He dressed and then returned to his bedroom to get the gift he'd wrapped that morning.

"You're not going to that party," his mother said, glancing at his father. Both sat in the small living room in the dark, the television providing the only source of light. Their faces flickered. His father laughed. "Oh, he'll have fun. The kids are really going to mix it up."

"Yeah. It'll be fun."

"You're not one of them," his mother said. "You can pretend. You always pretend." Then, she turned to his father, patting his shoulder. "Well?"

"Leave it alone, Boston," his father said. "It's the kid's party. You used to go to parties."

"What's that you've got there?" his mother asked. She got up from the couch, setting her beer down on the coffee table. His father reached over, turning on the standing lamp. Light came up. His mother looked gray, despite her colored hair. Even her skin seemed gray. His father looked like a wisp of smoke. It was all Owen could do to keep them from vanishing within the room.

Owen looked down at the box in his hands. "It's her birthday."

"You bought her something?" his mother asked, a grin spreading like blood on her face. He could imagine her dead, her skull cracked open like an egg. "You bought the Montgomery girl something? Working for tips at the Salty Dog and you bought the richest girl in the world something?" She shook her head gently. "Owen, you're always trying to impress someone with what you don't have." She said this sweetly, and he felt a tinge of love for her then. He almost felt bad for

280

what he'd done. He almost felt bad for what he'd stolen from his mother to put in the box.

He almost felt bad for what he was giving Jenna.

Almost.

2

The party was in full swing by ten at night. Every Nancy, every Skip, every Jess and Sloan, they all were there, poolside. The great curtains were drawn back, and the glass doors had been removed for the party. White tents had been erected along the yard; lanterns of every conceivable hue strung along the walkway to the Montgomery place, and balloons flew with some regularity from the back acre. The smell of cigarettes and perfume and gin and beer and money were there, too.

Watching it, you'd have seen nearly fifty teenagers dancing, laughing, shouting, a tall blond girl with flowing hair and limbs soaked from having been thrown into the swimming pool, the fat drunk frat boy vomiting over by the birdbath, half a dozen homely young women shining under the spotlight of boys' gazes—for lust and money and breeding and privilege all attract beyond mere looks. The Sound sparkled with moonlight, and summer was at its peak, the sun had only just gone down an hour before, and the smell of salty sea air mingled with the foam of mermaids' souls, lost from true love.

All these things Owen thought.

3

"Did you see Jimmy at the nationals? God, I hear he's going to be at Wimbledon someday. Soon."

"If he's at Harvard—"

"When he's at Harvard, I'm going to call him Jimmy McTeague of the Ivy League. Isn't that cute?"

"I think what's cute is his father. Have you ever met him?"

"Well, I've been in the store."

"Sports superstores never interested me. It seems crass to sell that kind of thing."

"I read in Forbes that his dad is worth several billion."

"Dead or alive?"

"Dead; then Jimmy's worth that."

"Jimmy McTeague is shallow. He is. He's not smart either," one deb said, her party dress ruined because someone spilled a Bloody Mary down the front. "He's pretty, but he's dumb. And my uncle went to Yale with his father, and let me tell you, that man was nearly kicked out for cheating, and once that kind of thing happens, you never know."

Owen stood back, beyond the lights that had been set up along the tents, and watched them all.

The small gift in its box, in his trembling hands.

"Smooth. Just be smooth," he whispered to himself.

He wanted to make sure Jenna saw the gift.

Saw what it meant.

4

Jimmy McTeague held on to a bourbon and water as if for dear life, and he laughed with his jock friends, and he eyed the other girls, and he thanked Mrs. Montgomery for the excellent whiskey. "People who have whiskey like this should own the world," and even when he said it, he didn't know what it meant; and when he saw Owen standing just at the edge of the party, he raised his glass and shouted, "Yo, Mooncalf, get your ass over here!"

5

Jenna Montgomery, in her own words:

Here are things I've read about and I really believe:

The happiest of people don't necessarily have the best of everything; they just make the most of everything that comes along their way.

Happiness lives for those who cry, those who hurt, those who have searched, and those who have tried, for only they can appreciate the importance of people who have touched their lives.

Love begins with a smile, grows with a kiss and ends with a tear.

The brightest future will always be based on a forgotten past; you can't go on well in life until you let go of your past failures and heartaches.

* * *

Okay, before you think I'm just some rich bitch who gets sentimental and gooey over romance novels, the reason I think about those things is because when you are beautiful and you have money, it's those simple things you have to remember.

And I was pretty happy for the most part, right up until last summer.

This probably began because Daddy didn't want me to open Montgomery Hill on Memorial Day like we always did. Mom was already up there, a week or two early, and I'd only just come home from finals.

I have gone to Outerbridge Island since I was about four, and I never miss a summer there. It's what I look forward to after a tough year in school, and since I would turn eighteen over the summer and I had just finished school—but I'd be entering Sarah Lawrence in September—I really wanted to enjoy what time I had left just to be a kid.

Daddy was in one of his moods, though, and I suspect that woman he knows was part of it. Mom told me all about that woman when she gave me the speech about sex and life and marriage when I was fourteen. "Men have problems with their bodies," she said, looking only a little embarrassed. "They all cheat. It's just something we put up with if we can. It's nothing about love. Don't even think that. It's just their biology. They have their good sides and their bad sides. And there are plenty of bad women, too," she added. "Like that woman."

That woman lived in Brooklyn, in a brownstone that my father had bought for her in the 1970s. I took the subway out to it once, and stood on the steps in front, looking through the windows. That woman had a nice chandelier and some paintings on the walls, but it was a fairly plain house in Park Slope. I sort of think I saw a little of her, too, walking up the street. She wasn't even pretty, which was sort of what amazed me. She wasn't like my mother. She was tall, with big feet, and red hair that needed some kind of style. Her face was nothing like my mother's, nothing like the women I knew. She looked Irish, I guess, sort of round and plain.

I don't really know if it was that woman I saw, but I suspect it was.

So just after high school graduation, I was all ready to go to the island, but Daddy was moody and told me that I needed to stay because of Jimmy, who was supposed to have been in town.

All right. Jimmy McTeague: He's a tennis player who goes to Wimbledon every year, he's practically a national champion, and his father owns McTeague Sports, the chain, although I never understand why they don't have stores in Manhattan. I met Jimmy when he was at Exeter, at some dance, and I was just thinking he was cute. Marnie called him the Leech for some reason I didn't quite understand, but I knew there was something interesting about him. He lived a different life than me, and I never really saw myself with that kind of Midwestern jock-type. He was always sweating, too, which I guess goes with the whole athletic thing, but not something that's pleasant to be around an hour after a match.

Still, by the time I was seventeen, I really liked Jimmy. And no, I had no thoughts of marriage or anything like that. We hadn't actually even been intimate or anything, just held hands a lot and went to dances and out to dinner. When I debuted, Jimmy shared the drudgery of that awful debutante season by being my escort; when I was really pissed off over not getting into Columbia, Jimmy actually flew in from the West Coast—where he had some important tennis match— and took me out to dinner.

Then, the night after I would normally go to the island, Jimmy told me we could sail there in this little boat he kept in Greenwich at the club. And that first night on the boat, I became a woman. We drank too many glasses of Chardonnay, and one thing led to another. Jimmy was never very aggressive in bed. He was kind of shy that way. So I pretty much had to seduce him, but once we both closed our eyes and let our bodies take over, we knew how to make love.

And it really was love. It really was. I felt it. We spent that first night on the boat. We got into the harbor at about 12 or 1 in the morning, and just slept together in the little bed. He snored sweetly. Not a hacking or sawing snore, but like a puppy dreaming. He did say something funny to me in the morning, something that struck me as odd, something about how maybe now we could think about the future more now that we'd mated, and I laughed at him and he looked a little angry when I laughed.

All right, I knew that maybe there would be trouble with Owen when I saw him on the jetty when we got off the boat the next morning. He looked like he'd been waiting there all night.

Like he'd been watching us.

The little turd. He really was. I care a lot for him, of course. We've known each other since we were both kids. He's the son of the gardener. His mother sometimes helps out with parties and laundry and other things. He's cute, which helps, too, because although I have nothing against boys that aren't very good looking, there's something about a good looking one that just makes you want him around all the time.

So I'm barely dressed, some tacky beach towel around me basically, and there's Owen at the shore seeing both of us coming up from the boat and the first thing he says to me is, "What happened?"

I felt all nervous and even giggly, like I needed a cigarette. I told him I didn't want to see my mother for a day or two. And then Jimmy just took over, like he always does. He has this way with guys—he always gets them on his side. Jimmy gave him a nickname and acted like Owen was Jimmy's kid brother and they just seemed to get along fine. It was like they'd known each other all their lives in about five minutes. Owen seemed to like all the ribbing and you know that sort of adolescent boy-talk they do. You know that. That way boys have of getting together and sort of sparring, and talking, and noticing each other's hair, or how one of them is sad, and they either peck it to death or get all brotherly. I saw it with Jimmy and his best friends at Exeter, too. The way they played like puppies. That's just what it was like—like watching two golden retrievers wrestle over a bone.

I didn't see Owen much during June. I guess he got the job down in town. Sometimes I saw him when we went to the Salty Dog, but he never waited on our table. Jimmy was virtually attached at the hip with me, which can get annoying no matter how much you care for a guy. I used to try and lose him in the mornings, after he'd go off to play his beloved tennis with one of the local pros or with my mother. My mother is excellent at sports, which are pretty much not my thing. I like golf a little, and sometimes I like to swim, but the whole girl-jock thing is beyond me.

So Jimmy would slip out of bed, and I'd just get dressed and go down to visit Marci and Elaine, and Elaine's brother, Cooper, down island. Sometimes we'd take whole afternoons just having brunch, or wandering the cove by Great Salt Pond. Jimmy would get all pissed off at me. He was a little jealous. Well, a little more than jealous. He thought that since he was the first guy I'd slept with that he somehow should've had more ownership of me. Or maybe I should've been more attached to him. I mean, I was attached. And he was, technically, the first guy I'd slept with, although I let Ricky Hofstedter press his fingers up there sophomore year, and then there was that time that I got drunk at Hollis Ownby's party and wound up making out with Harvey Somebody (he was a Somebody. I just can't remember his last name) until I woke up with a hangover and a major pain down there and I hoped it hadn't gone too far beyond basic, you know, petting.

But Jimmy had all these needs, and some days, particularly in June and early July, I just wanted to chill and hang out with some friends without worrying about whether I was paying attention to Jimmy and all his issues.

Purity

I didn't think of Owen much except sometimes I remember how fun he was when I was younger and exploring the beaches, or how I'd take him out in one of my dad's small boats, and he'd tell me all about his plans. How he was going to slowly start investing in stocks. I'd ask him how. And he'd look at me funny and laugh. Then, he'd tell me how his mother's father had been well off and when Owen turned twenty-one, he'd come into a trust fund. I knew he was lying, but I sort of liked his lies. They made the days go by. Sometimes the summer seemed short when I was around him, and by the time I got back to school in the fall, I felt renewed. I owed a lot of that to Owen.

But this summer, I've been distant from everybody. Part of it is Jimmy. And yes, it's sexual, I guess. But since I'm paying you by the hour, I guess that you're okay with me telling you, right? Well, Jimmy seems to not be all that aggressive in bed. I know that must sound weird since I'm not terribly experienced in that arena, either, but I've watched movies, I've read books, and I talk with my girlfriends about this stuff. This isn't like twenty years ago when no one ever talked about sex. My friends all say their boyfriends seem to put the moves on them constantly. With Jimmy, I have to literally reach down and grab him. And then, he just sort of you know, touches me here and there and then he—well you know—and then it's over and sort of unpleasant, even though it's not ghastly or anything. It's just not what I expected.

And then there was that fiasco with my birthday party. Christ, it was embarrassing. Mind if I light up? I'm hungry for nicotine at the moment. Ravenous.

Ah, that's better. I know everyone has to give up smoking at some point in their lives, but how nice not to have to give it up just yet.

So, the seventeenth was my big party, and I didn't even want Owen there—he didn't fit in with Jimmy's friends, and many of my friends found him a little cold. Plus, there was the whole problem of his mother, who's a force to be reckoned with. She's always looking at me like I'm the Whore of Babylon. She was helping us set up the party, and she kept giving me that look. You know that look. That mother look.

But Owen showed, and frankly, I was happy to see him. It was sort of a relief since I'd barely seen him all summer. Well, I saw him when he went swimming. In our pool, of course. In our pool. I called him Leech (funny that he and Jimmy both have been called that, huh?) when he wasn't around because he really is such a leech. I mean it in a funny nice way, not some awful way. I once slipped off a rock into one of the little ponds on the property, and my legs were covered with leeches. They don't hurt. You'd be surprised at that, wouldn't you? You'd think that something that sucks your blood would hurt, but they don't. It's just the fact that they're there that makes them bothersome.

So it was my little joke: calling Owen Leech. I care a lot for Owen, actually. We grew up together practically. My island boy. My father laughs whenever I call Owen Leech behind his back, but my mother, well, she doesn't understand that kind of humor. That ironic kind of humor. I mean it as an affectionate term. Sort of like the way Jimmy calls him Mooncalf.

It's a name. I guess it distances me from him or something. But it does get annoying when someone is always borrowing things or using your things or assuming things just because his father works in the garden. I like them. They're like family. I feel a lot for Owen, but really, he should've gotten over that Leech thing years ago.

I can hear my mother's voice in my head: That's cruel, Jenna. I know. I know. I get accused of cruelty all the time. Not physical cruelty. My mother means it's cruel to fault poor people for using our things.

My mother has this thing for him. Well, for all young men. She won't acknowledge it, and she thinks Daddy's the bad one, but I know she likes the boys who hang around me. And no, I'm not jealous of her. Why should I be? She's old. Her time has come and gone. My time is only just beginning.

Anyway, eighteen-year-old boys do not want forty-year-old women. It's embarrassing, really.

Even at the party, Mom is sauntering around in that green get-up she has that looks too glitzy for the island. We all go casual here, so she looked too much like Ginger on Gilligan's Island—too done up. Too too, as Missy Capshaw says. She's too too.

Missy came down from the Vineyard, and Shottsy had his cousin Alec with him, and pretty much the whole gang was there, except for the Faulkners who all went to Maine for the summer. I guess about sixteen of my friends came, and then six or seven of Jimmy's, and then Owen with his shirt that was so new it still had the wrinkles from the cardboard box, and Shottsy made a big point of letting everyone know that part of the plastic collar liner was still under the collar. Owen brought me this nice little gift, I mean that in an ironic way, and that's really the issue here.

But I was having some margaritas and just getting sort of high, and Marnie Llewellyn was regaling me with that story again, the one about her brother's professor and how he and two female students had gone off to Fenwick together and then got caught in the worst way, the very worst way possible.

And I saw what Owen was doing.

I saw that he had already cast a spell. Some kind of spell. Just like a witch.

Over Jimmy.

I saw Jimmy put his hand in Owen's hair, and I saw how they laughed, and I know it must seem irrational and paranoid, but the first thing I thought was:

That bastard is trying to steal my boyfriend.

You can imagine how I felt. I mean, I thought it was ludicrous. It wasn't like Skippy Marshall and that Donovan character from Harrow—they were both homosexual, and we all had known it since they got into the drama club and developed the perfect butts in the workout room doing squats.

This was different.

I thought it was absolutely ludicrous. But I grew livid as I watched them. Absolutely livid. Really, from the corner of my eye. I was working on my third or fourth margarita, and Missy kept talking and Alec kept eyeing my breasts like he always did, and I had my little circle, but they knew something was up, too.

They knew that Jimmy was not fawning on me, and I didn't really enjoy that. Frankly.

I suppose if I had not been drinking, I wouldn't have caused a scene. But I kept my eyes on the two of them, and I saw the touches.

Yes, that's right. Queerish little touches. Not the kind that boys do. Not normally. Owen touched Jimmy's elbow, and Jimmy looked at Owen's hand. And they laughed, and whenever one of them could, he took his fist and gently patted the other on the chest. Like old chums, yes, maybe. Certainly that's what I'd like to believe, but in fact, I saw Jimmy show Owen more genuine attention, not that needy attention he showed me, but the kind of attention every girl wants but never gets from a boy. That adoration kind of attention.

And Owen was milking it. I know he was. I asked Marnie later on, and she said I was imagining things, that Jimmy had been bedding girls since eighth grade, that it was just that boy thing. That's what she said, "That prep school boy thing where they get together and they touch each other and they tell dirty jokes and they check each other out. It's because they both want you. They need to check out the competition," she said.

But I don't know. I stood there, feeling embarrassed and humiliated, and at my party.

At my own party.

Finally I couldn't stand it.

Jimmy leaned forward and whispered something to him. It was like slow motion. I can remember it now like it's still in front of my face. I saw his lips move as he whispered, and I saw Owen lean into him, and Jimmy's hand was on Owen's shoulder, and maybe I was hallucinating or maybe I saw what I saw, but I think Jimmy McTeague placed the barest whisper of a kiss on Owen's ear, at my party, with me watching, with me having to bear witness to it. God, it's so gothic. It's so . . . Fire Island. It really hit me hard.

I began crying, without knowing I was doing it, weeping, just standing there, and Alec took my hand and said, "Aw, princess, what's up?"

And I shook myself free of that crowd, and I walked right over to those two horrible boys, that horrible Jimmy McTeague and I whispered, "If you embarrass me here, I will destroy you."

And then, of course, I had to go back to my party.

I had to.

I had an obligation to my friends. I was not going to let the boy who had been sleeping with me for nearly two months humiliate me in front of my friends.

It wasn't until the next morning that I opened the gift that Owen had given me, and that's pretty much why I freaked out, with my usual panache. I didn't want to see Owen again.

Ever.

But I knew that Jimmy would still be mine, no matter what we both went through to be together.

After all, remember these things:

The happiest of people don't necessarily have the best of everything; they just make the most of everything that comes along their way.

Purity

Happiness lives for those who cry, those who hurt, those who have searched, and those who have tried, for only they can appreciate the importance of people who have touched their lives.

Love begins with a smile, grows with a kiss, and ends with a tear.

The brightest future will always be based on a forgotten past; you can't go on well in life until you let go of your past failures and heartaches.

When I think of all I've had to deal with, particularly with Jimmy, these words bring me comfort.

Oh yeah, what Owen gave me for my birthday.

It was a gun. A crap-ass gun at that. It was tiny. It had some pearly kind of handle, and the safety looked like it had rusted out, and I couldn't get the little clippy thingy off if I tried. I thought it was a joke at first, but I guess not. It looks like something that you'd buy from some little old lady in Brooklyn, some little old lady with a thousand cats and one of those old fox furs, someone who chainsmokes and lives in a studio she's had since the 1950s.

Still, it was a gun, and I have to admit, it was the creepiest thing he could've given me.

He scares me a little.

I mean, what kind of psycho gift is that?

295

Chapter Five:
After the Party

1

Jimmy grabbed Owen's elbow, laughing, the smell of beer and tequila mixed in the air, and Owen giggled, too, and said, "Let's go to the jetty. It's beautiful there. You can see the North Star."

"You know the North Star?"

"Yeah. I know all the stars. I'm an islander. I know the dippers and Scorpio, too."

"You're a Mooncalf," Jimmy said, his grin big and goofy and not the controlled jock he'd once seemed. "God I wish I knew the stars like you. I want to just—just—look at the stars and know which ones they are, and where the earth is in relation to them."

The party spun around them, and Owen had a vague sense that Jenna's eyes floated around his every move. She'll understand, he thought. Someday, she'll understand. "She's a bitch," Jimmy whispered, as if reading his thoughts. "She and her friends and half these people here. All these quote unquote friends of mine, of ours, who are they? Damn it, who are they? And Jenna. Christ. Jenna."

"No, she's cool," Owen said. "Let's go. The jetty."

"God yeah, show me the stars," Jimmy said, and he kept saying it over and over again as they stumbled their way down the path along the bluffs, and every now and then Owen stopped and let Jimmy take his hand. Jimmy's hand was warm, and above them, the sounds of the party spun, and the smell of pine and sea mingled.

The moon cut a path for them all the way to the jetty, and by the time they got there, Jimmy had already grabbed Owen hard and pulled him close to him until their chests pressed together, their thighs met, and he pressed his lips to Owen's mouth.

2

Voices in the dark:

"It's all right, I know you. I know what we both want."

"Shut up. Just shut up."

"Come here. Come here. Let me help you. It's all right. It feels good."

"No, not like this. No."

"I've been so lonely."

"Oh."

"Wanting this."

"Oh."

"Since the first time I saw you."

"Oh."

"Does this feel good?"

"Ah."

"Will you let me take you?"

"Oh."

"Ask me."

"Oh."

"Ask me."

"Owen, take me? Owen? Take me."

3

Owen takes control

I had found my way to Jenna.

It wasn't much different than kissing a girl, and once I allowed Jimmy to feel as if he had seduced me, that I was the unwilling partner, it was easy to hold his attention. He told me to close my eyes and pretend he was a girl, to just let him do things to me, to just keep the image of a beautiful girl in my mind while he did things.

Jenna's was the only face I saw.

I knew that once I had Jimmy McTeague of the Ivy League in my arms, once I had pressed myself into him, owned him, dominated him, that Jenna would be mine.

I look at the boy that I was then: Owen Crites. Mooncalf.

He mounts the rich boy and he drives his point home.

And no, I'm not gay. I had no thrill from what I did to Jimmy McTeague, how I made him feel tenderness and acceptance and release that night. It felt less like sex to me than stabbing someone over and over while they curl around you.

How I caressed him as no one ever had, to the point that he wept against my chest.

It was purely because I thought of Jenna.

My love for her.

Love is purity.

My next decision, as I lay there with that puppy whispering his soul into my ear, was just how I was going to murder him.

Part Two: The Last of Summer

Chapter Six: Jimmy McTeague Keeps a Diary

1

1. Need to train better. Work on backswing, damn it. Wake up an hour earlier every morning. Run two miles. Then practice. Then row.
2. July was a waste. Feeling like I'm getting lazy. More strength training. Check out the sucky gym in town.
3. Jenna's a bitch. She thinks she knows. She doesn't know. She'll never really know.
4. Need to get back with Jenna. Need to figure this out.
5. I can't resist him. It's awful what we're doing. But I know I can stop. I know if I just stick with the program I can stop. I think he's evil.
6. What we did was wrong. I know that. What Jenna and I can build is right.

7. Call the Padre and Madre for more money.
8. Become a better person. Quit all the lying. Lying is bad. There's no reason. If you feel the way you feel, let it all out. Don't keep holding it in. Doesn't matter what Dad thinks. Doesn't matter if you know what you need from life. You can let it out. Other people do. Other people need those things, too.
9. Maybe it's not real. Maybe it's just sex. Maybe I shouldn't let it happen. But now all I think about is him.
10. Jenna and Mooncalf.
11. Mooncalf.
12. He told me something really smart. Just shows that you don't need all these prep schools and universities to be smart. He said, "Love is purity." It is so true. It's something I couldn't say out loud. But it's so true. But there's more to life than love. You can't survive on love. You can't have the important things in life just because of love. No one pays for three houses and European vacations and clothes from Italy and Rolls Royces with love.

2

My name's Jimmy McTeague. It's safe to assume you know that because you are me sitting here reading my diary. Since no one else is going to read this if I can

304

help it. It's also probably safe to assume that you'll burn these pages someday to make sure no one else reads them. But for now, writing it down seems right. My favorite movie is probably still *The Little Mermaid*, which I saw when I was nine years old and I still watch it on video once a year at least. Why? Because it was about sacrifice for what you wanted. I've always sort of believed in that. My dad doesn't understand why I watch a cartoon to inspire me. Sometimes I watch it before a match because it gets me going. I don't see why being smart and grown up has anything to do with abandoning the things you believed in when you were a kid.

I've wanted to keep a diary since I was about nine, about the same time as I saw that movie, but I didn't start 'til I was twelve, and then I threw it all out, so after another brief attempt at sixteen, I've decided now that I'm about to enter Harvard, it's time for me to keep one. I'm not only about tennis, anyway. I get tired of that dumb jock image. My SATs were through the roof. I get good grades and am totally wrapped up in Medieval History, which I figure I might pursue even after I graduate. If I graduate. If I make it through. If all the bad things that I've found out about don't happen in the meantime and it all ends.

This part of the diary is about my summer. Jenna and I were having a great year together, although I wasn't always there for her, I suppose, because of the matches I had in England and out in California, and then she spent Spring Break in Aruba, so that last week in May was really our first full week together, which is why I took the *Karenina* out of the yacht club and we sailed lazily up and down the coast for a few days. I was so pissed off at Dad over a lot of things. First and foremost was the talk he gave me, about how I needed to uphold the family and how I needed to look at life differently, not as a kid but as someone who had responsibilities and wanted to live a certain way with certain kinds of people. I didn't forget about Chip, but I guess that's one of those things I have to put aside. My dad says so anyway. Chip was really aggressive anyway, and the time we spent together wasn't really very meaningful because the whole time I kept thinking to myself: Where will this go? Two guys can't marry. I'll lose everything.

And Chip was all about loins, anyway. I shouldn't even write about it here. What if someone finds out? I'm not really gay anyway, I just get in these situations. I suppose I fall in love with people. And Chip turned out bad anyway. All that mess about fighting and arguing and him claiming I broke his arm when I didn't break it and if he fell it was his fault anyway for standing in my way and not letting me pass. He did that sort of blackmail thing too, but I showed him that I wasn't going to put up with that kind of shit.

I fell for Jenna pretty hard. I mean, who wouldn't? She's gorgeous and full of life and her brain is just amazing. And the money. To pretend it's not there is like not noticing her bra size. All the guys seem to want her, and I really had to fight off that bulldog from Choate with the Ferrari, but it wasn't too hard to dazzle her on the courts. She's a big fan of tennis, which helps, and that night we went for a walk back in the city really turned things around for me. I mean, we were walking down Fifth Avenue, and she was talking about what she wanted from life, all the wonderful things, to see the world and experience the best of everything, and how her trust fund was huge and she intended to always have the life her parents had, and my mind was turning a hundred little things around. I was walking with her under cloudy skies, and I was thinking about how this was right. Being with Chip was wrong because it was based on that one thing, that physical thing, and I thought, all right, I know where this will go with Jenna. We'll marry, we'll have children, we'll build something really solid. She has all this family land and properties and I'm really good at handling investments, so we'll be perfect together. And she wants kids really badly. So badly that she told me she wasn't even all that interested in college, and she wanted to just get out from under her parents and be on her own and make her own life. She has millions from her grandmother, and it's earning more millions every year, she said, so why should she have to go through college? She wanted to do some magazine work, one of those Condé Nast magazines, and her family has huge pull in that area, and she was smart enough.

It hardly bears comparison with a night spent on a dirty mattress in the back of some studio apartment in Chelsea with Chip, who fell on hard times after prep school. That sleaziness he had, like an air, like marijuana smoke in the back of a bus—that's what his place was like. He was slumming, he was degrading himself. His parents had cut him off, and he was willing to live like that. Hardly any furniture, a job that barely paid him per month what a reasonable man can live on. And still, he was willing to live like that for the sake of the feeling in his organ. I am never going to let that happen to me. I am never going to let people know how I am on the inside if I can help it. I got so mad at Chip I guess I ended up roughing him up a little, but he kept trying to ruin things, and I just won't let anyone do that. My dad is ruining things as it is, and pretty soon other people are going to know how he's ruining things, and I do not intend to be in that spot with him.

I remember clasping Jenna's hand, and listening to her optimistically go on about the life she intended for herself.

So I knew that if I just kept my eyes on her, it would all go in the right direction.

When we made love for the first time, it even felt right. She was overheated on the inside, it was like lava or something, it felt so natural.

I thought it would all turn out all right until I met Mooncalf.

I tried to fight it, too. I looked at him and tried. I tried not to look at his body. So well-developed. The way he spoke, almost sullenly. I didn't want him then, but I knew he had it in him to take me over. And I suppose he has.

There's even a dangerousness to him I enjoy. I find myself looking over Jenna's shoulder when we're at the beach or bicycling, hoping he's there, just out of reach.

And then, the party. It was like waking up for the

first time. It was like knowing that I'd been telling myself lies for years.

That I'd been foolish and wrong.

Now all I think about is Mooncalf and I wish we were in a different world, not one of secrets and half truths, but one where we could just be together.

I know he feels the same.

I'm sleeping pretty much on the boat now. I can't stay with Jenna. Not in her room. And her dad gives me those looks, which aren't pleasant, either. Jenna's been cold. Can't blame her. I know somehow it will all turn out okay. I know it will because I know life is not meant to be bad, and it's not meant to be confusing, and if we can all just get through this summer, it'll somehow work out because life is supposed to work out.

Sometimes, I get so lonely I want to just hold Jenna. As a friend.

I want to see him again, but he's been avoiding me since the party. I've had two weeks now, seeing Jenna and her family, playing a little golf, some tennis, taking the boat out when I can. Jenna's been good about this even if she's turned icy. She seems to handle my silences well. She really is a friend. I'm glad we can be this close and that she can be so understanding.

Most of the time, she seems to act as if the night of her party never happened, that I didn't go off with him. She won't really understand what it means, anyway. She'll think she'll know, but I'll let her know it was nothing. I'll get her thinking about us again, which is what she really wants anyway.

Chapter Seven: The Hurricane Approaches

1

There he is again: I see him. That boy Owen. He's been running down on the beach; swimming too much for his own good; working on his oxygen intake because breathing is the key; and he's felt a strength grow within him to match his body's power.

2

The weeks after the party went in a blur of moments and flashes in his brain—the sky clouded and then became unbearably sunny, the humidity soared and then dropped and then soared again; a tropical storm to the south had been upgraded to a hurricane, but it would not strike so far north as Outerbridge; and

311

once, in the dead of night, Owen lay in bed convinced he'd heard a gun go off somewhere on the island.

August was like that sometimes.

3

"Owen. Why?"

"Why what?" he asked, shielding his eyes from the sun.

Jenna had emerged from the deck all wrapped in a big yellow towel, and yet to him it was as magnificent as a summer dress. Her bountiful breasts poured in. The smell of the pool was intoxicating. He had just finished his morning laps, and he felt cleaner and stronger. Chlorine stank on his skin. He looked up at her. He wanted to kiss her; he wanted to touch her. They stood so close.

"Why the gun?"

"It's just a pistol. It's an antique."

"Why?"

"I thought you'd want it. I thought you'd like it."

"I'm not a fan of guns."

"No one is. But it has that inlay. It's mother of pearl. It seems feminine."

"You must be out of your mind. To give me that as a gift. On my birthday."

"It was my grandfather's."

"Well, I'm giving it back. God, I don't want it in the house, let alone in my hand."

"You need protection."

"From what?"

"Jimmy," Owen said. He sucked a breath in briefly. It was time to let it begin. He felt a curious shiver sweep through his body, as if he were on the verge of some delightful pleasure. "He told me . . ."

"Told you what? What did he say? Was it about me?"

Owen paused. He wanted her to feel the words as he said them. He wanted to make sure that she was completely focused on him. On his lips as he spoke. "No, it's nothing. I just think you should keep the gun."

"No, he said something," she nearly snarled. "Tell me."

"I'm sure he didn't mean it," Owen said.

"It made you think I needed a gun?" she asked. Her face went blank. She looked down at her feet for a moment. Then, she glanced up and looked him in the eye. "What's been going on between you two?"

"Nothing," Owen whispered.

"Owen, what's going on?" she said.

He looked at her and said, "Jenna, I want you to be safe. That's all. Look, I know you don't care for me, and that's fine. I can't make you like me. And I know I can't make you . . . care for me . . . in a way I happen to care for you. No one is magician enough for that. I've thought about you since we were both little kids. I've always considered you someone special."

"What?" she asked in a voice that was barely more than mouse squeak.

"I know that you'll go on to some really great college and you'll meet lots of guys like Jimmy and you'll come back to the island during the summer and be friendly with me, but you'll see me as the island townie who paints houses for a living, or perhaps works on boats. And you'll have a different life."

"What is this all getting to—" Jenna gasped, and then her eyes lit up. "You lost the island accent. You talk like one of us now."

She said it as if it was one of the most dreadful things imaginable. As if the "one of us" was the worst thing that could happen.

"That isn't true," Owen said. Then he glanced away from her, at the house and the beginnings of the roses his father so lovingly tended. "Look, I know I'm nothing to you. Just consider the gun some kind of protection. He's dangerous."

He walked away from her, his body barely dry from the swimming pool.

She called after him, but he didn't turn. He walked from the pool to the back lawn, and then disappeared down the path.

4

Another morning, he helped Mr. M with his golf clubs and luggage, driving the truck up from the ferry. Mr. M had almost missed the summer on the island. "Business takes a man over," he told Owen on the way up the hill to the house. He was the biggest man Owen had ever seen—like a bear, but slick, too, and shiny. He had on dark glasses and a rumpled blue oxford shirt; his skin was like pink snow. When Owen got to the door with the last of the bags, Mrs. M (he had to start thinking of her as Cathy if he was going to ever grow up) kissed her husband lightly on the nose.

"How's the summer?"

"Quiet," Mrs. M said.

"Where's that boy?"

"Which?"

"McTeague," Mr. M said.

"I think it's over. She's gone to Dr. Vaughan three times in two weeks. That's a record for her," Mrs. M said, and then turned to Owen. "Sweetie, can you go grab the mail?"

Owen nodded, feeling far too obedient, feeling his heart beating too fast, feeling too much within his frame, as if his muscles were about to twist and untangle and he was afraid for a moment that he had not heard what he thought he'd heard.

5

Owen sat by the koi pond, absorbing the last of an afternoon sun on one of his days off—the weather had gone back and forth, between brief bouts of showers and then sudden sunbursts. He was about to reach for Dagon beneath the placid green water when he noticed a shadow reflection move across the water.

He didn't turn, but knew that Jimmy had come up behind him.

"Aren't you ever going to talk to me again?"

Owen shrugged.

"I thought . . . I thought we could . . . we could at

315

least be friends," Jimmy said. "I think about you. All the time."

"Don't come here again," Owen measured his words carefully. The shadow withdrew, and Owen had the sun again.

6

Owen lay back in the grass and closed his eyes to the sun. As the violet darkness of his inner mind grew, he began to see the shadow sea of Dagon's realm. From the dusky waves, a form emerged, a magnificent sea god, its eyes round and without mind, like those of a shark, its body slick as oil with thousands of fins sprouting along its back; and as it grew, Owen knew what the god asked of him.

7

"I said peel the potatoes," his mother said, but he could see the look in her eyes. Her lashes wavered, and she didn't look directly at him. His mother was afraid of him. A little. Just a little fear. That was good.

"Don't use that tone of voice with me," Owen said almost politely, as he lifted the first potato and brought it to the small sharp knife.

"Something's missing in the house," she said, but his mother had begun saying strange things for the past few weeks—sentences that didn't go together, phrases that meant something only in her mind.

"You probably misplaced whatever it is," he told her almost nonchalantly. "You've always been like that, haven't you?"

8

And then, the storm came.

When storms come to Outerbridge, they usually have lost most of their power, they usually have been downgraded from hurricanes by the time they hit Bermuda to tropical storms when they reach Long Island, and by the time they make it past Block Island and start heading to the Avalons, it's usually high winds and warm rains but not much damage. The islanders who were over sixty remembered the storm of '53 that "took the hats off houses," as they said, and generally made a mess of the summer homes.

The storm that arrived the last week of August was not a terror, nor did it threaten to take the hats off houses. It was a warm palace of rain and wind, and it changed the geometry of the island with its shifts and movements.

The sky became a hardened gray, the rain was constant, and the koi pond overflowed. Owen ran outside with his father, newspapers curled over their heads, to try and save the fish as they flip-flopped along the mud and grass, their patchwork colors seeming to melt beneath the downpour.

9

Owen was on his way to work, using his father's truck to get to the Salty Dog, when he saw the figure standing in the pouring rain of afternoon down by the docks. Owen pulled the truck to the edge of the road and parked. He got out in the rain, opening his dark umbrella. The smell of fish was overpowering—it was a stink he was used to, but with the storm it was worse.

Jimmy looked otherworldly: He wore a shiny parka, and his face was pale beneath it. He nearly galloped over to Owen, and reached out to touch him on the shoulder, but Owen pulled back. Owen slammed the truck door shut.

"I'm going to work," Owen said.

"Mooncalf?"

"Leave me alone."

"I thought you—"

"You thought wrong."

"I've been waiting for you. At the boat. Every night, I watch you leave the restaurant and walk home. Every night I wish you'd come to me."

"You disgust me."

"Stop it. I know that's not true." Jimmy's shoulders began heaving. The sound of the rain became thunderous and sheets and blocks of it seemed to dump right down around then. "God. God!" Jimmy cried out, his arms going up to the sky like some clown, like some revival preacher clown; the rain pouring against his face. A thunderclap hid the sound of his bleating. "If only you knew! If only you could grow up inside me! Knowing how I've been pushed and pulled, first my father forcing me into tennis and basketball and soccer since I was six years old, the camps I've gone to every summer, and these schools I go to, and what it all means when inside . . . inside Owen . . . you know something about yourself that's like a doorway into a different world. Something that's like . . . I don't know . . . like a doorway out of this torture place and into this garden. When I was nine I had this garden that I helped create. It had vegetables and flowers in it, nothing pretty and nothing special, but it was mine. My dad dug it up in the middle of the night. He dug it up and told me that no son of his was going to be a goddamn gardener. That's what this feels like. Like someone is trying to dig up the garden I need to grow. And you know you need to go to that garden, but every single human being from your mother to your father to your coaches to your teachers to your friends to even strangers—every single human being—wants you to keep away from the one garden where you know you can just help things grow and where you'll feel calm for once in your life . . . where you will feel that what you have known inside your body, inside your heart, inside your mind, is the way God and nature and whatever it is that moves things within any human being—meant for you to be."

Owen nearly gasped, when Jimmy had finished.

"Jim, Christ, I know," Owen said, feeling as if he'd rehearsed the lines. He attempted a feeble smile. Part of him felt removed within his body. He was watching himself—Owen—react, seem gentle, seem kind. "It's

just like that." Then, he looked around at the tourists
coming off the ferry, their black and clear and red and
green umbrellas all blossoming above their head, and
there, beyond the Crab Shack were six of the island
guys he'd grown up with; and when he looked
through the thick rain, he saw other people he had
known all his life. "Look, we can't do this here," he
said. "Get in the truck."

10

Owen drove in silence through a rain-shattered
world—and followed the slick black island roads until they were nearly to the Great Salt Pond. Jimmy
seemed content with the quiet of the drive. When
Owen glanced over, he noticed that Jimmy pressed his
forehead against the window beside him, reminding
him somehow of a puppy. Finally, they came to the
end of road, which looked out over the enormous
pond. When he'd turned off the ignition, Owen
reached over and took Jimmy's hand in his.

"I know. It's difficult," Jimmy said. "I'm not like
this either. Not really. There are things I want out of
life. Things that have nothing to do with this. But
right now. Christ, right now, this is it."

"Other people can do this kind of thing, but I can't.
It wouldn't be right."

"No, it wouldn't be. But we can go somewhere that
it'll all be all right."

"Where?" Owen laughed. "Where would it be
right? My God. Where?"

Jimmy recoiled as if he'd been slapped. "Out to sea. In the boat."

"For how long, Jimmy? How long before your dad cuts you off, or before we move on? How long before you need to go off to your Ivy League school and then marry and meanwhile, I live in some kind of shame on this island. I'm not like you. I'm not like the kind of men who do this with other men. I'm just . . . just . . ."

"Just?"

"Just not sure what I feel right now."

It was easy to lie once Owen knew what he would do with Jimmy. How he would destroy him. How it would go easily once everything was in place.

"Oh, baby," Jimmy moaned, leaning over, into him, pressing his scalp against Owen's neck. Owen felt wetness along his throat. "You don't know how long I've hoped you'd say it."

"We don't need Jenna do we? Or girls like her," Owen whispered. "God, if I could, I'd kill her."

"Who? Kill? Owen?"

"I didn't mean that," Owen said, and kissed him on the top of his head.

The rain beat down in great sheets around the truck, and the great clouds roiled, and Owen knew that he had him now.

He had Jimmy right where he wanted him.

Where Dagon wanted him.

Chapter Eight: Dagon

1

"Owen?" his mother asked, holding it in her hand. The statue. It had always seemed enormous to him, but in her hand, it was only a foot in length. The base was cracked, some of its teeth had fallen out, and all it was in her hand was something that someone had carved and had left behind.

"Where'd you get that?"

"Where you left it," she said. She hefted it in her hand. "Where did it come from?"

"I . . . I found it."

"You found it?"

"Yeah, I did. It's mine." He held his hand out.

"Did you buy it?"

"That's none of your business," he said. "It's mine."

"Why did you put it in the fish pond?"

"It's an ornament. It looked nice there. Give it back."

"It's terrible looking. Its eyes. The skin on it. Who-

ever made that thing was sick. I think some kind of
animal was used. It smells, too."

"Mother."

"Don't mother me. You may be a young man, but
you have a thing or two to learn. I know you, Owen. I
know how you think. I saw you that morning."

"What are you talking about?"

"I saw you. You cut your arm and let it bleed on
this . . . this thing."

"That's crazy. Why would I do something crazy like
that? Like—what—like cut myself? And what—did
you say—bleed?"

"It's some kind of awful thing, isn't it? This thing.
It's some awful thing for you. The way your mind
works." She looked at the small statue in her hand,
and then back at his face. She squinted as if trying to
see him more clearly. "You've never been quite right.
You know that, too. You know how you're different
from other boys, don't you? Yes, you're crafty and
you look good in a suit and you can make your muscles talk for you. But I know you better than you
know yourself, Owen Crites. I know how cold you are
on the inside. I know how you believe different
things." He felt her closing in on him as she moved
toward him. "What exactly is this thing? Is this a toy?
Is this something else? Is this something you talk to?
Is this . . . is this . . . some kind of devil god? Do you
worship graven images now?" She said it in a half-
joking manner, and that was the worst of it. She
wasn't taking Dagon seriously. He could feel it in her
tone.

Owen felt as if his tongue had been cut out. He felt

a heat rash along his neck. He looked from the statue to his mother and back again. Then, he grinned. "Don't be ridiculous. You have such a small mind. You're so quick to judge me when you yourself are the one with the cold heart. You set a trap for Dad and now you punish him for that same trap. You can't even love your only child. And your imagination—your paranoid imagination—finding some carved art in a koi pond, something that you claim you watched me bleed over. Did you ever for a moment think that perhaps I hated myself so much I wanted to slit my wrists? But something made me stop. Something kept me from hurting myself. But it wasn't the thought of you, was it? It wasn't the love of my mother that saved me, was it? It was the thought that maybe one day I'd have a moment just like this. A moment when Dad is out of the house. A moment when you're at your worst. And then, do you know what I am going to do with you?"

"What are you talking about? Owen? Owen?"

"Give me that," he said, snatching it from her hand. "It's mine. Not yours."

She stood before him, trembling.

Owen cradled Dagon in his arms. He closed his eyes, and whispered a brief prayer.

When he opened them, he said, "Here is something I hope you think about until the moment you die. I am going to be your dutiful son as long as your years continue. But the moment that I get an inkling that you are old and feeble, I will come to your bedside one night, and I will press my hands over your nose and mouth until you smother to death. And in those last moments, you will look on me and know that everything you were ever afraid of was true."

His mother pressed her hands to her lips, but was unable to speak.

It was the power of Dagon, of course. It was there in the room.

The god was there with him.

Dagon whispered within his blood, "You will die like the bitch that you are."

Or had Owen himself said it aloud, in a whisper, to his mother?

2

This is how it will happen, the voice came to him. You will tell her things. You will tell him things. He harbors a madness. He is breakable. Then she will kill him. You will save her. She will kill him, and you will have her.

He slept that night with Dagon next to him in bed, and dreamed of the great realm beneath the sea, and he no longer felt his age, but felt as if he were again a child, and Jenna was with him, the Queen of the Deepest Fathom.

3

"Hello, sweetie," Mrs. M said. She had just finished the Sunday crossword puzzle, and looked up from the paper. "You all ready for four more days of this . . .

this tempest?" The kitchen was like a brilliant day compared to the murky rain outdoors.

Owen had come in through the back, his towel in his arms. "Up for a swim, Cathy?"

Mrs. M shook her head. "Feeling a bit downtrodden from the rain. Ask Frank, he'd probably love a race with you."

"Mr. M's around?"

"He's enjoying the summer here after all."

"That's great. I would've thought with the rain . . ."

Mrs. M didn't seem to notice his comment. She crossed her legs, one over the other, and Owen thought for a moment that it was the most luxurious movement he had ever in his life seen. "You here for Jenna?"

"I doubt she wants to see me."

"Owen," Mrs. M said, setting the paper down on the kitchen table. She arched an eyebrow. "Something's changed about you. What is it? Turn around."

Dutifully, he turned about and then back to face her again.

"You're different now. What's that all about?" She said it with a sweet amazement. "Are you in love?"

"No," he said, too quickly.

"Jenna's in her room. She sleeps later and later. Go call her if you want. She should get up. It's nearly ten. No one should sleep this late. Not at her age. Not in summer." Then, Mrs. M leaned forward, her breasts dropping slightly out of her robe. "Between you, me, and the wall, Owen, I think she's really depressed over something. But I'm the last person she'll confide in. I imagine it's about a boy," she whispered. "That McTeague character."

327

Then she said, lightly, "I always thought there was something not right about him."

4

"Oh. It's you," Jenna said. She was sitting up in her bed, the covers around her white cotton nightgown.

"Hi," he said from the doorway. The room smelled of sandalwood and vanilla.

"It's the rain. It does this to me," she said, wiping her hair back from her face. "I hate storms." She added, idly, almost as if he wasn't listening, "It's like my summer got stolen."

He remembered the love that he had nearly forgotten. He remembered why he loved Jenna so much. She was there for him, always. She had always been there for him.

"Okay if I come in? You know, like I used to?"

"Sure," she said, drawing her knees up. Then, "What is it between you two?"

He went into the bedroom, and sat on the chair near her desk. "Who two?"

"Don't be coy," she said unpleasantly. "Jimmy. Is it just sex?"

"Oh. That."

"Yes. That."

"I don't want to talk about it."

"I think you do."

"No, I really don't." And then, something within him opened up. It was like feeling a heat—a fire—in his chest, near his heart. It was Dagon. Dagon would inspire him. He felt that strength suddenly, just when he thought he would falter. Without even trying, tears poured from his eyes.

"Owen? Owen?" she asked, but he was nearly blind from the tears. She lifted the blanket, and patted a space next to her. "Come here. What's wrong? Owen?"

He bawled like a baby, and without knowing who—or what—had moved him, he found himself in her bed, her arms around him.

"Aw, Owen, what's wrong? What's wrong, my precious, precious, precious baby boy?" She held him close, and Dagon was there. He felt it. He was not alone.

Dagon was there.

The voice that came from his throat didn't feel like his. It was some small boy's. Some crybaby who shivered and spilled emotion across the girl he loved.

"He . . . I didn't . . . I didn't want . . . I can't talk about . . . I didn't . . . he just kept . . . he just kept . . . he kept . . . he . . . I tried to . . . fight . . . fight . . . fight . . . push . . . hit . . . but . . . he just kept . . . he just kept . . . he just kept . . ."

"Oh my God," Jenna said, her voice chilled and haunted. "No. He didn't. No. Did he? Owen? Did he rape you? Did he?"

"He just kept . . . oh God, Jenna, I can't face this . . . I wanted to . . . I wanted to . . . I wanted to . . . kill . . . myself . . . I wanted to . . ."

And so it began, and she said all the things she was meant to say; and Owen told less than he needed to tell because she made the connections herself, and he

329

sat with her for hours in her arms, and then, they made love.

5

He went to the boat that night.

It was over now. It was all over. Dagon was still within him, and he had won. He wanted to take it to Jimmy. He wanted Jimmy to suffer from it. If he could, he would've videotaped the afternoon, he would've tape recorded Jenna's voice saying over and over again that she loved him, that it was all her fault, that Jimmy should never have come to the island, that he was bad, he was evil, and they should call the police, they should do something. She even told him that if that bastard ever set foot on her property again, she would take that gun and shoot him right between the eyes.

The storm continued to rage, but in muted anger, across the gray mood of sky. The Sound and the distant islands that could be seen were like watercolor images, fuzzy and melting in the rain. Owen wore a bright yellow raincoat that belonged to his father. He was a fire in the darkness.

"Mooncalf, you look like a fisherman," Jimmy said. He wore cutoff jeans and a striped rugby shirt that was already soaked through, and his hair was like seaweed, hanging in his eyes. In his hand, a green bottle of beer. "Like, you know, a real New England clamchowder fisherman!" He had to shout over a roll of thunder and a crack in the sky; then the world lit up for a moment; it returned to gray.

Owen laughed, shaking his head. "You're drunk, boy."

"Want a beer?" Jimmy asked.

"Sure," Owen said. "How many you drink already?"

"Four. Maybe five. Who's counting?"

"Let's get out of the rain!"

"I like the jetty," Jimmy said, tossing him a small bottle and then leaping to the dock. He grabbed Owen's free hand. "No one's looking. We can hold hands, all right?"

"I don't know," Owen tugged away. He twisted the top off the Rolling Rock bottle and took a swig. "God, I'm sick of rain!"

"Me, too!" Jimmy tried to kiss him, but Owen stepped back to avoid it.

The rain lessened slightly; it was a warm rain; it washed across their bodies. "She's sort of expecting us," Owen said.

"Who?"

"Jenna."

"Jenna?" Jimmy laughed, and then looked sidelong up the hill to the Montgomery place. "What for? I thought it was you and me tonight."

"She's . . . she's pissed. I guess that's what it is." Owen shrugged. "She's pissed and she wants us to talk to her. I told her."

"You . . . you told her?"

"After yesterday, in the truck, Christ, Jimmy, I can't not tell her. I've known her all my life. She's one of my closest friends. I told her about us. About how we're going to go away together. How you love me now. How everything's all right."

"You . . . you . . ." he stammered. The bottle in his hand dropped to the rocky ledge, shattering. "You told her."

It was coming out now. The madness that they all had within them. Owen wanted to smile, but knew that if he did, he would give himself away.

6

The rain thinned. Minutes had passed while Jimmy had taken in what had just been said. Owen could practically see the thoughts in his eyebrows as they squiggled around, flashing anger and confusion, and the way he chewed his lip, and his eyes wouldn't stop blinking. Owen reached over and touched his scalp. "Sometimes I think I see a halo around your head. I do. I think you're some kind of angel," Owen said, and then scruffed his hair.

"You fucking told her?" Jimmy growled. "You goddamn fucking son of a bitch told her what we'd been . . . what we'd . . ."

"Do you think she didn't see?" Owen set his bottle down on the jetty, and put his hands on Jimmy's shoulders, pulling him into him. "Do you think she's stupid? We're her friends, for Christ sake. She can see. She told me she watched us that first night. She saw us. There was enough light to see our shadows, puppy. She told me it upset her, but she understood. She wasn't sure if it wasn't just one of those drunk boy things . . . or something else. I told her it was." Then, he added hesitantly, "Something else."

"You fucking goddamn son of a bitch gardener's son living in your goddamn peasant fucking world you don't even know what you've done!" Jimmy shouted. His face had contorted until it was more a mask than a face, a mask of pain and fury. It was no longer human. "You fucking think that," spit flew from his mouth, "that . . . that . . . you, you, with nothing to lose can just throw what we have in front of her, in front of—you know what you're playing with? You're playing with things you can't even understand!" Jimmy began stomping around in a circle, alternating his shouts with lion roars.

When he finally quieted, Owen said, "What happened to yesterday? You looking up at God and telling me how this all felt, how you felt on the inside. How you felt you needed to let this out? What happened to that?" He kept his voice low.

Jimmy's eyes lit up. "Don't you, you son of a bitch, use my words against me! I wasn't born to lose everything because I'm sleeping with some island townie pervert. I wasn't born to have this get out, to have this ruin everything I've ever built."

"Listen to yourself. It's practically a whole new century. You talk like it's 1950. You won't lose everything just because—"

"You think so? You little bitch, you think I won't lose everything? You don't even understand what is

going on here do you? You think it's about me wanting you. The stakes are higher! I'll tell you something,
boy, I want you, but I don't want you. You don't even
understand why I have to be with Jenna, do you? Do
you?"

Owen turned and walked toward the strip of
beach. "I don't want to hear."

"Well, you need to. Maybe living in some little caretaker's house gives you no perspective on this, but
Jenna Montgomery means I will not be some poor shit
like you."

Owen glanced back. "You're rich."

"Ha!" Jimmy cried. "You don't know the half of it."

"You're an heir to some fortune. Some sports store
chain."

Jimmy shook his head. "It's not like it looks. My father has these stores. That's all he has. But the business is changing. It's changing, and he's had some
setbacks. He isn't a good businessman, Mooncalf.
Never has been. All this stuff, this boat, the houses,
all of it, will be gone in a few years. It's coming. He's
going to be in jail someday, my father, and the IRS is
going to eat him alive. And I do not intend to live like
that. I do not intend . . ."

"Jesus," Owen gasped, and then began laughing.
"Jesus. You're just a golddigger. You are just after her
money. Jesus!"

Owen dropped to his knees on the wet sand.

"What's wrong with you?" Jimmy snarled, coming
over to him. "You feeling bad now?"

"I thought you loved me," Owen said.

Jimmy's voice had grown cold. "It's not about

whether I love you or not. It's not about that. But you've ruined even that now."

He grabbed Owen under his armpits, lifting him up to a standing position. "You've destroyed something for me, Mooncalf. You really have."

Then, he looked up the hill to the house. The lights were on along the pool, and the upstairs light—Jenna's bedroom—was dim.

"I need to set this right," he said.

"No, don't, Jimmy, it's—"

"I need to," Jimmy said. "I'll tell her that it was weakness. I'll tell her I love her. I love her more than anything on the face of the earth. I'll tell her that I couldn't help myself with you, but that it was nothing. That you were nothing." He nearly laughed, but it had a cry within it. "You're just a little manipulative piece of trash. She'll understand. She's not like you. She'll understand."

Then, he took off in the rain, bounding up the wooden steps that crept like a vine along the side of the hill, and Owen began following, but slowly.

He heard the shots ring out before he had reached the top step. Five distinct shots, and soon dogs down in town were howling, and lights came up along the waterfront.

7

The house was dark and silent when he went in through the glass doors by the pool. He walked past the shimmering water, flicking up the lights as he went. Entering the kitchen, he saw Mrs. M, lying in a pool of blood, and then Owen found himself moving more swiftly, his heart pounding—

—she resembled nothing of the mermaid she had once been; death had robbed her beauty; blood took away the magic of her form; her eyes were open, and fishlike—

Dagon, what is this? This isn't what was promised. This isn't what I prayed for—

And he ran up the stairs to Jenna's room, and found *him* standing there, the Colt in his hand.

On the bed, Jenna, bleeding, an enormous hole in her neck. Her hands moved as if she were trying to reach up to stop the blood, but could not.

She opened her mouth to cry out, but all that came was a rasping sound, and blood pulsed from her throat. He felt himself burning as he watched the last light flicker in her beautiful eyes.

Then, her eyes closed.

8

"Mooncalf, what did I do?" Jimmy said, his skin red, his eyes narrow slits, his shirt torn and bloody. Tears and sweat shone like diamonds on his skin. "What did I do? I . . . I came up . . . I wanted to talk . . . and she . . . she had this . . ." He held the pistol up. "She . . . she threatened me . . . and then her mother came up . . . I had grabbed it from her . . . I was going to leave . . . but they said things . . . her mother, too . . . they said things about me . . . and her father . . . About something . . . some lie . . . something you told her . . . something . . ."

"All of them?" Owen asked. "You killed all of them?"

Jimmy shrugged. "I guess so. It's kind of a blur. Funny thing is," he giggled in a way that seemed uncharacteristic, "it didn't really feel like me at all. It felt like something else. Like I got taken over. Maybe if she hadn't pointed this gun. Maybe if I hadn't been drinking. I don't know. It happened so fast. I was about to leave, but her mother saw me with the gun. She saw me and she was saying these things. And then I just wanted to shut her up and this thing was inside me. This feeling. Like something wanted me to point the gun at her mother. Just to scare her. And then: kabang."

"Jimmy?"

"And then her father starts shouting upstairs, and I feel this . . . this wild thing inside me," Jimmy said, and now the giggling was becoming annoying and seemed to increase between words. "And I just go running back up the stairs and down the hall and there's her dad, and I think of my dad, and I think of all the things I'm never going to have, and suddenly the gun is going off, and then Jenna's screaming and she's picking up the phone in her room because I hear that *beep beep* noise and I have to stop her, I have to tell her not to call, that there'll be a way to work this all out. And then, I feel it in me again. I'm moving faster than I'm supposed to—the rest of the world is moving slow—and I'm in her room and she has a look on her face like she doesn't understand how I got there so quickly, and I'm feeling this—power or something—and then I press the gun against her throat to shut her up."

He calmed slightly. He pointed the gun directly at Owen. "It's something you said to her. Isn't it? It's because you told her. But you said something terrible, didn't you?"

"Jimmy," Owen said. "Now, I know you're upset. I know this is difficult right now. But I want you to breathe. Take a few deep breaths. Come on. Just breathe."

Jimmy looked at him curiously for a moment, blinking. Then he opened his mouth and let the air in. Then, out. Then, in. Slowly, carefully.

Then, warmth returned to Jimmy McTeague's eyes and he said:

"Owen, I'm so sorry. I'm so sorry. I should never have come this summer."

Epilogue: Belief

1

I can look at this past summer now and see that it was all Dagon. Dagon was there. I had brought Dagon into our world, and Dagon had gotten loose. There is no madness except the madness of the gods. There is no purity except the purity of love.

Here is where he took me—down to the sailboat—and out to sea.

2

We sailed around Outerbridge, its cliffs and caves, around the Montgomery palazzo, shining green and white with the flashing of the lighthouse nearby, north and then east, beyond the Great Salt Pond, out into the diamond night where sea and sky met, and the storm howled around us, and Jimmy, gun to my head, calling me Mooncalf over and over again, forced me to whisper an incantation to Dagon of the purity and madness of human love.

Mooncalf, he said. Mooncalf.

BENTLEY LITTLE
DOUGLAS CLEGG
CHRISTOPHER GOLDEN
TOM PICCIRILLI
FOUR DARK NIGHTS

The most horrifying things take place at night, when the moon rises and darkness descends, when fear takes control and terror grips the heart. The four original novellas in this collection each take place during one chilling night, a night of shadows, a night of mystery—a night of horror. Each is a bloodcurdling vision of what waits in the darkness, told by one of horror's modern masters. But as the sun sets and night falls, prepare yourself. Dawn will be a long time coming, and you may not live to see it!

DOUGLAS CLEGG
THE HOUR BEFORE DARK

When Nemo Raglan's father is murdered in one of the most vicious killings of recent years, Nemo must return to the New England island he thought he had escaped for good, Burnley Island. But this murder was no crime of human ferocity. What butchered Nemo's father may in fact be something far more terrifying—something Nemo and his younger brother and sister have known since they were children.

As Nemo unravels the mysteries of his past and a terrible night of his childhood, he witnesses something unimaginable . . . and sees the true face of evil . . . while Burnley Island comes to know the unspeakable horror that grows in the darkness.
